I0534300

BURLESQUE BAD:

Book One
of the Destiny of Dance
series

NINA DAY GERARD

BURLESQUE BAD : BOOK ONE OF THE DESTINY OF DANCE SERIES © 2016 by Nina Day Gerard. All rights reserved. Printed in the United States of America. No part of this book may be used or reproduced in any manner whatsoever without written permission except in the case of brief quotations embodied in critical articles or reviews.

This book is a work of fiction. Names, characters, businesses, organizations, places, events, and incidents either are the product of the author's imagination or are used fictitiously. Any resemblance to actual persons, living or dead, events, or locales is entirely coincidental.
For information visit: www.ninadaygerard.com
Cover design by Tris Beezley Art & Design.
ISBN-13: 978-0-9984286-0-4
ISBN-10: 0-9984286-0-4

Dedicated to dancers everywhere...

Special Thanks:
My editor Elizabeth: thanks for
hanging in there with me!
My beta readers: your enthusiasm
inspires me to keep going.
My mom, the best beta reader
of them all—I love you, Mommy!

and

My husband—thank you for believing in me. You are
truly the wind beneath my wings.

Look for a review of *Burlesque Bad* by WOW! Women
on Writing, an ezine promoting the communication
between women writers, authors, editors, agents,
publishers and readers.
www.wow-womenonwriting.com

Fans praise *My Brother's Keeper*:

"…one of the best romance novels that I've read in a long time."
~ S. F., San Fransisco, CA

"Loved it. Cried. It was great. More! More!"
~ G.N., Los Angeles, CA

"From the second I picked up this novel, I could not put it down."
~ L.T., Millington, NJ

"Jack and Sam forever. MUST READ."
~ N.C., Los Angeles, CA

Prologue

Ava Riordan was Ireland's Cyd Charisse. At least that's what the American film producer said the night he came into the Swing Lounge in Dublin with his friend to see the late show. And drunk as he might have been, Sioban knew he spoke the truth. She could see it even from where she stood off stage.

That had been the one night Ava had agreed to let Sioban, all of twelve, come to watch the show. It was a jazz revue, "nothing too crass, you understand," Ava explained to her friend Peg, who was to chaperone Sioban for the evening. "And for God's sakes, don't breathe a word to Patrick."

Ava had reached down and smoothed her daughter's hair and looked at Sioban wistfully as she said it. Though Sioban knew Ava spoke the warning to Peg, she answered herself: "Never, Mam." Sioban had never felt closer to her mother in the secret they'd shared for months: that Ava was stealing away every Saturday night to dance in a club under her maiden name when she was supposed to be over at Peg's with the girls for cards, and had tonight taken Sioban with her. Poor Patrick O'Rourke thought that dancing was a hobby Ava had left behind when she met him and settled down to raise a family and be a wife. He was a good husband to Ava as far as Sioban knew in her young mind. He worked hard, never raised a hand to Ava, and kept his jaunts to the pub to three nights a week. But there was no way he'd understand this, Sioban thought as she watched Ava.

The gown was the color of cherries in winter and hugged Ava's body like a second skin. Though Ava's face was in shadow, the delicate crystal beads of it

1

glittered in the low blue light like a million tiny promises of the dazzling performance to come.

Ava stood in a jazz pose waiting for the music to start, her hands poised, one high, one low, in the black satin gloves that covered her elbows.

The first note of Tom Jones's "Delilah" popped from the band, and a full spotlight shone on Ava. Applause rose as she began to move. As the male singer for the evening belted out the lyrics in his best Tom Jones impersonation, Ava's body echoed every note, and retold the story of the dangerous Delilah all over again, and the audience followed her through every phrase and subtle nuance.

First the gloves came off; then Ava opened the outer slip of her gown and flung it away to a new wave of wild cheers from the audience. Two male dancers joined her in all black, and she sashayed between them in her black fishnets and red sequined bustier. They vied for the love of Delilah and tried to snare her in the black feather boa they held at either end. But the song rolled on, and Ava eluded their advances, snaking the boa around her own shoulders and leaving them begging in her wake as the singer wailed "why, why, whyyyy, Delilah?"

As if it were her destiny, Ava jazz-walked to a table near the stage where two men sat. One held a drink and a cigarette in the same hand and leaned in toward his friend, talking as if they were at a cocktail party instead of a show. But as Ava approached the table, the second man froze, and the drink he held stopped halfway to his mouth, which fell open when Ava reached the table. He nudged his rude talking friend away and Ava flung the boa around his neck. She shimmied the boa back and forth at his collar in time with her hips. Then, as the song rose toward its conclusion, Ava leaned in, kissed his forehead, and un-snaked the boa from his neck as she sashayed away. He didn't bother to wipe her red lip prints from his brow, but only stared out after her as she trailed the boa behind her.

The two male dancers had cast themselves down in despair, and now half-crawled, half-slithered after her on the floor. As the last note sounded, Ava gave one final glance back over her shoulder. She winked at her stargazer at the table. He reached up to touch his forehead where she'd kissed him.

No, Sioban, reasoned, her dear old da would never understand this. Sioban wasn't sure she understood it either, not fully. She only knew that her mam was magic.

Not long after Peg had shuttled Sioban back to the dressing room and left her to go home with her mother, Ava herself glided in, flushed and glowing. She was still half in her other world, the one she danced in. Ava never really left it completely, though she hid it well from Patrick and nearly everyone else. But not from Sioban, who could see the glimmer in Ava's eyes even when she wore her plain clothes, and did plain things, like scrub the loo or peel the potatoes for their stew. And there was no mistaking the lilt in her step, even when she went out to the post box or went around the living room pretending to make a difference with the feather duster.

Ava came right to her, and Sioban threw herself into Ava's arms.

"You were magnificent, Mam!"

"Who says I'm yer mam?" said Ava. She feigned shock and winked at Sioban. "Where'd I get a ginger girl from anyway?" she teased. They both knew that Sioban's shocking, poker-straight red hair came from Patrick, in spite of Ava's glossy raven-black waves.

"Well, I'm lost then, and you'll have to be my mam." Sioban played along and looked around the room in search of another suitable mother. "No one else here to take the job."

Ava laughed and pulled Sioban in for another hug. Just then, the club manager, Sam Cleary, entered the dressing room with a great sense of purpose. He raised an eyebrow at the sight of Sioban.

"Well, I hope we're not going to make a habit of this, then," he said.

"Not at all. She's been begging to see me perform for months, and I didn't see the harm this once," explained Ava.

"And let's keep it at that, right?"

"Fine, of course."

"Anyway, listen—"

Sam had forgotten to close the dressing-room door all the way, and a stage hand bustled in with Ava's gown and gloves draped over his arm. Upon catching Sam's perturbed glare, he tossed the garments unceremoniously over the privacy screen and scurried out.

"As I was about to say," continued Sam, as he reached to close the door to the room, "I don't usually bother with this kind of thing, but one of those two lads at the front table, the one ye tried to choke with yer feathers there, well he wants to see you."

Sioban stifled a snicker as Ava shoved her off of her lap in surprise.

"What for? Listen, I was just performing, you know I don't encourage any of that, I'm a—" Ava stopped herself. Sioban knew she was about to say that she was a married woman. They both looked at Sam and waited for his response.

"I know that. You seem like a fairly classy lady and all." He glanced warily at Sioban again. "But he was rather insistent. You can take care of it. Just don't let anyone see you leave the club with him."

"I'm not going to leave with him, Sam—"

"Look, like I said, I don't want to know. I hardly bother with this. But he wasn't gonna leave me be until I gave you this." Sam held out a white card to Ava. "Bloody Americans over here on holiday or some nonsense. They're drunk as monkeys to boot."

Ava took the card from him eagerly. "Says here he's a film producer in Hollywood."

"And I'm Brad Pitt, now, ain't I?"

"Well, and I'm sure you'd like to be. It isn't often I have an admirer. Send him back."

"Suit yerself. Just remember what I said." Sam shook his head, and walked out before either of them could say anything else. Sioban realized she'd been holding her breath when Ava flew into action.

"Hurry, get behind there," she ordered as she pointed to the privacy screen and reached for her robe on the ratty overstuffed chair in the corner.

"But I want to see the Hollywood producer!"

"Go on, do as I say—yer not too old for me to spank yer silly bottom!" Ava sounded her sternest, but they both grinned as Sioban ducked behind the screen.

Sioban's heart did a flip when she realized that she could see through the fabric of the screen if she put her face close to it. She glanced up at the gloves, and, overcome with a sudden urge, she snatched them down from the top of the screen. As she inched them on, a soft knock sounded at the door. Sioban pushed the gloves up her arms and became still as Ava opened the door.

"Yes?"

Sioban pressed her face as close to the screen as she could without being in danger of pushing it over.

The man appeared much younger up close like this. And he didn't seem drunk at all, unlike his friend.

"Good evening, miss. I'm sorry to bother you, I just...I just had to meet you."

"It's all right. Come in, then." Ava stepped aside and he ambled in. He almost seemed embarrassed to be there.

"Thank you." He turned and stood a respectable distance from her. Ava sat down at her dressing table again, and crossed her legs, giving the man another gander at the length of them in the black fishnets. Sioban feared he might faint, and suppressed a giggle. "I'm Justin Mars."

"So your card says."

"I-I'm a film producer. But you knew that. It says on the card. I mean, I'm mostly independent. I just— I'm always on the lookout for new talent, and I'm working on this new project."

Poor Justin rubbed his hands on his pants. He must be sweating bullets by now. Ava played the regal queen, aloof, but relishing the attention.

"Go on," she said, and gave him a winning smile that seemed to give him confidence.

"Well, Miss..."

"Riordan. Ava Riordan. But you may call me Ava."

"I, um...I'm working on this film. It's kind of a tribute, if you will. You see, I want to bring musicals back to film, in the tradition of Fred Astaire and Gene Kelly, but with more of a modern spin."

"Is that so?" Ava leaned forward slightly and her red bustier peeked out from her robe. She'd better be careful, Sioban supposed, or little Justin was going to keel over of a heart attack before he got to the end of his story. But Sioban already knew the end, and she suspected her mother did too.

"Yes, and I just can't believe, all the way over here, I see you—you're like a dream with your dancing. You capture the charm of a gone-by era, but with a totally modern sex appeal—"

Oh! Watch it there, little man, thought Sioban. Ava raised an eyebrow, channeling Sam for a brief moment. Justin demurred and gathered himself again.

"What I mean is, you're an Irish Cyd Charisse. 'The living end,' as my dad used to say. You're just the kind of girl I envisioned for my films."

Touché! Not even Ava could resist being perceived as a girl, and Sioban saw her mother's hand float up to her throat. She wondered if her da ever called Ava his girl anymore.

"Sure and that's awfully kind of you, Mr. Mars, but do you have any credentials besides this little card? Film credits? A contract to offer me?"

Well, you didn't trifle with Ava Riordan's dreams, and this lad had better be serious. But her questions had taken the wind out of his sails for sure. Sioban felt bad for him. He seemed like a nice young man.

"No, I don't, I...I just think you're beautiful...and incredibly talented. And if you ever decide to come to Hollywood, I'll put you in one of my films in a heartbeat."

"I see." Ava did see, all the hope he had in him. Sioban looked at both of them. She guessed that Ava had had the same hope about her dancing that Justin had now for his films before she married Patrick. "Well, rest assured, Justin, if I ever make it across the ocean to Hollywood, yer the first person I'll ring up." She gave him her most beautiful smile yet.

"I'll count on it. It's late—I'd better go before the club manager boots me out on my ass."

"I think he's more worried that yer friend's had a little too much whiskey."

"He's right about that, which is why I put him in a cab after the show. I couldn't have him messing up my chance to meet you, now could I?"

"I'm glad you did—come back to meet me, that is."

"I am too." He smiled wistfully back at her, and opened the door to leave, but turned back again. "You keep dancing, Ava."

It wasn't until he'd closed the door that Ava whispered her response. "I will, Justin Mars. I will."

Sioban could hardly contain herself. She leaped from behind the screen still wearing the gloves, and ran to Ava. She flung her arms around Ava's neck.

"Mam! Mam, are we going to be starlets in the movies in America?"

"Oh, you want to be a starlet, do you?"

Sioban wanted to cry, just then. Didn't her mother understand? The only thing she ever wanted to be was, well, Ava. "Maybe I can't be a starlet, mam, 'cause of my ginger hair and all. I just want to dance—like you."

Ava pulled Sioban onto her lap and hugged her close. Even though Sioban was nearly as tall as Ava, and her toes touched the floor as she sat there, Sioban felt like she was a little toddler again. They both began to cry. "Oh, my girl, you already are a starlet—you're *my* starlet." Ava pulled back from Sioban and gazed at her with watery eyes. "I wish we could go to America, my lamb."

"But why can't we, Mam? Ye've got to—you're meant to dance and be a star!" Sioban knew she'd just better not even mention her father.

"We can't. I can't. And that's just the end of it. Now, get yourself ready to go home, and I'll do the same."

Ava gently pushed Sioban off of her lap. But Sioban stood next to her as they both peered into the lighted mirror. Ava touched her own cheek as if to wonder if indeed she was a modern-day Cyd Charisse. Sioban reached out and touched Ava's other cheek, and they looked at each other in the mirror for a long moment before Sioban rose and they finally gathered themselves to steal home in the wee hours of the night.

That spring, Ava came to Sioban's school one afternoon and pulled her out of Mrs. McCarthy's math class, just as Sioban had prayed for her to do since the night at the lounge. By late that afternoon they were on a train to London.

Two days later, they were on a plane to Los Angeles.

By the end of the week, they'd discovered that Justin Mars's phone number had been disconnected, and that his office, which was really just a run-down apartment in Culver City, had been vacated. He'd taken his silly notions about filmmaking and gone back to wherever he'd come from just like every other person who came to L.A., the landlord said.

So Ava rented an apartment and auditioned for every non-union musical and dance production she could. But she never got the parts, and the money ran out. Within three months, she was waiting tables. Three months after that, she became the hostess at the strip club across the street from the diner where she'd been waiting tables.

By the following year, Ava was on the pole. Sioban went to school every morning and returned to an empty apartment each afternoon. She made herself sandwiches and huddled on the couch in front of the television until Ava stumbled in, sometimes at 4 a.m. Then Ava would shoo her off to bed, where Sioban would cry herself to sleep.

There were other clubs, and eventually the men started following her home. One night, just after Sioban's uneventful sixteenth birthday, Ava announced that she was going to marry a man named Jimmy, who owned a place called Club 29. She had to, or they'd be deported, she told Sioban. Besides, this would be different, a nice club, not like those other dives. But there was no wedding, or even a ring. Ava just came home from the courthouse one day and stuffed a bunch of legal papers in her dresser drawer.

In the end, there was little to no difference between Club 29 and the ones before, except that Ava had started drinking. And taking little pills. And apparently, her and Jimmy's was an open marriage, because Ava still came home with other men.

The third or fourth time Ava missed a night at work, Jimmy "encouraged" Sioban to leave school and come work for him. In other words, if she didn't cover for her mother at the club, Jimmy would divorce Ava and they'd both be on a plane back to Ireland. Sioban did it without a second thought. If she could just save enough for them to leave Club 29, then she could get Ava clean, they could both start auditioning again, and get in the union, and get cast in something good.

By the following Christmas, Ava was dead.

Neither Ava nor Sioban had ever heard from her father directly. There had been one letter from Sioban's aunt Rose, Ava's oldest sister, shortly after they'd arrived in America. It said how Patrick was beside himself, more hurt than angry, sobbing "why?" for days on end. Then, suddenly, he just became stony, going about his daily routine as if nothing had ever happened. Apparently, Ava and Sioban were dead to him, but Ava was still her sister, after all, Rose wrote, and may God keep her until she came to her senses and moved back to Ireland.

Sioban tucked the letter, along with Ava's black satin gloves, into the lining of her tiny, worn suitcase. She took a pole every night at Club 29, and rotated as hostess between sets along with the other girls. As long as she did her job and kept her mouth shut, Jimmy seemed happy enough. But Sioban made it clear that there'd be no booze, no drugs, and no men. She did what she had to do and paid her bills, setting aside what she could. Sioban was determined to keep Ava's dream, now her own, alive—and not to let it kill her in the process.

Chapter One

Sioban stared at Captain Johnny's, now closed down, through her vintage cat-eye sunglasses. The pink bubble she'd blown of her tired gum popped like a BB gun in the frigid January air. Chicago winters were nothing to be trifled with, she knew. Her mam would be scolding her right now for not having the sense to put on some decent winter clothes. But Sioban was who she was: an Irish girl raised in Los Angeles—part wildcat, part glamour girl, and all sass.

A gust of wind tore under her short plum-colored coat and equally short denim skirt to smack her bottom in rebuke, probably as her mam would have done, even though Sioban was a grown woman of twenty-nine.

The wind continued its assault, flying down her bare legs. Her black ankle boots were a poor defense against it. There hadn't been time to buy tights. Lord, there'd barely been time to pack her single bag and get herself on the plane before the hell that was on her heels caught up to her.

Sioban gasped as the wind whipped the thick curtain of her hair aside and sliced the back of her neck. Her breath caught as the sensation of Sonny Coniglione's hand gripping that exact spot returned to haunt her, and she froze on the spot.

"Hurry up, silly! Why'd you stop in the middle of the street?"

The voice reached her, but it sounded small. Then Sioban remembered—she'd been walking next to her best friend Vonda, and then following her across the street to the bar that had belonged to Von's father. Following Von to the bar that she was transforming into her dream club, to a new future for both of them.

Disoriented, Sioban stared at her feet, expecting to be standing on the sidewalk. But she had indeed walked halfway into the street and stopped there, caught up in her daydreams. She looked up at Von and a wry grin spread across her face. Von had grown up in Chicago, and hadn't let her years in Los Angeles dull her common sense. She was covered head to toe in fleece-lined suede boots, jeans, at least a sweater and a tee-shirt under her down jacket, and a wool hat from under which her fat blond curls spilled down her back.

"Come on, you crazy girl!" Vonda called to her again with a wide smile. God bless Vonda Douglas, Sioban thought. Without her, she'd have had no place to run to two days ago.

But an instant later, Vonda's expression changed to panic, and she was waving her arms wildly at Sioban.

The roar of an engine filled the air and Sioban turned to see that a large black pickup truck had rounded the corner and was heading straight for her.

"Oh, *shite*..."

Chapter Two

Danny secured his opponent's attack arm behind the man's back and had him pinned face down on the ground within seconds. After all, the dude had tried to stab him—or at least he'd pretended to.

The blue light of nighttime was lightening into day as Danny looked up at the window. He'd chosen to work combat training with Reece Gorman, his friend and fellow Rockford Security operative, instead of pumping iron that morning. By the look of the early morning winter sky, he had about another half an hour before he had to get cleaned up and head out with his boss to meet a new client.

Scratch that, an old client. Okay, a new client at an old location. The crowd at Captain Johnny's was a bit sedate for Danny's taste, but it was a good pub to have a beer and watch a game of whatever sport was in season now and again.

Apparently the owner had died and left the place to his daughter. Barry "Bear" Rockford needed him to go and meet with the woman to hopefully retain Rockford's contract with her. Johnny Douglas had been a Rockford Security client for years. Bear knew more about it than he did, but one thing was for sure. Danny was in no mood to deal with women. For one thing, they were always trouble—*always*. This Douglas woman would probably want twenty-four-hour guards, or want some spy shit installed in the joint that she really didn't need. Yeah, women just fucking annoyed him. The more he thought about it, the more pissed off he felt.

"Jesus, man, you're killing me here." Gorman's strained voice broke through the onslaught of annoyance that had taken over Danny's thoughts.

Suddenly he realized that he was focusing his irritation on the pressure point he'd created by driving his knee into Gorman's lower back. Even the slam mat couldn't be much help for the man with Danny leaning into him that way.

"Sorry," Danny muttered. He stood up and offered a hand to Gorman.

"Thanks," said Gorman as he stood. "If you'd smashed me any further into that mat, you would have ruined Priscilla's full enjoyment of our date tonight, if you get my drift."

Danny tensed again. Why did everything always have to be about a goddam woman? Nothing. But. Trouble.

"Really," he said. "Well, maybe if you'd get your mind off that tail you're chasing, you'd focus on what the fuck you're doing, and I'd be the one laid flat on the mat, now wouldn't I?"

Gorman had an incredulous look on his face, but Danny didn't stick around to hear what reply he might have come up with.

Danny plowed through the metal doors of the combat training room, and powered down the hall to the weight room. Thankfully it was empty, but it probably wouldn't be for long. Danny went straight to the free weights and picked up fifty pounds in each hand. One. Two. One. Two. He pumped bicep curls alternately with each arm. He was a big man at six feet four and two hundred and fifty pounds. But he didn't want to bulk up too much. He'd seen it too many times with hired goons that were as big as houses and could put their fists through a brick wall, but were slow as mud when it came time to pursue the bad guy. God forbid they should have to actually chase someone down.

No, long gone were Danny's days of trying to look like the Incredible Hulk. One. Two. One. Two. He'd only ever bulked up that way because women ate that shit up. Correction—*Caryn* ate that shit up. Hell, she ate *him* up. She'd text or call him just to tell him how hot he was. She'd talk dirty until they were both dying to fuck each other's brains out. She'd oil him up and rub him down, and they'd go at it for hours.

But there was more to her than that, at least for Danny. Caryn, with her sass and wit. Caryn, with her strength and laughter. Caryn, with her pale blue eyes and lush lips. Danny had met his match when he met her. She'd been everything he thought he wanted in a woman.

Until he found her in bed with a millionaire. His bed. Their bed. In the end, Caryn had chosen that bastard's fiscal assets over Danny's brawn. Not that he minded that she loved his body, but that had been all she loved, and that had hurt him to his core.

Once he'd thrown the asshole out, Caryn had tried talking to Danny as she gathered her things. He could barely hear her over the roar in his head until she came to him and touched his chest with her fingers. She raked her nails just hard enough so he felt them through his shirt. Just the way he liked it.

"You're amazing, Danny," she cooed. "It's been a nice ride, but you and I don't want the same things out of life."

Danny wasn't enough for her and he never had been. He couldn't provide her with the trappings she thought she deserved, so he wasn't worth more to her than a good fuck. She'd marked her meal ticket and lured him to bed—Danny's bed.

Danny was sweating now, and he was pumping with so much anger that he could have very easily hurled the weights through the plaster wall. Fucking

Caryn. It wasn't just that she'd cheated on him. That would have been bad enough, but he could have weathered that a little bit better. Instead, she'd done it brazenly in his own home, and then emasculated him.

Suddenly Danny stopped pumping. Breathing hard, he let his arms hang straight, then lowered the weights to the floor. Shit.

Realization hit him and he cringed inside. Gorman hadn't deserved to be treated so roughly, even in a rigorous training exercise. Nor had he deserved Danny's rude remark. But Danny had let the memory of Caryn's betrayal get to him once again. It only took him an instant to understand why it was especially bad this morning. He'd walked in on them exactly one year ago today, and normally it was a day he tried hard to forget. But as he'd read the paper that morning, and started to toss the Lifestyle pages to the side for more serious fare, the photo splashed on the front page of the section stopped his heart: the millionaire bastard and Caryn in all their wedding finery. She'd married him. Well that didn't take long, but as usual, Caryn's timing sucked. Or maybe it was perfect, depending on who you asked. Danny should have just come straight to the weight room instead of sparring with Gorman. Better yet, he should have called in sick and let Bear do his own little client visit. That would have been safer for everyone. Instead, he'd taken let all of his residual anger over Caryn rise up inside him again, and taken it out on poor Gorman.

Danny sighed in frustration and put the weights back on their stand. Most of the Rockford team thought of him as big brooding Danny. To them he was just an ex-Marine hardass. But Danny knew better. And so did Bear. He hadn't been himself since Caryn had cheated on him. He just used the ex-military badass part to hide it, and not very well at that. Well, hell.

He had just enough time to shower before he and Bear had to head over to Captain Johnny's. As the water sluiced over him, he couldn't help but remember Caryn's touch on his body. He wanted that touch again—not hers, hell no. But he wanted to be touched like that again, and to feel wanted himself. But not used that way, not ever again.

Danny pounded the shower wall with the edge of his fist, since breaking his knuckles wasn't on the schedule today. Caryn hadn't wanted him for who he was as a person. She hadn't loved him.

"Fuck," Danny muttered to himself. He laughed bitterly as he shut the water off. Love wasn't something he'd ever have, because no way in hell would he give any woman the chance to trash his heart that way again, let alone get close enough to love him.

There were ways for him to satisfy his needs, and there were the kind of women who would help him with that and disappear, no questions asked.

Danny knew he should apologize to Gorman. He also needed to mend his reputation with the entire team, he thought as he finished dressing and started toward Bear's office. There were a lot of things he should do, but right now it was enough to drag himself to Captain Johnny's with Bear, who was already pulling on his coat when Danny walked into the office.

"Ready?" Danny asked needlessly.

Bear raised an eyebrow. "Almost. Just let me put the file into my briefcase, Hoss."

Danny stood waiting with his arms crossed.

"I see you're in a good mood," Bear continued. "Want me to drive? We might get there in one piece that way."

"But we might get there sometime this year if *I* drive." Danny didn't change his stance or his facial expression.

"Fine, but only because I want to look over Johnny's file again on the way," groused Bear.

Danny wasn't much for smiling, but he almost did then. Bear was all business on the surface, but he'd also been like a big brother to Danny since they'd served together. He'd never been able to B.S. Bear, but Danny knew the other man would always have his back.

"I promise not to speed—too much." Danny smirked to himself as he followed Bear out of the office.

Chapter Three

Fear immobilized Sioban for almost an instant too long. But the sound of a horn finally motivated her to bolt forward. As she did, she glimpsed the two men inside the pickup truck. The man in the passenger seat seemed anxious, as if he were afraid that his friend behind the wheel might have actually wanted to hit her. As for the driver, his deep scowl conveyed that he wished he had. But his glittering eyes weren't lost on her. She felt a chill—or was it a thrill?—as she ran onto the sidewalk. Von clutched Sioban's forearms and pulled her further toward the door.

"That was close!" Von huffed out a long breath.

"Yeah, well, Dale Earnhardt Jr. there could have slowed down a tad. Jerk!"

"And you were standing in the middle of the street, so what does that make you, then?" said Von as she dug into her purse for the keys to the bar.

Out of the corner of her eye, Sioban saw the truck screech to a halt in front of the loading zone at the lingerie store two doors down from the bar. Sioban startled when the driver jumped out. He slammed the door and powered toward them. And boy was he big. He had to be well over six feet tall. His hair was jet black and hung just past his collar. And his eyes...now that she could see more clearly, they were the sharpest cobalt blue she'd ever seen. And they were boring into her as he came barreling toward them.

Meanwhile, the man in the passenger seat had jumped out as well.

"Danny! Wait—"

Von had the outer security gate open and was working on the first of the three door locks when she heard the man's voice and looked up. Then she observed the terrifyingly big man just as he stalked up to them.

"Oh boy."

"Don't worry, I'll handle this brute," Sioban said, and squared her shoulders. She didn't have anything to defend herself with this time, but he'd have to go through both her and Von by the time all was said and done, plus there were witnesses. Hell, it appeared as if the other man might even defend them if it came to that. He wasn't as tall, or nearly as bulky, but maybe he could hold the beast down long enough for Sioban to get in a few good licks.

"Are you crazy?" the beast bellowed. "I could have killed you!"

"We're very sorry, we—" Von sputtered in apology.

"Really!" Sioban laid a hand on her cheek in mock astonishment. "Well, this isn't the Indianapolis Speedway, for your information." With hands on her hips, Sioban stepped up so close to the hulking man that she could practically feel his heart beating, surprising as it was that he actually had one. Her nose twitched as she got a whiff of his aftershave. She tried to ignore how sexy he was, or had the potential to be if he weren't such an ass, as she tilted her chin up to look him in the eye.

"Back off, Danny," the other man warned. Sioban allowed her eyes to stray from the beast for an instant, hoping that he wouldn't use the opportunity to snap her neck. She saw that the second stranger's eyes were deep brown and much kinder than the beast's. He appeared as though he had a few years on his friend, because his sable-brown hair, which was cut in a military style, was greying at the temples.

Sioban also noticed that Von was staring at him. *Snap out of it, sister, these two aren't here to ask us out to dinner.* She hoped her silent message would somehow reach her friend's brain.

"Danny, this nice woman was unlocking the bar, in case you didn't notice. Which means we're here to see her. So take it down a notch. Make that about ten notches."

Von just seemed confused, but Sioban narrowed her eyes and glared up at the beast again. *How ya like me now?* she thought.

A low growl rumbled from his chest, and he raked his hand through his gorgeous mane of hair. Sioban mentally kicked herself for wanting to reach up and do the same thing. "Sorry," he muttered in Von's general direction.

"Good boy." *Oops.* Sioban didn't know what made her say that. She couldn't help herself. There was something about the man that made her want to kiss him and smack him at the same time. Since smacking him was out, and kissing him was definitely out, she had provoked him instead.

"Sioban!" Von swatted her arm. The beast grimaced down at her again like he wanted to bend her over his knee and spank her. And damn if she wasn't turned on by that idea.

"Okay, let's just press the pause button here." Von was going into command mode. Sioban couldn't wait to see how the beast handled five feet six of pure authority. Von wasn't tall, but when she got serious, you'd better listen. Von had never ceased to amaze Sioban with the way she'd basically run Jimmy's club for him without him even realizing it.

"One: my friend here shouldn't have been standing in the street like that—should you, Sioban?"

Sioban sighed in exasperation. "No, I shouldn't have." She was rewarded by a snort from the beast.

"Two," Von continued, "you said you're here to see me? Want to explain?"

"Yes, absolutely." The beast's handler injected the voice of reason once more. "Look, can we start over?" Sioban made note of the fact that the man and Von were engaging one another's attention as if she and the beast were invisible. *Huh.*

"Of course we can. I'm Vonda Douglas." Von held out her hand and he took it warmly.

"I figured. I'm Barry Rockford. Folks call me Bear. I did the security for your father." He pointed at the door, where a Rockford Security sticker was stuck to the glass. "I'm very sorry for your loss, Ms. Douglas."

"Oh..."

"And this," he said as he clapped his hand on the beast's shoulder, "is my associate Danny Sheridan. He seems to be lacking in manners today, but generally speaking, he's a good guy."

Jesus. Black Irish. Sioban should have known, with a temper like that. Danny the Beast held out his hand to Von, and ignored Sioban altogether.

"Sorry, ma'am. I let my temper get the best of me."

Ya think?

"Well, we all have our bad days. No harm, no foul."

This was ridiculous. Sioban thought she just might puke if all these achey-fakey pleasantries went on much longer.

"Listen, can we take this little party inside? It's freezing out here."

"Excellent idea." Von turned to finish unlocking the door. "I'll put on a pot of coffee."

"Thank you. We appreciate it," said Bear.

Von made quick work of the locks and stepped inside, followed by Bear. It wasn't lost on Sioban how he placed a hand on the small of Von's back as they went in. Before she could step in behind him, the beast leaned down by her ear.

"It might not be a bad idea to ditch the elf boots and the raincoat for some real winter clothes."

Sioban fisted her hands at her sides. God, she wanted to slug him, even if she would break her hand in the process. He strode in front of her then and didn't even bother to hold the door open for her in his wake.

She stood there with her mouth open. The nerve of that guy! Not only was he a class-A jerk, but he had the gall to comment on her wardrobe when all he wore was a leather biker jacket. That stopped just above the pockets of his jeans. Which were perfectly filled out by his killer ass.

She snapped her mouth shut at that mental picture, along with a silent rebuke to herself. What was wrong with her? The guy was clearly an asshole. So why did he have to be so sexy? *Cool it, O'Rourke.*

And cool it she would. Danny the Beast might outweigh her by a hundred pounds or so, but when it came to acerbic wit, the Neanderthal was no match for her.

§

Danny stewed as he took a bar stool, while Vonda started up the coffee pot behind the far end of the bar. He narrowed his eyes as he glared at his boss, who seemed to be checking out the Douglas woman's backside quite intently. What was that about? Never mind Bear—what was wrong with him? He knew Bear was right to scold him for over-reacting. And hell, he hadn't meant to just walk in front of the redhead, nor had he meant to let the door close in her face. *Asshole.* But there was something about that

24

woman. He wanted to throttle her one second, and throw his jacket around her the next. It pissed him off that her coat was practically up to her ass, so the whole world could see those beautiful legs of hers. And she was Irish, God help him. He wanted to plunge his hands into that curtain of fiery red hair, and...*what the fuck? Snap out of it, Sheridan!*

Jesus, a woman like that would probably stab him in his sleep. But he couldn't stop himself from wondering why she hadn't come inside yet, which was followed closely by feeling irked with himself for caring about how cold she was out there. He didn't have to wonder for long. In the next instant, she burst into the bar. She strode forward, and, ignoring him completely, slammed her purse down on the bar top, and jerked the silly sunglasses off of her face.

"Von, is there a tea bag to be had in this place? You know I don't drink that sewage."

Danny ground his teeth together. She was a rude little cuss of a woman. Why had he even bothered concerning himself with her well being?

"Sure, hon." The Douglas woman grinned at her; she seemed to take her friend's temper in stride. "I got some tea as soon as I knew you were coming."

Danny kept still, afraid that if he said anything, it would be rude. Then she might slap him. Then he might have to kiss her.

In a flash, Vonda had placed a tea bag into a clean mug, filled it from the hot-water tap on the coffee maker, and put it on the bar in front of Sioban before she placed Danny's and Bear's coffees in front of them. She climbed onto a stool that had made its way behind the bar, and took a sip of her own coffee as she looked at Bear with anticipation.

Sioban dangled the tea bag up and down twice and took a loud sip of the scalding liquid. "Och, we have to get some proper tea, this stuff's rubbish."

Vonda just snickered and sipped her coffee. Danny, however, couldn't contain his irritation with the wench.

"Do you put that accent on just for insults?"

Sioban set her mug down carefully, although Danny could tell she wanted to slam it down, or throw the hot liquid into his face, one or the other. Then she flashed her green eyes at him, and he thought he might fall off of his stool. If she could have fired bullets out of them, he'd be a dead man. *Shit*.

"You know, for a Yank, you certainly have retained all the arrogance of your Black Irish ancestors. As for my *accent*, it's more pronounced when I'm *provoked*." She nearly spat the last word at him. Bear and Vonda eyed them like their unruly children.

"Settle down, you two," Vonda scolded, but she was looking at Sioban when she said it.

"Danny, may I remind you again that we're here to conduct business, and that means that we need to conduct *ourselves* in a professional manner?"

Danny met Bear's flashing eyes, and knew that he'd come close to angering his boss, who was also his friend, for real. But before he could apologize, Sioban spoke up.

"Well, if you'll excuse me, I'll just wander around a bit while you all conduct your business." Sioban picked up her mug again and walked to the other side of the room. Danny watched her intently as she sat at a table near the window, and turned her chair so she could see out of it. He could see her shoulders slump, and since her back wasn't completely turned on him, he thought he could see her face fall. God, he hoped she wasn't crying, or he'd never forgive himself. As irksome as she was, Danny actually respected her for not taking his bullshit. When he'd yanked on the ponytails of girls in school as a kid, he realized later that he'd liked them, but hadn't known how to go about letting them know. He'd met Sioban not even ten minutes ago, and that was hardly enough time to have any definite feelings about her one way or the other. All he knew was that she'd gotten under his skin the instant he saw her standing in the middle of the street. He hadn't had a woman under his skin in a long time, and even then, none of them had been like her, making him want to shout at her and hold her all at the same time.

Danny turned his gaze back to the bar where a mug of steaming coffee sat in front of him. He took a sip, and the strong liquid sobered him. Not only was he here to do a job, but he couldn't allow a woman, any woman, to get to him that way. Not today, not ever. Getting over Caryn was one thing. But letting himself get riled up over a strange woman was not an option, especially this one. Clearly, she was nothing but trouble.

Chapter Four

There was just enough mental space now between Sioban and the others as she sat apart from them, just enough quiet, for the nightmare of what had happened in L.A. to rush back in. The previous two days had been filled primarily with rest (she'd slept like the dead once she'd gotten to Von's), food, and catching up with Von, even though they'd only been apart for a couple of months.

But even the knowledge that Chicago was her new home now didn't change the fact that Sioban had to tell Von the whole story of what had happened, and soon. She had to face it. For the first time since she'd gotten on the plane, Sioban allowed herself to retrace the entirety of the problem at hand.

§

There had only been one strand of green garland, and it was just long enough to go around the television screen once. The red and gold ones Sioban had purchased to drape around the place were still in their packaging and lying in the dingy armchair where she'd tossed them days before.

Every strand of the dismal collection of lights had stopped working, either because she'd accidentally crushed a bulb under her shoe or because of a faulty wire. Who could be bothered to test the spare bulb in one hundred and twenty-five tiny little sockets? Sioban had simply yanked one strand from the outlet on the wall when she couldn't get the bloody thing to stop blinking. *Too bad you couldn't grind them up in the garbage disposal*, she thought grimly.

Burlesque Bad

Her last attempt at holiday cheer was to make popcorn and string it. After the third time she'd stabbed her finger with the needle, she gave up and devoured the whole bowl of it. Nothing was any fun anymore without Von. Sioban threw a handful of popcorn at the television as Jimmy Stewart yammered on about what a wonderful life it was.

"Did you put the tree up?" Sioban could hear the hope in Von's voice when they'd spoken the other day. Their official Charlie Brown Christmas tree sat on the coffee table. Poor Von. What did Sioban really have to complain about in comparison to her friend, besides the loss of a parent, which she remembered only too well. She and Von had talked often in the weeks since Von's departure. They were still there for one another and that should have been a comfort to Sioban. Vonda had all but begged her to come to Chicago, not just for Johnny Douglas's funeral, but to live, saying she had a plan for the bar she'd inherited from her father, and that they'd resume the pursuit of their dreams to be dancers, only without Jimmy and Club 29.

But Sioban had shut her down on both counts by explaining that things had gotten dicey for her at the club, making it hard to get away, even if Von did spring for the plane ticket. This only made Vonda worry more, so Sioban promised to try to get some paid vacation time out of Jimmy after the holidays.

She took the bowl, which now only held the un-popped kernels, and tossed it carelessly into the kitchen sink before returning to the living room. Lord, *Miracle on 34th Street* was starting up. Was there no end to this sugar-coated holiday nonsense? Sioban clicked off the TV, almost relieved that it was time to go to work.

Disgusted with herself, with Christmas, and with life, she pulled on her coat and snatched up her purse. As she strode through the living room, her purse on its long strap flew out behind her and toppled the Charlie Brown tree. The little red glass ball cracked against the coffee table and shattered. Sioban willed the tears that threatened to fall back into hiding.

She still hadn't found a replacement roommate, and so there was no one else besides her to care about the dishes she left in the sink. Or the bedraggled, broken little tree, or whether or not she ever got out of Club 29. *Nothing for it now*, Sioban thought bitterly. She turned her back on the mess inside and went out into the rainy night.

Club 29's main bar room was slick, well appointed, and posh, even, if you hadn't been there day in and day out ever since you could legally serve drinks to every horny man who walked in the place. Assorted black round and square tables dotted the main floor, each with a votive candle. There were four large rectangular tables along the outer perimeter for larger groups, and booths along the two walls that framed the stage. The stage lighting was dynamic and the sound system was technically on par with any contemporary club. Jimmy had even hired two experienced DJs in the city to run the music on alternating nights. It could almost pass for an upscale nightclub. Almost.

The poles, recently polished, still pierced the room at intervals from floor to ceiling. The women in the club were shackled to those poles with invisible chains by Jimmy's cruel and selfish design. So many of them were like Ava had been, desperate for work, their dreams, if they ever had them, dashed by the need to survive. And like Ava, Sioban would be back on the pole again at the end of her shift.

Burlesque Bad

Gone, or nearly so, were the shows that Von had choreographed. There was only one per night now. Gone as well was Von's protection of the girls. Jimmy had put them all back on the poles within days of Von's departure. It was only because of the extra two girls he'd let Sioban hire that she'd been able to claim the role of lead hostess. She'd proven to Jimmy how good she was at hostessing, and so only stepped down to do the one stage show each night, and to take the pole just before closing time.

"Yeah, they like you as hostess, but they also like to see that spicy ass swinging on a pole," Jimmy had said. "You're the only redhead I got."

So Sioban did as she was told without complaining, because she'd rather swing on the pole than go behind the curtains. Every single booth was now enclosed by heavy crimson velveteen curtains. They stayed tied back until one of the girls came and took the customer's drink order. Small circular stand tables had replaced the full-sized ones. The new ones were just big enough for a couple of drinks at most, and didn't get in the way of other activities that took place in the booth.

Along with curtains, Jimmy had installed semi-circular white leather couches in each booth. And once drinks were served, the gold ropes that held the curtains open were released and customers were not disturbed until they opened the curtains themselves to order more drinks or take their leave.

Sioban shuddered as she tidied up the hostess stand and settled in for the club to open. She hadn't wanted Von to know just how quickly things had gone downhill in the last two months, or how precariously close she was to the edge that Ava had fallen over headlong. But another part of her longed to pour her soul out to Von every time they talked, and beg Von to let her come to Chicago as she'd originally offered.

But pride, perhaps, kept Sioban where she was. When she did visit Von in Chicago, she wanted to bring her own success with her, not come dragging in like some stray cat with a sad story in tow. So stay she would, and somehow get out of Club 29 on her own, and not the way Ava had. Sioban took a deep breath of resolve, but as she exhaled, she caught Jimmy's eye from across the room. He gave her the grin of a man with no good intentions and winked at her before he turned and walked toward his office.

The club was teeming that night, but Sioban didn't notice. Or rather, she didn't care. The nights were just something to be survived. Not even the show excited her anymore. She did her best to maintain Von's standards. But the best girls had quit when Von left, and the new ones either had no aptitude for learning the choreography, or no desire to learn it. They got better tips working the poles (and the booths), and wasn't that what Jimmy had hired them for, anyway?

Now the trick was just for Sioban to do her time on the pole and get home. She went to other places in her mind when she had to dance on the pole. Like all the places Cyd Charisse had danced. Like the heaven she hoped Ava had finally found.

Sioban noticed Darlene coming toward the hostess stand to take over for her. Darlene had been at Club 29 almost as long as Sioban had, and might be attractive for all anyone knew, but there was no way to tell with the pounds of makeup she wore, and the tarantulas she put on as eyelashes. Then again, no one was looking at her face, were they? Sioban reminded herself.

She started to move off as Darlene stepped up, but when she glanced over at the poles, Sheila was already where Sioban was scheduled to be. For an instant, the promise of possibility surged through her: maybe she could go home early for once; maybe she didn't have to do the poles anymore; maybe...

"Jimmy wants you in his office. Right away." Darlene had a smug look on her face when she said it, as though she were at last rising from her station in life. *But what she doesn't realize,* pondered Sioban sadly, *is that no one rises, as long as they work for Jimmy.*

"What does he want?" Sioban asked.

"He didn't say." Darlene pretended to peruse the table chart on the hostess stand, and Sioban headed for the back, where Jimmy's office waited like a wolf's lair.

She tried to maintain her hopeful notions in spite of the prickle under her skin. And when she got to Jimmy's office, he wasn't alone. Sonny Coniglione sat in one of the guest chairs opposite Jimmy. They both looked up when she came in. Sonny turned in his chair and smiled lecherously at her.

Club 29 had become Sonny's favorite night spot when he was in town from Vegas. From everything Sioban had observed, Sonny was on his way to running his own part of the Vegas underworld. The way he dressed was flashy, but not quite classy. He always pulled out a big roll of cash, even when he was only buying one drink. And he and the meatheads he brought with him clocked more time behind the curtains than any other customers.

Sonny's eyes scanned her from head to toe as if she were a wench for sale. Sioban's heart galloped as an image of her mother flashed through her mind.

"Listen, Jimmy, if you're in a meeting, I can—"

"Come in, Sioban." Jimmy spoke in the voice he used when he intended to get his way. "I've kept you off the poles most of the time because you're special, Sioban. And you never want to give up something special to the masses; you save it for just the right time, and just the right place."

Sioban started to shake, and Jimmy's next words nearly brought her to her knees.

"Well, the time is tonight, here. My most special dancer for my most special customer."

For a moment, Sioban considered giving in to the dizziness and letting herself faint. But images of what they might do to her while she lay unconscious, and of never waking up again, like Ava, were as good as any smelling salts. She caught herself and gripped the back of the empty chair next to Sonny for support.

Jimmy seemed to move in slow motion toward her from behind the desk. He stopped next to her and grabbed her arm. "Don't fuck this up, sunshine," he whispered in her ear. "Not only is Sonny paying a lot for this—for you—but if he's happy, he'll start bringing his colleagues to the club. If he's not happy, then I lose. And if I lose, you lose. Big time. Understand?"

Sioban cringed at his hot, damp breath in her ear, but she nodded.

"Good." Jimmy released her arm, leaving a red handprint, and turned to Sonny. "Enjoy your evening— let me know if you need anything else."

Sioban couldn't bring herself to look at either one of them, but she felt Sonny's eyes on her. "Thanks, Jimmy. I've got everything I need right here."

Suddenly, Jimmy was gone and a new wave of panic overtook her. This situation was beyond dangerous. Living through the night now meant dancing for Sonny instead of on the pole. But if she did survive this night, Sioban vowed to herself then and there that she was never coming back to Club 29. The money be damned. She'd live out of her car if she had to, until she found another job. Until she found her dream.

"Let's get this party started, sweetheart."

Sioban flinched as Sonny's fingers grazed her arm. He raised the remote to Jimmy's stereo. Robin Thicke's "Blurred Lines" came out of the speakers. It didn't matter as long as she could move, find a rhythm, and escape in it. She faded mentally, falling into another place, becoming another person. She was Cyd Charisse. She was a girl dancing behind her mother across the living room floor. She was Ava in her Dublin dressing room.

Following her mind with her body, Sioban danced backward, away from Sonny and into the center of the room. She smiled at him as another woman, a starlet who still had the world to give through dance. But he only grinned his wolfish approval as her hips swerved out in time with the words that had caused such a media stir. He looked straight through Sioban, and that was fine with her. He'd never have her. A man like him could never have a woman like her, a woman like Ava had once been.

But Sioban made the mistake of closing her eyes and turning, turning. And then Sonny locked his arms around her from behind. He swiveled them both and walked them back toward the desk as he pressed himself against her.

Oh God, he was turned on. The reality of what was about to happen made her stomach drop. *A special dancer for a special client...paying a lot for this—for you...I have everything I need right here.*

Instinct kicked in and Sioban tried to break free. But Sonny was strong for his size, and apparently schooled in how to subdue women, because he quickly had her bent over the desk. "Where do you think you're going?" He pressed against her harder with his entire frame so she couldn't move, much less gain enough purchase to kick him or round on him.

"Did you think you were just gonna shake your hips at me a few times? Uh-uh. For five grand, we're gonna *dance*, baby. All. Night. Long." He yanked her hair to one side and pushed her down onto the desk with her neck in a vise grip before forcing her legs apart with one knee.

Mother Mary, what do I do...? Sioban couldn't have stopped the tears if she tried.

"Now be a good little girl, or I'll have to refuse payment and that will make Jimmy very, very unhappy," said Sonny through gritted teeth.

This was where the road ended for her. She might not die tonight, but she might as well.

Sonny moved his hips back just enough to slide his other hand between them and work his fly open. In another few seconds, he'd have to lift another fraction to pull his cock out of his pants.

God, girl, it's your only chance, Sioban told herself silently. It wasn't a very good one at that, but she had to try. She had to fight as hard as Von would want her to, and harder than Ava had.

With the side of her face plastered to the desk, Sioban rolled her eyes as far as they would go in any direction. She searched for scissors, a letter opener, anything she could use to attack Sonny. Through the blur of her tears, she spotted the marble panther next to the phone.

Their next movements seemed to happen very slowly and very quickly at the same time. Sonny edged back to pull himself out of his pants. She knew it would hurt, but Sioban jerked her head back and cracked Sonny in the chin, and tried to jam the spike

36

heel of her shoe into his foot. She missed with her heel, but the pain in his chin pissed Sonny off royally.

"Bitch!" He tried to shove her back down, but Sioban rested her elbow on the desk and held herself up enough to grab the panther with her other hand.

Now! Sioban rammed her backside into Sonny's cock hard enough to cause him discomfort. That bought her both the space and the instant she needed to twist around and smash the panther into the side of his head.

Sonny gave a long groan and slumped on top of Sioban as she now lay on her back across the desk. She pushed him off and he crumpled to the floor. She stood up and caught his stare. He seemed to register her standing above him, but was not able to respond in any way. Blood trickled from a gash on the side of his head. He groaned again before his eyes fell closed.

This was it. There was no more time. Sioban dropped the marble jungle cat on the floor. She wished she had time to wipe everything down like they did on TV, but that was a ludicrous notion.

Instead, she bent down and fished out Sonny's wallet from his pants pocket. When she only pulled out a few hundred, she searched the other pocket, where she found his standard roll of bills. She clutched it all to her bosom and ran to the door.

When Sioban opened the door ever so carefully, she saw Jimmy's thug of the month standing at the end of the hall. He peered over at her, and she narrowed the opening of the door until not much more than her face showed. When she crooked her finger at him, he lumbered over until he stood at the door. He craned his neck trying to see into the office.

"Hi, um, I need my purse from under the hostess stand." Sioban craned up too, until he looked down at her.

"What?"

"Listen, Mr. C. didn't bring any protection... He's ready to party, and Jimmy's gonna bust us all if we keep him waiting."

The thug narrowed his eyes at her, but turned and ambled off to the main room. Sioban closed the door almost shut and watched anxiously until he returned with her purse. She tried not to snatch it from him too quickly.

"Thanks...um, hate to ask you, but Mr. C. needs you to go and find his guy. He needs his pills—gotta wake things up, if you know what I mean."

"What the hell? Do I look like a servant to you?" The thug was pissed, but Sioban had to get him out of the hallway again so she could make her escape. So she turned on her Irish temper, which was a risk, but she couldn't think of anything else to do at the moment.

"Now see here, let me remind you what an important client Mr. C. is. He's quite indisposed at the moment. Do you really want me to tell him *you* said he should get off his arse and get his own damn pills?" He stiffened in irritation, but seemed to know she had him beat.

"I'll be right back," he grunted.

As she watched him amble back down the hall, Sioban shoved the money into her purse. She realized with regret that she'd have to leave her coat behind; it was still shoved under the hostess stand next to where her purse had been. It was a good thing she had the old suede one in the closet at home. As soon as the thug cleared the door to the main room, Sioban vanished.

Burlesque Bad

§

Rain continued to pour, and Sioban was soaked by the time she pulled up in front of her apartment building. She darted in, having barely been able to unlock the door with her hands shaking so badly. No time, she told herself as questions whirled through her mind like dervishes. What if Von wouldn't let her come to Chicago now? What if Sonny was dead?

She snatched her tiny suitcase out of her closet and shoved in some underwear and tee-shirts. Then she shed her clothes and crawled into a dry shirt and a short denim skirt. Lastly, she stuffed her feet into a pair of ankle boots, and pulled on the purple suede coat. She didn't give herself the chance to think about what she was leaving behind as she closed the door to her apartment behind her for the last time.

The rain finally slowed as Sioban drove to a nearby Holiday Inn. She parked in the lot behind the hotel. When she noticed a couple coming out of the back entrance, she asked them to hold the door open and ran inside, since she had no key card to let her in.

Once she made her way to the front lobby, Sioban stopped in the women's bathroom to straighten herself out. It took several paper towels to dry her hair and wipe the streaks of mascara from under her eyes. She looked awful, and it angered her all over again that the goon at the club hadn't seemed to notice her obvious state of distress or show concern for her. But for now, she was as safe as she could be, away from the club and from Sonny, until she reached her final destination.

She gave her hair one last pat-down and smoothed the wrinkles in her coat as best she could.

She strode out into the lobby to the curb in front of the hotel as if she'd just checked out. The attendant came over to her with a startling readiness.

"Airport, miss?"

"Yes, thank you." Sioban gave him an appropriate smile of gratitude, and otherwise tried not to look him in the eye. Thankfully, he waved over one of the two waiting cabs without further comment.

§

It was blessedly quiet at the gate. She'd sat there for two hours already, and must have looked over her shoulder fifty times to see if Jimmy or one of his "associates" had somehow caught up with her. It wouldn't be hard for Sonny to guess that she'd go to Von, and he'd probably send someone after her either way. But flying was the fastest way out of town. Besides, her car would never make the cross-country trek. The question of Sonny, and whether or not he was still alive, was too much for her to contemplate, and she shoved it aside. Nor could she dwell on how much of the cash she'd spent for a last-minute plane ticket. Now all that was left was to make a call. Sioban took a deep breath and dialed Von's number. It rang twice before she answered.

"Sioban? Is everything okay?" Vonda was groggy, but obviously concerned about having Sioban's number pop up in her caller I.D. so early in the morning.

"Yeah, it's me. Sorry to call you at this hour." *Do not cry. Do not cry.* "Von, I…"

"Spit it out. What's wrong?" Vonda's voice was still scratchy with sleep, but she was on high alert now.

"I need to leave L.A." Before Sioban could bring herself to form the next words, Von spoke the answer she'd prayed for.

"Come to Chicago. Now."

Sioban closed her eyes in relief. "My plane leaves in an hour. I land at O'Hare at noon." She heard shuffling, as if Von was getting out of bed.

"Jesus, I need coffee. Text me the flight info."

"Von, thank you..."

"Shut it, and get your ass on the plane. I'll be there when you land."

And she was. Then somehow they were in the living room of the house Johnny had left Von, and Sioban was holding a steaming mug of tea. Although she'd never be able to recall the ride from the airport, she supposed maybe they'd both been silent, just waiting to get to the safe haven of home—Von's, and apparently hers now too—where Sioban could finally let go.

The tears came in earnest then, and Vonda, who had been sitting across from Sioban, settled in beside her and hugged her tightly. Sioban couldn't even speak at first, but hiccupped on small sobs, as her best friend comforted her.

"Shh...it's going to be okay, Sioban. Really, it will."

Sioban looked at Vonda with wonderment.

"Why, Von? Why didn't you leave Club 29 sooner?"

"I just kept thinking...that it wouldn't be that much longer until I could have saved enough—until we could have saved enough—to get out and start something together. And I suppose part of me was afraid of whether or not I could really make it on my own, or even in someone else's legitimate burlesque club. Hell, I still don't know if I can make this work. But the bottom line is that I couldn't really just leave you behind. Until I had to."

Sioban gave that a thought before she answered. "I hope you won't come to regret that I came to you now."

Vonda pulled back and gripped Sioban by the shoulders. Her own eyes were filling with tears now. "Silly woman, don't you know how glad I am that you're finally here? And it's where you belong, I might add."

Vonda yanked a succession of tissues from the box on the coffee table and pushed half of them at Sioban, who set her mug down and honked her nose into one of them.

"Whatever happened in L.A.," Von continued, "we'll figure it out together. Just take a couple of days to settle down and then we'll talk. Okay?"

"Okay." Sioban dabbed at her eyes, and Von decided they both needed a break from reality, so she ordered pizza and put their favorite comedy, *Austin Powers*, in the DVD player. They both laughed until they cried again, and fell asleep bundled in blankets, Sioban on the couch and Von in Johnny's BarcaLounger. Just before she drifted off, Sioban finally noticed that one Christmas decoration remained in Vonda's living room: the official Charlie Brown Christmas tree sat perched on the mantle.

§

A movement in her peripheral vision brought Sioban back to the present, back to herself. It was subtle. She knew the three others were talking among themselves, but she heard the scrape of a bar stool and *felt* Danny shift his attention to her, an instant before she turned her head to look at him.

Sioban didn't want to believe the hint of kindness she saw in Danny's eyes. She couldn't afford to believe it. Not now, when this terrible thing loomed over her head. As tempting as it might be to let a man like Danny into her life, to let him help her and maybe even be there for her, the memory of what happened to Ava when she let a man in—too many men—crippled Sioban's faith. Never would there be trusting any man for Sioban. She arched her eyebrows at Danny in a challenging glare.

§

The minx, thought Danny. What on earth gave him the notion that there was any vulnerability under that crackly exterior, much less that she might actually need him for anything, he didn't know. But he was here to do a job for Bear and for the Douglas woman, who didn't seem to have the same scales for skin that Irish did. Beyond that, he didn't have time to keep that little tempest inside her teapot. If she wanted to square off with him, there was only one thing she had to do, in his mind: *Bring it, baby.*

Chapter Five

"Right, Danny?"

Bear's voice reminded him that he was supposed to be part of this conversation, which was essentially a client meeting. "What?"

"Jump in any time, now. I was just telling Ms. Douglas here about our services. We can just continue the new club under Johnny's contract."

"Club?"

"Yes, as I was just explaining to Mr. Rockford here—"

"—call me Bear."

"I will if you call me Vonda. Anyway, I was just explaining to Bear here that I'm renovating the bar. It's actually going to be a burlesque night club."

It took every ounce of control for Danny not to choke on his coffee.

"Right," continued Bear. "Aside from a few extras, the system configuration will be basically the same. And I can recommend some decent contractors for the renovation."

Danny nodded in agreement. It was about all he had to contribute at the moment. One thing was for sure, though: he was going to harass the hell out of Bear for the way he was looking at Vonda—*again*.

"That all sounds great, but can I afford this?"

"Like I said, we'll just continue under your father's contract," Bear assured her. "It's paid for several months still."

"But what about the extras you mentioned?"

Danny decided to finally add his two cents to the discussion. Clearly Bear was anxious about helping the woman. Maybe she needed extra convincing. "I'm sure we can come up with a plan that will work for you."

"That's absolutely right, of course. But I don't want you to feel pressured. Take a little time, just think about what we've talked about today. We're not going anywhere." *What you mean is,* you're *not going anywhere*, Danny thought.

"Thank you, I really appreciate this. At the very least, I have a place to start." Danny saw Vonda's gaze connect with Bear's before embarrassment took over. She tried to bury her blush in her mug by taking a long sip of her coffee. What the hell was going on around here?

"Well." Bear had always been good at wrapping things up, especially if there was tension or dead air. "Thank you for your hospitality, and for considering keeping us on as your security firm. We should get out of your hair now, and let you go about your business."

Danny and Bear stood simultaneously, and Vonda set her mug down to come around and see them out. As the three of them moved toward the door, Danny glanced over at Sioban. She didn't move, just continued to stare out the window. Bear noticed too, but was too courteous to say anything. They needn't have worried, because Vonda covered for her friend beautifully.

"She's...been through a lot lately," Vonda said in a hushed tone, then added more loudly, "Take care, gentlemen. I'll be in touch." She shook hands with both of them, and locked the bar door behind them.

Danny had barely gotten the key into the ignition before Bear started in on him.

"Are you going to tell me what's going on with you?"

Danny glanced at the lingerie shop next door. An emerald-green bustier in the upstairs window caught his eye. *That's the last thing I need to be thinking about right now*, he told himself as he pulled out into traffic. "Sure. You first, though. What's going on with you?" He did glance over at Bear then, who had an indignant expression on his face. "Heh. Yeah, I caught you staring at the Douglas woman. Here to help her and all. Very chivalrous of you, boss."

"I don't know what you think you're talking about, but let's just focus on the issue at hand here."

"Oh, there's an issue, to be sure. But it's not the only one." Danny took the opportunity that the red light afforded him and looked Bear dead in the eye. "Her father didn't have a contract with us, did he?"

Bear sighed and turned away from Danny. "Not on paper, no."

"Aha! I knew it!"

"Light's green—pay attention, will you?"

Danny laughed as he drove forward. He had the upper hand now.

"So what do you have to say for yourself?"

"What I have to say is," Bear said slowly, as he turned a leveling gaze back to Danny, "I know Johnny would have wanted things to go smoothly for his daughter. So I'm doing what I can to see that they do. Let's just leave it at that."

Danny wasn't stupid. There was only so far he could push, so he stifled a smirk and concentrated on driving. Clearly the woman had gotten to Bear on some level, and he could understand that, having had such a strong reaction to the other one. Danny realized that Bear could probably no more tell him why he was feeling so protective of the Douglas woman than Danny himself could explain why he'd behaved so badly around her friend. It was best to just leave the whole subject alone for now. He thought they could maintain a friendly silence for the rest of the drive back to the office, but he stiffened when Bear spoke again a few seconds later.

"Now are you going to tell me what the hell is wrong with you, or do I have to beat it out of you when we get back to the office?"

Danny's jaw ticced as he gritted his teeth. If he kept this up, he'd grind them to powder before this whole thing was over. His grip on the steering wheel tightened as he tried to think of what to say.

"Yeah, well, you know what they say about me around the office."

"Yes," Bear agreed, "I know all about that, and the fact that nobody wants to be around you much of the time is definitely worth having a discussion about. But right now, I want to know what's got you in such a bad mood that you're snapping at clients."

"Technically, that crazy redhead isn't our client."

"Danny, that's bullshit and you know—"

"It's the anniversary." Danny took a moment and let that hang in the air before he pressed on. "I found Caryn—in my bed—with that bastard Harrison Baxter. A year ago. Today."

Bear huffed out a breath. "Jesus, man. I'm sorry. It just wasn't on my radar."

"And she married him. Their wedding picture is splashed on the front page of the Lifestyle section this morning.

Bear whistled.

"Yeah, perfect timing as always. Not the best day to meet with a client."

"So it's just women in general you're angry with. Because I know you never would have acted that way around Johnny."

"Probably not. But like I said, you know what the team thinks, I'm just one grumpy asshole."

"Not really, but I'm starting to see that the two are related. I knew you were hurt by Caryn's cheating on you. I just didn't realize it was having long-term effects on you. It had to be hard to see that news in the paper this morning."

"I'm not one to chat about my feelings."

"I get it. But you know the team's got your back. And so do I. If you ever find yourself wanting to 'chat' over a few beers, no one's going to hold it against you."

"Roger that."

"In the meantime, you need to find a way to get along with her."

"What? *I* have to find a way? Did you not hear the mouth on that woman? Strutting around the place, flinging her hair around like that. I could just—"

Danny was brought up short when he realized that Bear was chuckling. When he looked at Bear, the man wore a grin as wide as Lake Michigan on his face.

"She's a handful. And part of you likes that about her, am I right?"

Danny cursed under his breath before ceding the point to Bear. "Maybe she's not all bad. If she would just not be so damn defensive and ornery about everything!"

"Well, you've got two choices. You can either just ignore her for the most part like Vonda does, or just give it right back to her when she dishes it out."

"That's what I did! I gave her as good as she gives out!" Danny knew he sounded like a little boy who'd had his train set taken away, but he couldn't seem to help it at the moment. Damn it, the woman wasn't even here and she was still driving him crazy.

"But you have to do it without tearing her down completely. Remember what Vonda said on our way out—that she's been through something lately."

"I know that, damn it!" Danny closed his eyes and tried to get a grip on himself. He knew Bear was right, if only from a business standpoint. He needed to find a way to conduct himself professionally. "I know," he said again more quietly. "I'll work on keeping things under control."

"That's all I ask," said Bear, who, Danny could see, was still grinning at him.

"That woman's trouble."

"I'm sure she'll come around once she's dealt with whatever happened to her. But even if she doesn't, you've got to be a man about this."

"Right." There was no use arguing about it. Bear was right: he and Danny had a job to do, and no matter what he thought about Sioban, he couldn't let anything get in the way of that.

"Come on, I'll order in lunch for us, and we can start going over the schematics of the bar."

They got out of the car, and Danny followed Bear inside with the mission—and its women—heavy on his mind.

§

Sioban heard Von lock the door behind Danny and Bear, and she knew she'd have to answer to Von now for her ornery behavior, and the trauma of the last few days was still no excuse to be downright rude to someone.

But when she rose and turned toward the bar, Von was pouring another cup of coffee for herself. "Hey there," she said to Sioban as she looked up. "How about bringing your mug over here for another

49

cup of sub-standard American tea?" Von's smile restored some of her confidence.

"So, you're not cross with me, then, for being so bitchy to the Hardy Boys?"

"I didn't say that," Vonda giggled. "Your behavior was completely uncalled for. But I thought we could talk about it like civilized friends over our soothing hot drinks, instead of me dragging you through the ringer."

"Drop a pinch of schnapps in that swill you call tea, and you've got yourself a deal." Vonda winked at her, and added a splash of the stuff to Sioban's mug, and then a splash of Bailey's to her coffee.

Sioban settled herself on the stool where Danny had been sitting as Vonda eyed her over her own steaming mug of coffee.

"I know I've got to tell you everything."

"For now, why don't we start with what gives with the guys from Rockford today. There just didn't seem to be any rationale behind you lashing out like that against Danny—"

"It's just the stress of everything—"

"—and not Bear."

Well, shite, Von had her there, now didn't she. "You're right. It's really got very little to do with what happened to me in Los Angeles," confessed Sioban. "Except for the fact that I'm still in a state of emotional exhaustion, and the way he barreled around the corner in his assault vehicle, and nearly ran me down, *on purpose* if you ask me. And not even taking into consideration that I might be otherwise traumatized in some way, as if I stand in the middle of the bloody street as a daily habit. On top of that, insulting my personal appearance, my clothes! But then—the way he pushed in front of me going into the bar, and let the door drop right in my FACE! That's it. That's the end. Just let him try and show his arrogant face in here again!"

For a brief instant Vonda just stared at her as if she'd completely lost her mind. Well, it was clear, wasn't it? Sure, maybe she'd been a little cross, but the man was a brute, a complete bastard...and why in Christ's name was Von laughing at her? Sioban realized in that moment that she'd not only stood up in the heat of her indignation, but had accidentally slopped some of her tea on the bar.

"Oh. My god." Von was still laughing at her as she wiped up the spilled tea with a bar towel. "This is worse than I thought."

"What do you mean? I admit I was feeling cranky this morning, but HIM—he was completely out of line!" Sioban vocalized what she'd just been thinking a moment ago in the midst of her tirade, in hopes she'd get some empathy from Von.

"It's true, he gave as good as he got. I'm not condoning his behavior, but both of you need a time-out. I wonder what Bear makes of all of this?"

Sioban knew her mouth was hanging open, but she didn't quite know how to respond.

"I don't know what we're going to do with you two," Von concluded.

Then it came to her. In order for Sioban to derail this line of thinking that was certainly pointing to an outrageous conclusion on Von's part, she'd have to shed light on her friend's own behavior that morning.

"If anything, I think I should be worried about what to do with you."

Von stared at her incredulously. "I beg your pardon?"

"Oh sure, don't think I didn't notice. Mr. Rockford's brute of a sidekick and I might have kicked up a bit of storm, but you were quietly pouring the coffee all hostess-like, and you were totally enthralled with the ins and outs of alarm systems and contracts—or was it his brown eyes you were getting lost in, then?"

"Well, I wouldn't say I was enthralled, exactly, and it had nothing to do with his eyes!"

"Uh-huh. Whatever you say... Why are you so trusting of him anyway? It's not like you to make rash decisions."

"It's more like Johnny trusted him. And I haven't signed on the dotted line yet, I still intend to do some investigating. I mean, they did drive all the way over here to meet with me in person."

"Right." Sioban knew she'd ruffled her friend, but it wasn't enough to throw her off the path for long.

"And don't 'right' me, missy. Don't think you're going to distract me from the issue here, with your fantastical observations."

"'Fantastical' is not a word."

"It is actually. But the point is, if indeed I do keep Bear—Rockford Security—on, in all likelihood, Danny will be working very closely with him on every aspect. Which means he will be showing his 'arrogant face' around here, as you put it, quite a bit. Which means you two are going to have to find a way to get along. Besides, he seems to know a lot about the business; he had some intelligent input to offer during our meeting."

"Okay, okay. I'll play nice. But Rockford better put a muzzle on him before they come back again."

"I'm sure Bear is having the very same conversation with Danny."

Sioban only snorted in response, leaving room for Vonda to get in one last dig. "Glad to know you'll try to behave—no matter how much you like him."

"What?—like him? Are you *mad*?"

Sioban's hackles rose again, even though she knew Von was only teasing her. Vonda threw up her hands in mock surrender.

"Okay, sorry, enough about you and Danny—for now. How about the nickel tour of this place?"

"Much better."

Von washed out the mugs in the small kitchen off the bar while Sioban took in the space in amazement. Even though the bar had been closed for over a month, and dust had definitely gathered, she could see the love that Johnny had put into the place. The furnishings weren't the newest, but the bar top still shone as if you could eat right off of it.

As she looked around the room, the photos on the walls seemed to whisper a history that was full of life. There was comfort to be found here, and though Sioban couldn't quite grasp Von's new vision for the place, she knew that there would be just as much love poured into it as Johnny'd had when he first bought the place. Sioban caught sight of one photograph in particular of a very glamorous woman. It hung on a narrow column of a wall just to the left of the bar. She had crossed to it and carefully taken it off of its hook to examine it more closely when Von stepped up beside her.

"That's Sally Rand. She was one of the best burlesque dancers back in her day. She came in here a couple of times, long before I was born." Sioban looked up at Von for a sign that there was more to this story than she was telling.

"Oh no, did your dad…"

"God no, nothing like that. He was completely in love with my mother. But he'd seen some of Sally's shows long before he got married. He just always admired her. I'd taken a bunch of different styles of dance lessons—ballet, tap, even jazz. I came close to finding what I wanted to pursue, but it wasn't until I saw her picture that I really knew."

"She inspired you the way Ava inspired me. Until Ava veered off the path, that is."

"Exactly."

Sioban's heart filled with gratitude as she hung the photograph back on its hook. How lucky was she, how lucky were they both, to have met, and now to have the opportunity to help each other's professional dreams come true?

"Come on then, show me how we're going to bring this place back to life." Sioban took her friend's arm as they went around the room together. Von showed her where she wanted to build out a stage, and described a color scheme that included blue velveteen curtains and cushioned chairs. For one instant, Sioban's stomach dropped at the memory of the curtains in Club 29, but she knew Von would never entertain a use for them other than to adorn the windows. There were no booths here. And there would be no mobster clientele.

"I've got enough from what Johnny left me to do most of what I want, and I have another small loan that I took out on the house for the rest—I have plans for the house too. And last but not least, the name: it's going to be called The Velvet Room."

Sioban had let her mind drift again, to possibilities she hadn't thought about in years. The possibility that maybe she could finally become the dancer she'd always wanted to be nearly overwhelmed her.

"Earth to Sioban. Did I lose you again?"

Sioban's eyes had filled with tears again. Lord, was she ever going to stop crying?

"No, you haven't lost me, girl. I'm right here. Standing in the Velvet Room with my best friend, and not believing that I've been given this incredible chance. That *you've* given it to me."

"I'm so glad you're here. I couldn't do this without you, and I wouldn't want to do this with any other friend at my side." Von hugged her tight again. "I don't know about you, but I'm starving. I think we should have lunch, and do some shopping for some decent winter clothes for you."

"You won't get any arguments from me. But can't we start next door?" Sioban fluttered her eyelashes at Vonda playfully. She'd noticed the lingerie shop next to the bar right before Danny came careening toward her in his black truck.

"I should have known you'd want to go there first. Fine, but we're only staying a few minutes."

Excitement filled Sioban as she ran and grabbed her coat and purse. At least if she had to bury herself in sweaters and such, she could have fun with what went on underneath.

Chapter Six

Lady Eve's was the polar opposite of Captain Johnny's in every respect. Victorian accents and a pale plum wash of paint contrasted greatly with the dark-hued browns and greens of Johnny's pub. And certainly the salty old guys who stopped in for a pint would never be caught dead sniffing around such a place as Eve's, although if they were honest, almost all of them had slithered in there to buy a make-up gift for a wife or girlfriend they'd angered. For such occasions, Eve carried every manner of gift: from the sexiest and classiest French lingerie to a variety of imported toiletries and cosmetics, and even a small section of stationery and couture chocolates.

As Sioban followed Von into the main room on the first floor, she almost wanted to take her boots off and squish her toes into the thick lavender-colored carpet. There seemed to be a lingering lavender scent in the air as well. Sioban was in awe and hardly knew where to start first.

The first displays they encountered were of nightgowns of various styles and lengths, all extremely elegant. They came to teddies and undergarments next. A large modern counter with two registers stood in the center of the room about three-quarters of the way back, and the remaining space around it was devoted to soap and perfume on one side and stationery on the other, all the way to the back wall. A modest dressing room was off to the right, with four cushioned chairs outside it.

A broad staircase led to the open-plan second floor. Later, Sioban would lose herself on this naughtier, racier floor, which was decorated in deeper purples with splashes of animal prints here and there, including the throw pillows on a plush deep-purple couch in the center of the room, which faced the back, where another dressing room lurked. The second floor housed all manner of bustiers, more exotic fragrances and body oils, a small chocolate salon, an espresso machine, and other stationery more fitting to the tone.

"This place is nothing short of amazing," cooed Sioban. "Please tell me you are getting some pieces here for future costumes."

"It is amazing, isn't it? I'm not sure I can afford anything in here for myself, let alone multiple dance costumes, but I should definitely see if Eve has any lower-end distributors she can steer me toward."

As they moved through the first floor, Sioban fingered every garment within reach. She breathed in, and the lavender scent gradually gave way to a spicier mixture that at first seemed to be coming from the soaps and perfumes as they moved further toward the back. But suddenly she caught sight of a small woman pouring boiling water into an infuser over loose tea that had the appearance of potpourri, and then dropping a cinnamon stick into it. The woman herself seemed just as exotic, with glossy jet-black hair cut into a '30s bob with bangs. It had one white streak in the front. She was casually dressed in black pants and a chic fuzzy yellow sweater.

"Welcome, darlings, I've almost got our tea ready," said the tiny woman, without even looking at them. She couldn't have been over five feet tall, thought Sioban.

"Hey, Eve." Vonda smiled knowingly, and winked at Sioban.

"But how did she—"

"I am all-knowing, my love," said Eve in a smoky voice that didn't seem to fit her petite frame. She finally looked up at her and met Sioban's eyes with her glimmering dark ones, before she laughed loudly. "All right, I confess, I see this darling girl at least every other day. I also knew she'd be bringing you to the bar today, so the odds were in my favor that you'd be by here. As for the timing, it's just my good luck that I'd boiled the water right when you girls walked in."

This was a woman Sioban liked instantly, which was saying a lot, given her zero-trust policy toward most individuals. And it wasn't just that Von knew her. Eve had a verve and a sass that very much reminded Sioban of her mother. But she also exuded a motherly love that Sioban realized came through in every aspect of the store, and in the way she made tea for those who wandered into it.

Eve placed three mugs in varying shades of purple onto an ornate white tray, along with the necessary condiments from the cabinets and mini fridge below the tea table, and a few cookies and chocolates. Sioban and Vonda followed Eve to another small table that stood near the plush chairs outside the dressing room.

"How are you today, darling?" Eve asked Vonda, as she held the cookie plate up for the girls to choose a confection.

"It's not a bad day—at least not as bad as some have been, especially before Sioban arrived."

Even the tea had a slight taste of lavender, and rose, too, if Sioban wasn't mistaken. And even though she was used to much stronger stuff, she was quite enjoying it. She closed her eyes and inhaled the comforting vapors. When she opened them, she found that Eve was looking at her again, this time with great tenderness.

"Ah, yes. Sioban. I hear it's been quite a journey for you."

This caught Sioban unawares. Maybe the woman really was all-knowing, even though Sioban hadn't even told a fraction of the whole story to Von yet.

"Not to worry," said Eve. "I don't know that much. I'm just glad you're here with our Vonda now; it's bound to be as good for her as it is for you."

"Heck, she hasn't even told me everything yet," added Vonda.

"All in good time. It takes a minute or two to get settled into a new situation." Eve glanced surreptitiously between the two of them.

There was a moment of silence as they all sipped on the rose-and-lavender tea before Eve spoke again. "So what brings you in today?"

The all-knowing woman now seemed to be lacking in information. "Von wants costumes for her new show," Sioban blurted before she gave herself a chance to think about what she was saying.

"Actually," Vonda said, glaring at Sioban, "this is the first stop on a much-needed shopping trip for Sioban. What she really needs is winter gear, but I knew I'd never hear the end of it if we didn't stop by today."

Sioban sank back a little into her chair and tried to hide behind her teacup. She'd never be able to afford anything in here, but there was no harm in getting Eve, who clearly cared a great deal about Von, to think about how she could help with costumes. The problem was that Sioban had assumed that everyone in Von's circle of friends here knew about her plans for the old bar.

"Well, this sounds intriguing," said Eve. "I knew you'd be renovating next door, Vonda dear, but this sounds too delicious. Do tell."

Suddenly it was Vonda who acted as if she were being chased by a story she didn't want to tell.

"It's a work in progress, Eve. I'll tell you more when I know more. Listen, we were on our way to lunch, anyway. I promise we'll come back soon, but we really need to get going."

"Nonsense," answered Eve, much to Sioban's relief and delight. "I'll order lunch in for us from that nice little Thai place around the corner. There's plenty of time to buy boots and sweaters. Besides, I know little Sioban here is anxious to get into something that can go underneath her new winter wardrobe." Eve winked at Sioban. She didn't mention costumes or Vonda's plans again, and Sioban gave her credit for that. Eve clearly knew when to pull back and when to push her motherly guidance. She was also extremely observant, and there was a chance she'd collect more information today simply by watching and listening. It seemed everyone had a story to tell, perhaps even Eve herself. They'd all have their turn. Sioban knew hers was coming that night with Von, but Von would have to open up to the world about her vision for the club. As difficult as it was, the only way to get support was to tell people what you were up to—in other words, to make yourself vulnerable.

Before Vonda could protest, or Sioban could get too lost in her tea-induced reverie, Eve turned in her chair and called up to the second level.

"Chy, darling, can you come down, please?"

The most interesting, and quite possibly the most exotic, young woman Sioban had ever seen appeared at the top of the staircase. She'd obviously been moving stock or working on displays, because she wore jeans and a tee-shirt, and held scissors in her hand. But she looked like a princess from a foreign land. Her hair fell from a natural side part in a glossy black sheet nearly down to her bottom. Her skin was a dark nut brown, so naturally lovely, and not from a tanning booth at all. And her eyes...even from that distance, Sioban caught the drama of them. They were blue-grey, a shade that she'd never seen in a human being, or any living creature for that matter.

"I thought I heard voices down there. Hey, Vonda." Her smile was a pretty brilliant white, too, Sioban noted.

"Hey, Chyenne," said Vonda. "How are you today, sweetie?"

"I'm good. Did you need me, Eve?"

"Yes, darling, just set aside whatever you're doing. We're going to order in lunch, and I need you to cover for a few minutes while we eat. I'll get yours as well, and you can eat once I've done."

"Okay, I'll be down in a sec."

Eve had barely put the tea things in the back sink to wash and retrieved the takeout menu from the Thai place before Chyenne came bounding down. She'd exchanged her tee-shirt for a black long-sleeved blouse with rhinestone buttons, and her tennis shoes for black flats. She looked wonderfully casual-chic. Once they'd all chosen what they wanted to eat, Eve led them to the back while Chyenne took up her post at the front counter, where she placed the phone order.

Even the back of Eve's store was charming. A round wrought-iron table sat to one side of a small kitchenette. The cabinets were painted in the palest periwinkle, and had fleur-de-lis fixtures and knobs. Eve pulled out sparkling water from a second mini-fridge as they all settled in and waited for the food to arrive.

"Thanks for lunch, Eve. You really don't have to do this." Vonda sighed as she sat back in her chair. She put up a good front, but Sioban could still see the strain and sadness around her eyes. "You've been spoiling me ever since I've been back."

"It's my job to spoil you. What kind of friend would I be to Johnny if I didn't?" Aha, thought Sioban, when she saw a shadow pass over Eve's face for the first time. She did have a story. Her affection for Vonda had even deeper roots in the one she'd shared with Johnny.

The three of them made idle chitchat in the short time it took for the food to arrive. Though Von's house wasn't in delivery range of the Thai restaurant, Sioban confiscated one of the menus. The food was fantastic, and if they were to be spending hours at the bar, or rather the club, over the next several weeks, Sioban would be eating Thai food quite often, she decided.

True to a shop-owner's work ethic, Eve finished her lunch in ten minutes. "You two relax and enjoy. I want to relieve Chy so she can enjoy her food as well. I think she's dying to meet Sioban in earnest and chat with you both as well."

Eve whisked out of the room, and almost as quickly, Chyenne peeked her head through the crystal beads that hung in the doorway. "Okay if I join you?"

"Come on in, girlie, we don't bite. At least I don't," Sioban joked.

"Hey, I've never bitten her, have I, Chy? But I might bite you, if you keep it up. You are so impish today!"

Chyenne demurred and came to the table. She swept her curtain of hair over her shoulder as she peeked into the containers of food.

"Oh, I love this one—bo satay." She extracted the remainder of the chicken dish with pineapple, spinach, and peanut sauce onto an empty styrofoam plate.

"Sorry, darlin'," said Sioban. "If I'd known you liked it, I wouldn't have scarfed it down like a lonely truck driver."

Sioban and Vonda exchanged a mischievous grin.

"Isn't it great? Peanut sauce is the best," said Chyenne around a mouthful of food.

Sioban smiled at Chyenne. She remembered the boys at her grammar school talking with food in their mouths at the lunch table. She'd thought it was a disgusting habit back then. But somehow when this little chickadee did it, she looked adorable. Maybe it was because you could see the soul in her eyes. The gold flecks in her irises twinkled with her delight, but there was also a depth to their blue-grey that was beyond her years. Too late, Sioban realized she was staring.

"Wha?" Chyenne grabbed a napkin and dabbed at her mouth with it before she swallowed.

"Oh, nuthin', darlin'. Just got lost in my own head for a moment."

But Chyenne guessed what had their attention. "Sorry, I'm just really hungry. My mom would smack my mouth if she saw me eating this way."

"I know what you mean," Von chimed in. "My mom wasn't around growing up, but heaven help me if my dad caught me forgetting my manners. But don't worry, you're among friends here."

Chyenne gave a soft laugh. "Thanks...Miss Eve says she misses your dad—um, she says the whole neighborhood does."

"Yeah." Vonda pressed her lips together and started to clear her and Sioban's plates. "We all do."

"Well, um, I know we have a lot of shopping to do today," said Sioban in an effort to move past the moment. "But I'd really like to see what's upstairs before we leave."

"Ooooo!" Chyenne started waving her hands up and down in front of her face as if she'd just swallowed a cup of lava. "Omigod, there's something I have to show you, Sioban. You will *love* it."

"But what about your lunch, sweetie?" implored Vonda. Chyenne waved her off as she covered her plate.

"I can always heat it up later. This will be way more fun—come on!"

Before they could protest, Chy had run out of the room, beads dangling in her wake. Clearly she expected them to follow.

"Well, come on, Von, let's not keep the child waiting." Sioban didn't even try to contain her excitement as she practically ran up the stairs to the second level, followed by a smiling Vonda.

§

All Sioban could do was stare. She didn't believe her eyes, nor the feelings evoked by seeing herself in the bustier, which was far from your average department-store lingerie. It was a work of art. The green was a rich emerald satin that shone like the Irish countryside beneath black velvet pinstripes and buttons of green faux crystals. The sweetheart neckline perfectly accented her décollatage, and was lined in ruffles in the same sumptuous black velvet. Decorative green crystal buttons dotted the front in a shimmering straight line. The back, she observed when she turned and looked over her shoulder, was her favorite lace-up structure, with black velvet ribbon ending in a luscious bow at her rump. Sioban wore a pair of black lace hose with a small, elegant floral pattern. Chyenne had insisted that she needed to try on the bustier with hose to get the full effect, and Sioban had made it clear that she'd be buying them. After all, at least she could afford the hose, and they would remind her of the glory of what she could have when she got on her feet financially.

Chyenne was in a perfect state of glee having shown her the beautiful piece. Vonda just grinned and shook her head. Eve had joined the party and was hiding her knowing smile as she held her fingers up to her lips.

Sioban realized that she probably would have stood there in a state of awe for the rest of the afternoon if Von hadn't cleared her throat pointedly and loudly. Sioban whipped her head around and met their amused gazes.

"Holy fucking Christ, I look amazing, don't I now?"

At that they all dissolved into peals of laughter.

"I knew you'd love it!" squealed Chyenne. "You've got to have it."

Sioban reached for the price tag on the side, already knowing it was well beyond her financial reach at the moment.

"And no doubt I will someday, but for now I'm only going to have it in my dreams," she sighed. "But go ahead and ring me up for the hose. I think I'll wear them home—they'll keep my dreams alive."

Chyenne was crestfallen as she started to unlace the back of the bustier. Eve glanced sideways at Vonda, who returned a knowing glance to her, before she stepped over to her best friend.

"Listen, sweetie, I know we haven't had a chance to discuss anything yet, but now is just as good a time as any to tell you that I don't just want you to dance at the new club—I want you to be my talent manager and co-choreographer."

"What?" Sioban stared at her friend intently. "I... Oh my God, Von." She could feel the tears trying to push their way out from behind her eyes.

"And I'm putting you on the payroll starting today."

Sioban just kept staring at her.

"Which means, you can get the bustier—I'll deduct it from your first paycheck."

"Oh Vonnie, it's too much, I couldn't...I can't."

"You can, sweetie, and you should."

"She's right," Eve chimed in. "Obviously you've been through a lot lately. You need to treat yourself to something wonderful—it's part of your new beginning. Besides, you're Vonda's family now, so I'll give you the family discount. That way you might get to keep a little bit of that first paycheck."

"I don't know what to say, except thank you. Thank you both." Sioban pulled away from Chyenne long enough to hug Vonda tightly.

"So you're getting it?" asked Chyenne with ends of the ribbon still in her hands. She didn't bother waiting for confirmation. "Yes!"

Downstairs, Chyenne rang up the sale at the discount Eve had specified. Sioban dabbed at her eyes again when she read the reduced amount, but she chattered animatedly with the girl as Chyenne boxed the bustier with all the trimmings as if it were a gift.

"Seems to me like your young protégé has found a new best friend," said Vonda.

"She certainly has." Eve paused and gave Vonda a penetrating look. "A club, you said? Choreography? Well, good for you. I can't wait to hear more about what you have planned. But we will be talking soon, and you will let me help you with whatever I can. You know how I feel...felt about your father. And how I feel about you."

"I know. I wasn't trying to keep you in the dark. I've barely roughed out the plans in my own mind. But yes, we can talk."

"You know, I can do some brilliant costumes for you."

"Oh, no doubt," Vonda laughed. "But even with your generous discount, I don't think I could swing that."

"We'll work something out." Eve winked at her.

Sioban smiled inwardly. It seemed that more than one person was willing to "work things out" with Vonda to see that her dreams finally came true.

Chapter Seven

They were still laughing as they emerged from the highly polished passageways of the mall into the darkening parking garage. As for Sioban, she'd have a hard time later remembering everything that had them in stitches that afternoon. There was the elderly lady in Victoria's Secret who was absolutely bored, she'd declared, with the lack of red lace undergarments; then there was the poor kid in the video game store who'd been so flustered by the combination of Von's beauty and Xbox acumen that he nearly peed himself putting her *Call of Duty* 4 into the bag. Oh, but they couldn't forget how Sioban had stumbled into a book display and sent the whole thing crashing to the floor—they'd scrambled out of the store giggling and snorting before any employees could see what had happened.

Sioban sighed as she settled herself into the passenger seat of Von's car. God, it had been fun, almost enough to give her hope of outliving and outrunning the mess she'd left behind in L.A. But even better, she'd surprised herself with how much she'd enjoyed shopping for her new clothes. She still had some of the money she'd left L.A. with, and she didn't feel shy about spending it, since Von was officially putting her on the payroll within the next week. It was amazing how much a few new outfits could raise a girl's spirits. And even though they'd only been shopping for regular underwear in Victoria's Secret, since Eve only carried specialty items, Sioban had relished choosing new bra-and-panty sets in deliciously bright colors. She smiled as she thought of the purple set she'd actually worn out of the store. Though it was buried under her new jeans, turtleneck sweater, and three-quarter-length down coat, Sioban felt sassy, sweet...beautiful.

"What are you grinning about?" asked Vonda as she put the car into gear. Though they'd gone to the mall with the intent of getting Sioban a more suitable winter wardrobe, Vonda hadn't been shy about getting things for herself. She'd told Sioban that she'd been so preoccupied with settling Johnny's affairs and making plans for the Velvet Room that she hadn't had time to put much effort into her wardrobe. As a result, she'd come away with almost as many sweaters as Sioban had, along with two new pairs of jeans. And they'd both indulged in new leotards and dance-workout clothes. It was a wonder the trunk closed with all the bags in it.

"Oh, just pleased as punch with my new jeans. And sweaters. And coat. And boots."

"Yes, but which pair?"

Sioban had chosen a fun but practical pair of waterproof boots, along with a pair of black suede dress boots, and a third pair of casual brown leather flat boots, which she'd worn the entire afternoon.

"All three!" Sioban laughed again. "Now don't pretend you didn't score some major swag today too, missy."

"You're right. It does feel good, doesn't it? I didn't even realize how much I needed new underwear. Too bad there's no one to enjoy seeing me in it but me," said Vonda.

Sioban caught her eye, and it was one of those moments when each knew what the other was thinking, but neither wanted to say it out loud.

"You never know—keep hope alive," quipped Sioban, with a raised eyebrow.

Vonda narrowed her eyes. "I will if you will."

Sioban smirked at her and looked out the window. "Now there's where I should be right now," she said as they passed a gym. "Even though it's only been a few days, my leg muscles are tighter than rubber bands."

"I'll do you one better," answered Vonda as she steered the car into the parking lot of a strip mall. "We'll get to the gym too, but what you really need is to stretch and do some real dancing. So I'm taking you to a class with one of my favorite teachers."

"What? Why didn't you tell me?"

"I was afraid you'd chicken out."

"Are you kidding me? After Club 29, I'm dying to do something like this, body and soul. Plus, we get to break in our new dance stuff."

"Yeah, I thought you'd like that. Here we are." Vonda brought the car to a stop in front of a modest studio named Dance with Iliana. Sioban swallowed hard. *Iliana Gregoriev. Sweet Jesus.*

"Yes, it's her," Von continued, as if to read her mind. "Another reason I didn't tell you, and another reason I was afraid you'd chicken out."

All that could be seen from the front was a reception area, and a door, out of which came a young ballerina who was probably eight or nine at the most.

"So are we taking up kiddie ballet then?" asked Sioban as they stepped out of the car, in an attempt to calm her nerves. She followed Vonda around to the trunk so they could dig through their bags to get at their leotards.

"Hardly," laughed Vonda. "Iliana doesn't even teach the young girls any more. She says she doesn't have the patience, so her staff takes the children's classes. Ana still works with professional adult dancers, though, mostly jazz and modern."

"Oh God, am I even a professional? She'll probably send me back to the kiddie class."

Vonda grabbed Sioban's elbow. "Hey—I don't want to hear that kind of talk from you ever again, do you hear me? The venue doesn't make the dancer—you are not Club 29. Got it?"

"Got it." Sioban said it because she knew it was what Von wanted to hear. And she wanted to believe it herself. And when they got inside and made their way to the changing rooms, Sioban wanted to move, needed to move again. But at her core, she was terrified. This was the real dance world, the one she'd wanted to be a part of for so long, but one she still wasn't sure she belonged in.

It didn't help to see all the beautiful dancers they passed in the hallway. They all seemed so confident and poised.

Just as Sioban considered fleeing the studio, Von led them into a small, empty dance room.

"Class starts in fifteen minutes. We can get warmed up in here," said Vonda.

Sioban avoided the bar in front of the mirror and took to the floor to stretch. The fluorescent lights suddenly made her appear washed out and pale, or perhaps fear had just drained the color from her face and left the building with it. It would have been silly to have her back to the mirror, so Sioban put the mirror at her right side. She was doing a good job of ignoring her reflection until the door opened just to the right of the mirror and a tallish older woman wearing a red scarf over most of her head like a turban and a black leotard and tights came in. It had to be Iliana. Her bare dancer's feet made no sound on the floor as she made her way toward them—or rather, toward Von.

"Vonda, darling," she said in a thick Russian accent, her voice husky with matronly affection, or hoarse from yelling at her students, one or the other. She clasped her hands as if she were pleased to see Von at least. "You've been hiding from me. I haven't see you since your father's wake."

"Ana."

As they embraced, Sioban could see the snow-white bun of her hair peeking out of the top of the turban scarf. The legendary dancer bestowed a kiss on Von's cheek. Her lips were almost as red as her scarf. She was magnificent.

All Sioban wanted to do was disappear, and she tried to keep her knees from shaking as the teacher turned to look at her.

"Iliana, I'd like you to meet my friend, and a very talented dancer, Sioban O' Rourke." Vonda beamed like she'd just presented the woman with a new puppy. More like a new lamb to the slaughter, thought Sioban.

"It's a pleasure, madam. So honored to be studying with you today." Sioban extended her hand and when Iliana took it in her icy grip, Sioban could hardly keep from gasping. Time seemed to stop as Iliana caught Sioban's gaze. The woman's dark eyes bored into her intently for what felt like an eternity. Sioban was sure that Iliana could see into her soul like a crystal ball.

"So happy Vonda could bring a friend for her return to my studio." Iliana smiled, but it didn't have nearly the warmth that Von's held. She dropped Sioban's hand unceremoniously, but her eyes lingered on Sioban a moment longer before she turned back to Von. "I'll let you get back to warming up. See you in class—it starts in precisely ten minutes."

She nodded at Von and walked out.

"Lord save me. You never thought to mention that you had studied with a legend? And still are? Christ, Von, what have you gotten me into?"

"Calm down, hon. I don't know why I never mentioned it to you. I haven't had cause to drag my credentials out for a long time, and they certainly would have been lost on Jimmy, so I didn't think about it. Ana is marvelous, though. You're going to love class today."

"Of course she is. Of course I'll love the class—just like I loved my last trip to the dentist." Von just laughed at her as they continued stretching.

Exactly eight minutes later, they filed into another, much larger space. A temporary sign taped to the door read "Jazz 6:00." Von chose a spot near the middle, but there was no way Sioban was going to embarrass herself, so she stayed to the back. Unfortunately, Iliana zeroed in on her the moment she walked in a few seconds later. She nodded at Sioban as if to say "Fine, stay back there, but you can't hide from me."

Instead, she brought the class to heel right away. "All right, picking up from last week, the first half of the routine. Newcomers, watch as we run through it, then fall in on the second run-through. We'll do it several times, then we'll start putting together the second half."

The dancers fell in as Iliana pointed a remote control at the sound system. Von stepped slightly behind her line so that she could observe and shadow without anyone tripping over her. Sioban did the same, but moved as close to the back wall as she could get. She wasn't even sure she'd be able to fall in after the first run-through.

The first note of "Big Spender" leapt out of the stereo and caught Sioban's heart. The sheer relief that she knew it, and had seen at least one routine choreographed to it outside of the original Broadway-recorded production, battled with a pang she couldn't tamp down.

She and Ava had shadowed the original routine one night in the living room. A BBC special about Bob Fosse was on the television. She and Ava had used the back of the couch as the makeshift bar. Aunt Rose would have died if she'd seen Ava teaching her daughter a dance routine about hookers. But Ava herself wasn't concerned about it, and neither had Sioban been. The music was all there was, and they both let it lead them. Of course Ava was so much better than Sioban at it, as well she should have been, since Sioban was only twelve at the time and hadn't had much in the way of formal dance training.

Ava had always stared at some point in space, beyond the television, that had only been visible to her. She beckoned at someone just like the dancers did on the television. But as Sioban had watched her and tried to make the same connection to the song, she realized that the being Ava beckoned to embodied more than just a well-paid night of passion. He was everything to Ava in that moment: he was dancing and beauty and light, everything she'd come to Los Angeles to harness. He was her reason for living. And Sioban had seen just as clearly in that moment how elusive he could be. Many women wanted him, but for the wrong reasons, and even fewer were meant to have him, even for one night.

Sioban had prayed for her mother that night, as she prayed for herself now, that Ava be allowed just one glimpse, just one taste of fulfillment. She'd missed the first several seconds of the routine in her reverie, but Iliana's voice brought her back to the room.

"Faces, everyone! You were looking, but you've found him—now make him want you!"

The only bar was the one in front of the mirror, but Iliana's choreography didn't require it. Every move captured the call and anticipated response of the predator and her intended prey. Each dancer sashayed back and forth along an imaginary sidewalk, pointed, reached to her mark, swung her hips, then turned and did a low grind to show what she could offer. And then the brief coquetry of innocence—fun...fun...fun—before the hip thrusts that could sink an eight ball in the corner pocket by sheer kinetic will. Let me show you a—*good time*!... I can show you a—*good time*!

Sioban shadowed them, almost unaware of herself and how the story had drawn her body into its telling. When the first run-through was over, barely a beat passed before the music looped again. Iliana drove them forward like a rogue madam calling to her best call girls.

"Fall in! Again! Get him this time, get him to spend his last million dollars on you, my darlings! Power!"

Sioban tingled. She hadn't memorized the first several bars, but she didn't care, only let her body move intuitively through the story. She was vaguely aware of Iliana moving through the room and stopping to correct an extension or foot placement. There was some praise amidst a barrage of scolding, but Sioban couldn't give in to the fear. She just had to keep moving no matter what. She couldn't be wrong, even if her steps weren't one hundred percent right.

The first time she felt Iliana's long fingers on her, they were warm from touching the other dancers, but her grip was unforgiving. Sioban's arm was placed completely incorrectly and she almost hit the dancer next to her in the face. Iliana let loose what had to have been a curse in Russian. The second time, she grabbed Sioban's hips from behind and nearly propelled her into the dancer in front of them. Again, strong words in Russian, but Sioban chose to hear a hint of approval in them.

They did the routine another two times, and were allotted a brief break to take a few swallows of water while Iliana changed the music and explained the second part of the routine. On the surface, it seemed shorter and simpler than the first part, but required them to move in synchronicity into a specific formation. Sioban concentrated with everything she had, and she was at least able to follow the steps. Iliana never came to her again, but every verbal correction, especially the ones in English, seemed to be directed right at her. She hardly thought any of the praise was for her.

Finally, the class ended and the dancers toweled off and filed out in clusters unceremoniously. And Christ in heaven, Iliana came right for her almost before she could catch her breath.

"You obviously have something," Iliana pronounced. "Whom have you studied with?"

"Well, I...my mother was a dancer and she—"

"Forget about her. Focus on what you have to offer." Iliana's eyes drilled right through her again as she spoke. "Perhaps I will see you again next week."

Sioban was staring even after Iliana was gone— and so were most of the other dancers before she noticed Von standing next to her.

"She's something else, isn't she?" Von was positively glowing. Sioban had been trying so hard not to mess up that she hadn't even seen Vonda dancing, but she was sure Von had been fantastic. "What did she say to you?"

"Um, basically that I didn't suck." Sioban wiped at her brow with the towel, not wanting to look Von in the eye.

"Interesting...you know what she said to me?"

Sioban did look up then, to see Von smiling at her proudly. "She told me to bring you back—and soon."

§

By the time they stumbled in the door that evening, the two best friends were once again exhausted from shopping and, finally, dancing. But it was a happy exhaustion, and as they collapsed on the sofa with mostly Sioban's bags of loot falling around them, they laughed as if they had not a care in the world. Sioban still wore her skirt and the new lace hose she'd bought at Eve's, but they were covered by her new parka and the fleece-lined boots that came all the way up to her knees, leaving her ankles a mystery.

"So, what'll it be tonight? Chef Von Douglas is still on strike."

"And Chef Sioban O'Can't Cook is not a viable stand-in. How about Thai?"

"Perfect. I'll call it in." Before Vonda could get off the couch, Sioban reached into her purse and whipped out her wallet. She held out some cash to Vonda.

"Here, I'm not out of money yet. Besides, I've just scored this awesome job at a club, and I'll be a millionaire soon, so feed my pride and let me buy us dinner."

Vonda smirked at her, and snatched the money. Within the hour they were happily devouring pad thai and spring rolls at the living-room coffee table, accompanied by the light from a sandalwood candle and two glasses of red wine. There was no comedy film blaring from the TV, and they both knew it was time for Sioban to tell Vonda what had happened in L.A. Vonda didn't push her though, and when Sioban had taken her last bite, she scooted up from her position on the floor to the couch with her wine glass in hand. She stared into it intently as if to find the best way to tell her story in the pool of red liquid. She took a breath. There was nothing for it but to dive in at the deep end.

"I was almost raped," she began. Von nearly jumped out of her seat, but instead stayed quiet and allowed her friend to continue. Sioban quietly completed the tale over the next hour, and without looking up at Vonda, she knew there were tears in her eyes, just like there were in her own *again*. Jesus, Mary, and Joseph, would she never be able to stop crying?

"We'll figure this out," Vonda finally said, wiping at her eyes.

"I know." Sioban's voice was quiet, but unwavering. "But not tonight. I had to tell you, I know that, but I don't want to bloody think about it anymore right now. It'll be staring me in the face again sure as shite when I open my eyes in the morning."

Sioban drained her glass as they both rose to clean up the remains of dinner. Anxious to change the subject, she ventured to get Vonda to talk for a change.

"Von, why did you freak out when I said you'd want costumes from Eve's shop? And why haven't you told her about your plans?"

"I'm...afraid, Sioban. Suddenly, I have everything I need. Johnny's blessing, God rest his soul, along with the means to finally achieve my dream thanks to what he left me. But all that bravado I showed Jimmy—what if it's all bullshit? What if I fail? I failed in Los Angeles."

"Excuse me, you did not fail in L.A. You kicked ass in a horrible situation. You had Jimmy by the balls and he knew it. It might have taken you a while, but eventually you would have saved the money and found a venue. But this is better. It's going to be fantastic."

"You're good for my confidence. Or my ego. Or something. In spite of the circumstances, I'm glad you're here."

"Me too. We're good for each other." Sioban sighed. They both had mountainous challenges to overcome, but the opening of the Velvet Room would give them something positive to focus on.

"I know it's important to Eve to help me," Vonda said thoughtfully. "I planned on telling her soon; I wanted it to be a surprise. I'm just trying to get my head around the whole undertaking enough to share it with others."

"It's clear she's excited. She's got almost a motherly pride about it."

"You're not far off the mark," Vonda said, as she grabbed the wine bottle along with her glass. Sioban followed her back into the living room to hear what was obviously a juicy story.

"I couldn't believe I didn't see it coming, even living in L.A.," began Von, as she sank back down onto the couch.

"See what?"

"Eve came up to me at the wake, after all the guests had gone. I thought she was just staying behind to help me clean up at the bar."

Vonda went on to tell her how Eve had confessed that her friendship with Johnny had become much more. They'd kept quiet about it, mostly at Eve's insistence. She didn't want Johnny's friends giving him a hard time for taking up with the local lingerie-shop owner. It couldn't be good for a tavern owner. Of course Johnny didn't care deep down, and most of his close friends already knew. But he didn't see any point in parading his personal life in front of the customers, and it was easy (and preferable) for them to meet after hours.

Eve might stop by for a cup of coffee of an afternoon. Or a sherry after she closed the shop in the evening. But Johnny waited until at least an hour after he'd locked up to make his way into the private back entrance to Eve's apartment above the shop. Of course, after she'd taken in Chy and her mother, Eve had started staying over at Johnny's house several evenings a week, to give them all more space.

"I think it's brilliant," declared Sioban. "Seems like they were practically married there at the end, don't mind my saying so. How people didn't catch on is beyond me. People can be clueless about what's right under their nose."

"Hey, I happened to have been one of those clueless people. Even from across the country, I should have been picking up on all the times Johnny told me he'd just seen a great movie with Eve, or tried a new restaurant with her, or repeated some silly joke she'd told him."

"Well, it's understandable, you were focused on surviving."

"True enough. But there's one thing I'm not clueless about."

Sioban darted her eyes at Vonda. "Oh? And what's that?" Sioban had the sudden foreboding feeling that she'd be sorry she asked.

"You should have seen yourself trying on that bustier."

"Um, I did—in the three-sided mirror that was standing right in front of me."

"No, smarty-pants, what I mean is, the look on your face. You seemed surprised at how sexy you looked—how sexy you *are*. And then you got into it."

"Well, admittedly, it's been a long time since I felt like anything other than some stranger's eye candy, or jerk-off fantasy. I haven't believed I was sexy, as in beautiful, well, not ever, really."

"But you did today."

Sioban tried to hide her grin by taking another sip of wine.

"Yeah, so what of it, then?"

"I just think it's a good thing, that's all." Vonda traced the rim of her glass coyly, making it sing slightly. "And if someone else finds you beautiful too, well, that's a bonus."

Sioban nearly choked on her wine. "Like who?"

"I don't know. Just that you seemed pretty radiant in that moment, almost like you were modeling for someone."

"I think the wine has gone to your head, woman. And I just realized how tired I am. Enough of this silly talk. I'm off to bed."

Von had taken over Johnny's room and her old room was free for Sioban. As Sioban lay there praying for sleep to come, she couldn't quiet her restless mind. God, was she that transparent? Or was Von just some kind of mind reader? She blushed at remembering her own train of thought that afternoon as she'd stared at herself in the bustier. She realized for the first time in her life that she could stop comparing herself to Ava's dark beauty, and that she had a fiery gorgeousness that was all her own. And then, shockingly, she'd remembered how Danny Sheridan had looked at her that morning, first as he swerved to avoid hitting her in the road, and then the two or three glances he'd spared her when he thought she wasn't paying attention. Sure, his eyes had been cold, filled with annoyance and even anger. But there'd been something else there, a subtle heat. He'd found her attractive, even if he wanted to throttle her. Or maybe that's just what she wanted to think, because God help her, she couldn't help imagining what he'd think of her in the bustier, how he'd admire her in it, how he'd run his fingers down her neck until they reached the plunge between her breasts... Jesus, if Von hadn't brought her back from that fantasy, well, she was afraid to find out how far she would have let it go. She couldn't even begin to think of having a man in her life, even in her fantasies, with the mess she was in. And even if she wasn't on the lam from Sonny Coniglione, she could only focus on launching the Velvet Room with Von, and maybe, just maybe, finding out if she could be the dancer she'd always dreamed she could be. The only problem with that intention was that the minute she drifted off to sleep, Danny was there in her dreams, admiring the emerald bustier, and taking her fantasy where she'd dared not let it go before.

Chapter Eight

Danny had a tight grip on the steering wheel—again—as he made his way through the West Town neighborhood in the early morning hours. Bear and the rest of the team would say he needed to relax. Danny knew he should have been cool as a cucumber, business as usual, as he made his way through the Chicago streets to his first appointment of the day. The problem was, Danny could still hear their lunchtime conversation of yesterday in his head. Bear might as well have been sitting right next to him again, going over his very specific instructions for Danny as far as the Douglas account was concerned.

Danny grumbled to himself as he brought the truck to a halt at a red light. He drummed his fingers on the steering wheel as the end of their lunch meeting rang in his head again.

"And I take it you want me to be the one to meet with the Douglas woman about the first round of equipment to go in?" Danny had asked, thinking he'd better just volunteer before Bear asked him to do it anyway. Bear had tilted his head and given him a funny look.

"You take it right. I don't want to reschedule my meeting. This client could have international business for us if this goes well."

"And you'd rather send your second in command on this errand than help you win a high-level client?"

"That's not it and you know it. I don't even know if I want this guy as a client yet. Today's meeting will be short and will be mostly him pitching himself to me as a client, though it won't seem that way to him. And when I'm ready to accept this security assignment, you'll be there to solidify things, just like you were at Captain Johnny's yesterday."

"Fine."

"Which is why I *trust* you," Bear continued, "to lay out stage one for Vonda—Ms. Douglas, in a way that makes her comfortable. She's still not sold on Rockford to handle things for her new club."

Danny bit back his comment about how the Douglas woman would still prefer to see Bear anyway, especially when her best friend wanted to claw his eyes out.

"And that includes making Ms. O'Rourke comfortable with the plan as well." Danny knew he'd winced at that remark. "Or at least not making her uncomfortable."

But it was really what Danny himself had said that had his blood pressure up more than anything Bear had said. He'd *volunteered* to meet with Ms. Douglas, for fuck's sake. Sure, Bear would have sent him anyway, but he'd initiated the idea. And he'd done so because, he realized, he wanted to see Sioban. Fuck.

An angry horn sounded behind him, and Danny gunned the truck through the green light. He actually wasn't far from the bar now. Only he wasn't going to the bar. Too bad, because there, he would have stood a chance at avoiding Sioban, or at least surviving her claws when they came out. But no, he was headed straight to Ms. Douglas's home, just a few blocks away from the bar itself. She'd agreed because he had to get her approval of stage one of the plans, then gather the equipment before meeting her, along with a few trusted contractors Bear had recommended for her, to begin work. Now he'd have to see Sioban in a different setting, and he wondered if she'd be less confrontational and more vulnerable. Like she had been in his dreams last night.

Burlesque Bad

Danny knew he'd been thinking of her way more than he wanted to after their encounter at the bar yesterday. But he had no idea that his subconscious was so full of her he'd dream about her. And not about her sassy, brassy vixen side either, damn it. That would have just been a nightmare. No, the Sioban of his dreams had come to him, not exactly soft and willing, but needing him. There had been signs in her eyes of things he knew existed beneath her prickly surface. Things like kindness, tenderness, and even humor. And she'd come to him wearing that damn outfit he'd seen in Eve's window when he and Bear had left the bar—sultry, hot, and wanting him. Shit.

He sighed in resignation as he pulled up in front of the Douglas home. He might be an ex-Marine, and a security expert, but he had no idea how he was going to survive the next hour, much less this entire project.

§

The hot, strong tea coursed through Sioban's veins, further waking up her body from its delicious repose. She took another sip and closed her eyes as the steam from her mug wafted around her face. She was completely relaxed, with her wet hair still wrapped in a turban towel, and snuggled in one of Von's plush robes. It had been the best sleep she'd had in days, probably months. Being safe here in Chicago with Von, the yummy food, the wine, the dreams... *No!* She fairly slammed the mug down onto the table in front of her, sloshing the scalding tea over her hand.

"Damn, shite, hellfire!" She had to get hold of herself. The beast had worked his way into her dreams, damn him, and she had to find a way to banish him from her mind for good. Fat chance of that, when she was supposed to be helping Von open the club, and

85

Danny was supposed to be helping Bear with security. With her luck, she'd have to see him every bloody day.

"Sioban? Are you okay?" Von called in from her post at the desk in the living room. She was sitting there at the computer, fully dressed, when Sioban came down, looking like she'd been up for hours.

"Oh, fine, just scalding myself with my own tea." She half waited for Von to come rushing into the kitchen to make sure she was okay. But whatever she was working on was far more consuming than her burning hand.

"Okay," Von replied distractedly.

"What are you doing, reprogramming the nuclear launch codes?" Sioban reached for a napkin and patted her hand dry before opening the newspaper. At least she wouldn't have to read about the fallout at Club 29. She could still pretend that the news in Los Angeles and its consequences couldn't find her here.

"Hmm?"

Sioban was about to get up and see what Von was so absorbed in when the doorbell rang. With Von in her state, Sioban was certain she hadn't even heard it.

"Earth to Von!" Sioban stalked into the living room and threw open the door to find Danny Bloody Sheridan standing there. *Shite.*

He didn't have his usual scowl. Instead, he had a look of dread on his face, as if he'd rather be anywhere else than standing in front of her. He crossed his arms and gave her a wicked, predatory grin. *Say something!* she admonished herself. Sioban knew she should invite him in, but all she managed was a dose of her typical sass.

"And just what do you think you're looking at?"

The familiar coldness returned to Danny's eyes.

"Well, I can make out nice warm living quarters behind that hive on your head. I'm thinking it would be nice if you could let me in before I freeze to death."

Sioban grumbled and took a step back to let him in.

"Von! Your appointment is here."

"What?" Vonda finally looked up from her computer screen. "Crap, it's nine o'clock!" Sioban heard her toss her glasses on the desk and close the laptop. In an instant, she was there to greet her guest.

"Danny, good morning! So sorry, I was caught up in what I was doing."

No doubt she had been Tweeting, or Friending, or one of those ridiculous things.

"Morning, Ms. Douglas. Thank you for seeing me so early. It'll be great to go over stage one of the plans with you, so that I'll have everything I need when we get to the bar later."

"Glad we can get a head start. And it's 'Vonda,' okay?"

"Yes, ma'am." His voice was pure butter—hot, melted butter—when he wasn't growling at everyone.

Vonda just shook her head.

"We'll work on the 'ma'am' thing later. But your momma raised you right, so you get points for politeness. Speaking of which, please come in and sit down. I'll put a fresh pot of coffee on."

Sioban knew she should follow suit, and be polite and welcoming, if for no other reason than to be supportive of Von. But oh Lord, how he filled the room, and the sight of him had her speechless. He swiped off his grey knit hat to reveal those gorgeous black waves of hair again and Sioban felt her heart begin to tap dance in her chest.

"Sioban, if you're not going to at least say good morning to the man, could you keep him company while I get us some coffee?"

Keep him company? Oh no, she had to get out of there, and fast.

"Are you mad? You might have at least warned me we were expecting…company!"

At that, Sioban turned on her heel and ran up the stairs. She was sure she felt Danny's eyes burning the back of her neck as she went. She hurled herself into the safety of the bathroom. She didn't need to see her face to feel the flush of heat on her cheeks.

Less than twenty minutes later, Sioban was dressed, and blow-drying her hair. With only a few damp strands remaining, she shut it off. The two of them must have gotten over her outburst, because she could hear their muffled voices below. She envied Von her ability not to let the big hulk get to her. Then again, she was fairly certain that Von wasn't having dreams about him, either. And crap, she was also jealous of the congenial tone of Danny's voice. If only she could stifle her impulse to be such a witch around him, he might speak kindly, or at least civilly, to her, too. And that was it, wasn't it? This thing he'd awakened in her, this need to be cared for by a man.

God, that was dangerous right now, she thought, as she blended foundation over her freckles. It was a feeling Sioban didn't know if she'd ever be ready to handle or accept. In the time it took her to plump her lashes with mascara and dab peach-flavored gloss over her lips, the meeting downstairs had concluded. She took a breath as she heard Danny say his goodbye and close the front door behind him, and tried to gather the courage to go down and face Von's ire.

But it wasn't Von's ire that was waiting for her. Danny was leaning against the mantle, studying Von's personal family photos just a nonchalant as you please.

"What the devil are you still doing here?"

"Hello again. Well, Vonda rushed out, she said she had to take care of something, and that I could let myself out." The man was grinning at her now. The insolence of him!

"So why the hell didn't you, then?"

"Well, I had this strange notion that since we'd gotten off on the wrong foot before, I'd stick around and offer to drop you at the bar. You could even come with me to get these things if you were up for it."

"Have you lost your mind? You just decided to stick around, never mind that you might scare me half to death knowing I'd be expecting to find Von still here. Then you offer me a ride under the pretense of pushing a shopping cart behind you for the next however long. Well, I don't need a ride, thank you very much, Von will be back for me. Besides, I wouldn't get in that killing machine of a truck with you anyway, not with the way you drive."

Danny didn't say anything at first. He looked down at his feet and sighed in resignation.

"No problem." She could see that his jaw was clenched as he raised his head and turned toward the door without looking her in the eye. "Glad you were able to get some warm clothes. Chicago winters can be brutal. See you later, Irish."

Danny closed the door behind him, leaving Sioban rather stunned. He hadn't growled. He hadn't made fun of her in any way. Rather, he'd offered her a ride and a chance to build a normal rapport with him. But she rationalized to herself that it was better to keep him at a distance. But with him being almost kind to her the way he had just now, it would be harder than ever to keep him out of her dreams.

Chapter Nine

The outer lobby of Rockford Security was impressive. The website hadn't done it justice, Vonda realized, as she waited for Bear to finish his meeting. There was no receptionist, but a lone sign on the desk read "Please wait for assistance." She wondered how anyone would know what kind of assistance she needed, until she spotted a camera just above the door that must lead to the back office. Of course, it was a security firm. They didn't need a receptionist to announce visitors; they were just alerted by top-of-the-line surveillance.

Within minutes, a very large man wearing a headset and carrying a clipboard entered the lobby. He certainly fit the part of a security expert in black cargo pants and a very tight black tee-shirt. Vonda wondered what his background was. No team members' names appeared, of course, and neither did the website specify how many personnel were on the payroll, but Rockford boasted openly about the qualifications of its staff, including extensive experience in either military or government security agencies. There hadn't even been a photo of Bear, and he wasn't listed as the proprietor, either. There'd just been an address on the home page, and a phone number to call for an appointment. But Vonda had opted to just show up, especially after she clicked through the website. There was a tab for residential and small-business services, and another labeled "corporate and international." Instinct told her that was the page she wanted, but when she clicked on it, there was a single message on the screen saying that this page of the website was still under construction, but that interested parties should call for an appointment. Well, she was interested, but if her instincts were right, and Bear could help her, or rather Sioban, then there was no time to make an appointment.

"Welcome to Rockford Security. How can I assist you today?" The man smiled at her, but he was still so imposing. She stood, hoping that doing so would help her not to feel so small.

"Good morning. I'm Vonda Douglas, and Bear is handling my account—or rather my father's account, but since he died recently, I guess it is mine." Good grief, she was rambling, and that wasn't going to help her in the slightest.

"Of course. Captain Johnny's. I'm familiar with the account. Your account. I know it's one of Rockford's top priorities right now. Bear's in a meeting at the moment, but he should be wrapping up soon. I'll let him know you're here."

"Um, great, thank you."

He disappeared behind the door again, and Vonda plopped back down on the leather sofa. She let out a sigh and sent up a prayer. She'd do anything to help Sioban, and she just hoped that Rockford— Bear—could handle the situation Sioban found herself in, and on top of that, he'd agree to take the case. Vonda didn't know what she'd do if he refused, or how she'd go about finding another firm she could trust. No, what she was really afraid of was that she wouldn't be able to find another man she could trust. Because if she were honest, it wasn't just Rockford's website or the polished appearance of their headquarters so far that made her feel safe, and comfortable bringing Sioban's situation to them. And it wasn't just the fact that Johnny had trusted them with his livelihood, the bar. It was Bear, and the way he was so respectful toward her, almost reverent. Bear and his reassurances that he could handle whatever changes would be required in converting the club, and that he would work with her on costs. Bear and his warm, strong hand on the small of her back as she walked him and Danny to the door yesterday—

And right then Bear stepped into the lobby with his other client. While his words were for the man with him, Bear's warm, chocolate-brown gaze fell on her as he spoke.

"Thank you, Harrison. I'll call your office and set up an appointment for next week. I'll get you a complete proposal then." Bear's gaze left her then, and Vonda tried to focus. So Rockford was expanding, and if this slick businessman in a designer suit was any indication of the new clientele they were after, maybe she and Sioban had a chance.

"Sounds good. I'll wait to hear from you." The man returned his best corporate smile and shook Bear's extended hand. But the way his silver hair almost matched his suit perfectly made him seem cold.

The chill she felt, along with her focus, evaporated when Bear turned back to her and smiled.

"Well, good morning. What brings you here? Everything go okay with Danny?" She was having more trouble standing this time. Bear held out his hand for her, not to shake it, but so that he could help her up, so she let him. "This couch is too damn cushy for its own good," he said.

"Yes, of course. I mean, yes, the meeting with Danny was fine. I'm looking forward to getting things underway at the bar."

"Thank goodness. I was afraid he'd been a bully to your friend again, and you'd decided to fire us." At that Vonda had to smile, as Bear opened the lobby door and held it open for her.

"Well, I'm afraid it was Sioban who acted out again this morning. But she's...been through a lot. That's sort of what I'm here to talk to you about this morning."

"That's fine. My door is always open. Come on into my office."

Vonda hadn't even realized that they'd traveled the short distance from the lobby, and she quickly glanced around as Bear ushered her into his office. The suite was small, and there were several cubicles in the middle, another office on the other side, and a conference room at the other end. Another door next to Bear's office must lead to the kitchen, she thought. She noticed the man who had greeted her seated in one of the cubicles, where she glimpsed two large monitors showing what appeared to be several views of the property. Two other formidable men dressed in similar black attire came out of the other room and headed for the lobby, giving her and Bear a nod as they passed.

"It's humble, but it's mine. It's quiet right now. Most of the staff is out in the field," he said, as if to read her mind. "They only report in periodically. Not too many desk jobs in this line of work."

"Of course." Having been caught in her curiosity, Vonda stepped quickly inside, and Bear closed the door after them. It wasn't as posh as the lobby, but neither was it like the shabby offices portrayed in detective and spy movies. She settled into the chair Bear offered her, and tried to think of how to tell him about Sioban's predicament.

§

Bear leaned his forearms on the desk across from Vonda and tried to remain calm about whatever had brought her here. Clearly she needed something beyond a few extra security cameras and a new alarm system, and that had him worried. Everything about her body language told him that she was assessing what she observed of the firm to see if Rockford was up to the task, whatever that was. He wasn't happy at all about the fact that she might have already encountered trouble at the bar before he and Danny had even had a chance to really make it safe again.

"How can I help you this morning, beyond the stage one plans that Danny's already gone over with you?" Bear eyed her intently as she stared down at her lap. After a moment she met his gaze, and he didn't like the uncertainty he saw there.

"I was perusing your website this morning. Your staff—they're all ex-military or former government agents...you're not just in this business to install burglar alarms, are you?"

Well, well, well. This must be significant if she'd researched the firm. Even though there weren't many details on the website, there was enough there to clue in people who knew what they were looking for. He didn't know whether to be glad she'd come to him or worried about why.

"It's true, I've been moving toward expanding to include—another level of clientele. What's going on, Vonda?"

"I...this isn't about the bar. I don't even know if you can help me, if you'd even want to help me with this, but I don't have any other options right now." She fanned the edge of her notebook. She was nervous, scared even, and he wanted nothing more than to ease her mind and let her know that whatever problem she had, he'd take care of it. He wanted to tell her that everything would be all right.

"I'll do whatever I can to help. Just take a deep breath and tell me what the problem is."

"It's Sioban. She...left kind of a mess behind, and I'm afraid—she's afraid that it will follow her here."

Well, that much was obvious. Now if he could just get her to explain the rest of it. But he had to tread carefully with her fragile trust.

"Go on."

"Sioban—we met back in L.A. We worked in the same nightclub as...dancers. The owner, Jimmy, was an asshole, but I convinced him that I could help him improve business, so that kept me off the poles, and running a dance show I produced myself. I was saving up to buy my own venue, and I was going to take Sioban with me."

Bear had picked up a pen from the desk and was biting the end of it. The idea of Vonda getting anywhere near a strip pole made him want to hurt someone—and right this minute, he wished it was the club owner she'd worked for.

"Sorry," she continued. "This isn't about me. I just wanted to give you a little background. Anyway, when my father died, I had to leave her behind. I tried to convince her to come with me back then, but she made every excuse in the book why she couldn't break away from him.

"Without me there, Jimmy just reverted to his old ways, and worse. He started to allow illicit activities, and for a while, Sioban managed to keep herself out of it. Until one night, when Jimmy promised one of his clients a private dance from Sioban. She...avoided doing it, but in the process, she got the client drunk and took a large sum of money off of him, which she used to escape. She knew she couldn't ever go back there. You see, Sioban's mother Ava was a dancer at Club 29 too. She tied herself to the wrong people, then came the drinking and pills. They found her dead one day of an overdose."

Bear just stared at Vonda. He had no doubt that he could help her and Sioban. He wanted to protect Sioban—and Vonda—more than he probably had a right to. And something was missing from her story, instinct told him, but he'd revisit that later. He was almost too full of consternation to speak, but he knew if he didn't say something to her, she'd take it as a sign that he wouldn't help her.

"Of course I'll do everything in my power to help you. I'm going to need you to go over some of the details again, and then I'll figure out the best approach. Obviously, I'll want to put some additional surveillance on the outside of the bar, and at the house too. I won't put a tail on the two of you—yet—until I'm clear on what we're dealing with."

"Thank you." Vonda nodded at him, and over the next forty-five minutes, he had written as much information as he could on a yellow legal pad. As much as she would tell him, that is. She claimed not to remember the name of the client, which he would bet his next case Sioban had told her. And she was still holding back on exactly how Sioban had avoided performing for said client and gotten away, with his money no less. But fear did strange things to people, and in his line of work, it always took a little time to get to the bottom of things. Bear stood, and they both moved toward the door.

"That should do it for now. I know you're both very concerned, as you should be, but I'll put two of my men on getting the needed surveillance up at the house as well as the bar, since Danny may not have gotten what we'd need in this morning's equipment purchase."

"Thank you again, Bear. I feel like I can manage everything Sioban and I are facing now."

"I'm glad you came to me. It's going to be okay, Vonda."

"Well, Johnny trusted you. And so do I." Her beautiful blue eyes looked a lot more hopeful to him now than when she'd walked in, and he was glad of that. They'd reached the lobby, and he held the door open for her to leave. "See you at the bar in an hour or so?"

"Yes, sounds good."

"Okay, drive carefully. And if either of you notices anything that makes you feel uncomfortable, anything at all, call me right away."

"Will do. See you soon." She smiled at him then, and his heart beat just a little faster. He meant it when he told her he was glad she'd come to him with this situation. Exactly why he felt so glad was something he'd have to figure out.

§

She should be stressed, frantic even, Von thought as she drove away from the Rockford Security building. She had a million things to do at the bar. And her best friend was still facing the very real threat of having assault charges brought against her, or, worse, that Sonny Coniglione could come after her out of revenge for the wound Sioban had inflicted on him in self-defense. Yeah, she should be freaking out. But she wasn't. Because Bear had handled everything for her. He'd taken seventy-five percent of the worry about the Velvet Room and put it on his own shoulders, going way beyond the scope of his contract as her security provider and helping her procure contractors and designers that he had connections with and trusted for the renovation. Basically, all Vonda would have to do would be to approve various elements along the way. And now, when she'd come to him with the mother of all curve balls, which had even less to do with the club, he'd caught it one-handed.

Somehow, she trusted him. Implicitly. With her life, and Sioban's too. Bear made her feel safe, and not just from the long arm of Sonny Coniglione, but safe about everything in her life. And wasn't that the problem? she mused, and sighed. Her shoulders hadn't been this relaxed since Sioban had called her in the middle of the night from Los Angeles. Vonda had been afraid to focus fully on her plans until she figured out what she could do for Sioban besides give her a bed to sleep in and a job. And now that she'd done that there was nothing left for her to really lose sleep over. Except maybe this. Feelings she had thanks to Bear. A heady mixture of warmth and safety—and desire, damn it—that she hadn't experienced with any man up until now.

Bear was a perfect gentleman, but there was heat in his brown eyes when he looked at her and told her that everything would be okay. He'd never push her where she didn't want to go. But he wasn't really the problem; Von was. Not only could she see herself going wherever he wanted to take her, whether it be into his arms, into his bed, or into his life, but hell, she *wanted* to go with him.

"It's impossible!" she wailed aloud. And even though she was alone in the car, she could hear Sioban's voice in her head saying "who do you think you're fooling?" It echoed her own thoughts that she'd tried to bury since she'd met Bear.

Who was she fooling? Beneath her fear that he'd refuse to help Sioban, Vonda had wanted to see him again. There had been butterflies in her stomach when she'd walked into Rockford this morning. She wanted him to be the one in whom she confided about Sioban's situation. And she loved feeling the kindness in his eyes, his warmth. Vonda might just as well have had his handprint tattooed on her lower back where he'd touched her as he gently ushered her into his office, because she wanted to feel it there again.

Vonda realized it was her turn at the four-way stop. She gave a wave of apology into her rearview mirror and urged the car forward. The only thing that would take her mind off of Bear was working out how she'd tell Sioban that she'd just hired Bear for all intents and purposes to protect them both from Sonny Coniglione.

When Vonda pulled up to the house, Sioban was already sitting outside, looking as if she'd been waiting for Vonda for hours. *Poor girl*, Vonda reflected. *So much to deal with, and now I have to tell her I've hired Bear...* Vonda stopped her own train of thought when Sioban stood up and waved. She half expected to hear her friend's voice again: *And what about who you're attracted to?*

Sioban came briskly down the walkway. Vonda barely waited for her to close the door and fasten her seat belt before she pulled away from the curb. Her only distraction now was driving. And hoping Sioban wouldn't make her wreck the car when she told her what she'd done.

"Those jeans are great on you. And that purple sweater looks so soft."

"It is. And the jeans are so comfortable. So, where'd you run off to?"

Of course. Darling Sioban, who always got right to the point.

"Right. Enough small talk, then."

"Or we could talk about why you left me behind with that beast."

"Well, he's not a beast. And I was in a hurry. Besides, deep down, I bet you didn't actually mind being left alone with him."

Sioban snorted. "So then why were you in such a hurry that you had to leave me alone with that beast?"

Vonda sighed. She felt sorry for Danny. She was used to Sioban, but at the moment, she knew how frustrated Danny must be. The woman's tenacity could drive a person insane, and Vonda was feeling it right now. But she couldn't let herself be distracted by it.

"I was at Rockford Security."

"But aren't they meeting us at the bar anyway?"

"Yes, but I had to ask Bear about something else."

"What about? Wondering what color you should paint the security cameras?"

"No, but in about thirty seconds, your pass for being a brat expires."

Sioban turned from the window and pulled her sunglasses down on her nose, and peered at Vonda over the top of them.

"I asked for his help with your...situation. I asked for Rockford's protection."

Sioban went rigid and answered so faintly that Vonda almost didn't hear her.

"Jesus, you told him, didn't you?"

Vonda pulled over to the curb almost recklessly. There was a fire hydrant, but she'd take her chances. She threw the car into park and turned to Sioban.

"No. Not that part, never. That's not mine to tell, and if you don't know that I'd never do that... Sweetie, we're in over our heads on this one. I think you know that too."

Sioban nodded. "And?"

"Of course he said he'd help. He's going to do some digging, and implement some extra precautions at the bar and the house."

Sioban took her sunglasses completely off and swiped at her tears.

"Bloody hell, I've been coasting along in some kind of dream land, thinking I could just lose myself in your plans. He could come after me, Von. And now you're in danger too."

Vonda took her hand.

"It's not a dream land, Sioban. You really are here, and you really are part of the plans for the Velvet Room. It's not just my new adventure, it's yours too. As for the other, it's scary, but that's why I went to Bear. It's going to be all right—he'll make sure it is."

"Thank you." Sioban gave Vonda's hand a squeeze.

"We'd better get going now." Vonda put the car back in gear. "Bear's here to help us. And so is Danny."

"I know."

Sioban dabbed at her eyes again with one of her mittens and turned back to the window.

Chapter Ten

Some of the tiniest cameras in the world could fit into the coolest objects. Danny had always wanted a pinhole adapter camera. Then again, the GPS data logger could help him find out if his wife was cheating, if he had a wife. But he hadn't needed a gadget to find out that his ex-girlfriend had been cheating. And he didn't need any of this stuff now. What he should be doing was getting the surveillance cameras on his list and getting over to the bar.

But a mental conspiracy wouldn't allow him to focus. Images of Sioban were obscured by thoughts of Caryn and how she'd had so much of what he'd glimpsed in Sioban. That had hit him like a punch to the kidneys the other day, and then again this morning. When he'd finally left her at the house to head over to Rockford he was rattled enough as it was. Then, on his way in, he'd seen none other than Baxter leaving the building. And if that wasn't enough still, Gorman had told him that Bear was in his office with Vonda Douglas, and the coffee he'd drunk in the car roiled in his stomach. Apparently he'd have to wait to talk to Bear about any of this, so he did an about-face and made tracks for the spy store, as they called it, with all of this shit in his head.

Caryn hadn't just broken his heart. She'd tank-rolled over it. And since then he'd shut down anything that had the potential to become a real relationship. The next thing he knew, Sioban was standing in the middle of the street not even a day ago, legs from here to forever and that sad excuse for a coat, her curtain of bright red hair cascading over it. She'd been in a trance when he turned the corner, and she'd mesmerized him, too, so that he almost didn't slow down in time, before she came to herself and ran up on the sidewalk. She'd pulled those ridiculous sunglasses down onto her nose to peer at him and he knew he was in trouble. Because as pissed as he'd been that she'd been standing there like she had a death wish, he'd also had the impulse to throw a blanket around her. Then when her eyes fell on him, he knew she'd give him hell either way.

And that was what scared him. Caryn had taken him by storm just that way, with her deep-blue eyes, dark, silky hair, and smart mouth that she used to say whatever the hell was on her mind. Danny had eaten her up like candy. And the minute he realized that Sioban was part of the package on the Douglas account, he'd started an internal campaign to push her as far away as possible by any means necessary, including being an ass to her. Except it wasn't working. Oh, he'd succeeded in pissing her off, and probably hurting her, without a doubt. But that did absolutely nothing for the attraction he felt for her, or his sheer fascination with her.

God damn it, get a grip, Sheridan! he thought as his cell phone rang. It was Bear. Danny pushed the call answer button on his Bluetooth.

"Sheridan."

"You got the stuff?" Bear sounded anxious, which wasn't good.

"Yeah, I'm on my way in."

"Listen, the ladies are already here. Meet me at the coffee shop over on James Street. I need to fill you in on some stuff."

"I hope that includes why that jackass Harrison Baxter was coming out of Rockford when I got there this morning." Danny disconnected before Bear could answer. Jesus, he really did have to get it together. Snapping at Bear wasn't going to help; neither was being an asshole to Sioban. And now he was faced with the possibility of running into Caryn again if her dick husband had hired Rockford.

Bear had already gotten them a table, and Danny sat in the empty chair across from him with as much calmness as he could muster.

"I'll go first. Sorry about snapping at you. Things were...interesting between me and Ms. Douglas's friend this morning. Then I stop at Rockford on my way to the supply store, and not only do I see that asshole leaving the building, but Gorman tells me you're in a meeting with Vonda Douglas. So near as I can figure, she wants me to steer clear of the bar for the duration if she hasn't fired Rockford outright because of me, and now you're sending me onto whatever detail Baxter has hired us for as punishment."

Bear just laughed at him. "Here, I got you an egg sandwich. I probably should have gotten you two, but you can't have mine." Bear pushed a brown paper bag and one of the paper coffee cups across to Danny.

"Listen," Bear continued. "Nobody is fired; nobody is in trouble. Although you do need to get it together where Vonda's friend is concerned, especially after I tell you why Vonda came to see me this morning. As for Harrison Baxter, I didn't want to tell you I was meeting with him until I knew if his bid was legit, which it seems to be. It's a straightforward contract for security personnel at his new corporate branch. I'll meet with him again next week with the final proposal. It's uniformed staff, and you won't have to get anywhere near it."

Danny took another bite of his egg sandwich and washed it down with a swig of coffee as he contemplated what Bear had just told him, as well as what he obviously still had to tell him.

"So that's it? Out of the clear blue sky, Baxter just called Rockford?"

"He did his research." Bear paused uncomfortably. "And he said that Caryn told him Rockford was the best in the business, and that he should give us a shot. We're one of his three final bids."

"What the hell is she up to?"

"Maybe nothing. Or maybe she just wants to make amends and doesn't know how to go about doing it."

"Well, fuck that."

"So picking up the phone to make her apologies would really work, would it? Anyway, I doubt Baxter would even consider contracting us if his wife was trying to reconnect with her old flame. I don't think he has any idea you work here, and I'm sure as hell not going to bring it up."

Danny snorted in derision. "Next! What did Vonda Douglas want?"

As Bear filled him in, a different kind of unease began to churn in Danny's stomach. Sioban had been...accosted in some way that made her uncomfortable, made her run. She was potentially in real danger, and this wasn't something a new winter coat and some boots could protect her from. He'd never heard of Sonny Coniglione, but he knew more about the mob than he wanted to.

"Christ, Bear. So what do we do first?"

"Well, put a rotating man and some better equipment at the house for one thing. I'd already tricked out the plans for the bar interior pretty well, but I want to add to what I'd thought of for exterior cameras. And I want a van out front until we know more."

"And?"

"And you're going to make a little reconnaissance trip out West."

"Because you think I could use some time away from the bar?"

"That, and if taking on Baxter Industries as a client is a way for Caryn to get to you, it'll be easier to put her off if you're out of town," Bear said with a slight grin. "And I know you want to be the one to do this—whether you realize it or not."

Danny crumpled the bag that had held his egg sandwich and downed the last of his coffee. The next however many weeks on this new side of the Douglas case were going to be hell. But mainly he just hated it when Bear was right about him.

"Well, whatever it takes, if Sioban is in danger."

"In this case, they could both be in danger." Danny registered the frown of worry that came over Bear's face as they rose to leave. Apparently Danny wasn't the only one who had a personal investment in the situation.

§

The rest of the day at the bar passed smoothly enough, if not completely without tension. There was simply too much to be done. Sioban had busied herself in the office making phone calls for Vonda, where Danny was mercifully out of her sight. She and Von had even eaten their lunch in the office, leaving the outer bar to Rockford personnel. The few times she did venture out to check with Von on something, he was too busy installing surveillance cameras, or talking with the guys. But late in the day, she saw one of the Rockford men come in and hand two small boxes to Danny, after which he made a beeline to the bar, where she sat with Von going over some design samples.

"Hey, Danny. How's everything going today? I've been so buried in my own work, I'm sorry I haven't really checked in with you yet."

"Don't worry, do what you've got to do. Bear and I are here for the rest. A couple of potential contractors have been by to look at the space. Bear thinks he's going to settle on a recommendation for you. And these just came in for you. Bear wants you to use these cell phones temporarily, in light of the current situation."

So he knew. She couldn't fathom what he must think of her now. Even though Von hadn't told Bear every detail, now Danny probably thought she was just one bratty pain in the ass. Von took a breath to speak but Danny didn't let her.

"These are Rockford phones, so there's no cost to you. You can return them to us when this is all over, but Bear didn't want any traceable activity on your own phones for the time being."

"Well, that's smart," Vonda said. "We certainly appreciate it."

Sioban knew she should say something, preferably without insults or complaints. She finally forced herself to find Danny's gaze. "Yes, thank you. Thank Bear for me. I'm sorry for the trouble."

Danny's eyes held hers, and she couldn't look away even if she wanted to. "It's no trouble, it's our job."

"Oh. Well. I'll try to stay out of your way as much as possible."

"You won't be in our way. We've almost got the interior cameras in. Bear will oversee the installation of the exterior equipment, as well as what needs to happen at the house. There'll be a van out front here starting tonight."

"I see," said Sioban quietly.

"Well, you guys are certainly very thorough, I'll give you that."

"Yes ma'am."

Sioban blurted out the question that was in her head before she could stifle it. "And which part will you be supervising?" At least she could know when and where to avoid him.

"None of it. I'm leaving for Los Angeles tomorrow."

And just like that, the atmosphere thickened with her own disappointment. She should be relieved, but instead she felt like a balloon that someone had just popped. There was no way she could let that show, but the way she'd felt pinned by his gaze for that brief moment before he left would haunt her until he came back. His eyes seemed filled with things he wanted to say, but dare not. She saw the desire to claim and protect—along with just plain desire. She was drawn into the cobalt of his determined stare, and she wanted to stay there. But there was no sense in dwelling on the impossible.

"Well then. Have a nice trip." Sioban hopped off of her bar stool, took up her mug of tea, and went back to the office.

§

The bar seemed quiet, even though the new contactor had started two days ago. Bear had been checking in on a regular basis, and there was always a Rockford presence, especially since Vonda had revealed Sioban's predicament. But today, the security team was busy working on external reinforcements, and they had teamed up with the contractor and his crew to remove all unwanted furniture. Most of it was being donated to a used furniture store, but some pieces were just too worn to salvage. Vonda had chosen one table—the one Sioban favored for daydreaming—and two of the older chairs to take back to the house. Eventually she'd have a small home office in the basement and the setup would be perfect to work on her laptop and sip tea.

She fought back her tears as she surveyed the emptiness. Only by cleaning and preparing for the big renovation had she realized how worn down the place had become. Vonda couldn't help wonder how worn out Johnny must have been just before he died, maybe lonely too. Thank goodness for Eve, but Vonda still felt guilty as hell for having left Chicago in the first place. Still, she'd met Sioban in L.A., and now they were here together finally building her dream. It was as if Johnny had been waiting for her to come home all along, waiting for her to realize that her dreams could come true right here.

And as for Captain Johnny's, as run down as it might have become, it was still a wonderful place, beloved by the neighborhood and the regular customers. It had been, until she'd gutted it, anyway. What if she failed just like she had in L.A.? What if no one came once she re-opened the doors? It was a stretch at the moment to think of calling it the Velvet Room. Maybe in another few weeks, when the stage was built and the new décor was in. Maybe once she had dancers. The thought of having to find talent almost sent Vonda back home to bed. But she swallowed hard and wiped at a tear that was falling down her cheek.

Just then her security-issue cell phone rang, startling her from where it sat on the bar. The caller I.D.

read "Rockford 1." It was Bear. Vonda cleared her throat and answered.

"Is this the head honcho of Rockford Security checking up on me?"

"Yes, it's me, Bear. What's wrong?"

"What do you mean?"

"You sound...upset." Shit. He could tell she'd been crying.

"No, just...a little overwhelmed by what I've undertaken here."

"Anything I can do?"

Oh, she could think of a few things. Take her in his arms, kiss her senseless. Jesus, it was a good thing he wasn't there in person for her to see the concern that was certainly flooding those chocolate-brown eyes of his.

"No, I'm okay."

"Well, in any case, I'll be there before too long in case you think of something. And I have news."

"Oh?"

"Sonny's alive. Wounded, but alive."

"Thank God!"

"Well, yes, it means Sioban won't have to prove self-defense in a murder case. And I hardly think he'll want the attention that bringing assault charges against her would draw."

"But he could still come after her himself, or send someone after her, as revenge."

"Yes." Vonda didn't really know what to say to that. "Vonda, it's going to be okay," Bear continued. "That's why Danny went, to pick up on what Sonny's next move is going to be. And the Velvet Room is going to turn out okay too—it's going to be wonderful. Do you believe me?"

"I want to."

"We'll work on that together. See you soon."

Vonda laid the phone back down on the bar, and smiled. It wasn't hard to believe anything Bear told her. She sighed and glanced up at the picture of Johnny she'd had framed for the wake and then hung near the bar.

"Was he part of your plan too, Johnny?" Vonda didn't realize she'd spoken aloud until Sioban looked up from her newspaper.

"What are you babbling about?"

"Sorry, nothing." Vonda poured another cup of coffee and moved down to the end of the bar where Sioban sat. "That was Bear on the phone. Sonny's alive."

Sioban froze for a moment. Vonda could see her eyes darken as she processed the information. "Danny's seen him?"

"Yes. Apparently his wound is still obvious."

"Well at least I won't be sent up for murder. That's something then. How long until the bastard comes after me?"

"His next move is still unclear. That's what Danny's trying to get a handle on." Sioban just nodded and turned back to her newspaper. "Danny didn't call me either, hon. It's probably protocol for him to communicate with Bear, not to mention easier. And Bear probably thinks it will also be easier for you to hear whatever news there is from me."

"I know." Sioban looked at her again with worry. "I just didn't even give him half a chance. I wouldn't know how to have a normal, civil conversation with him, even if he did call me directly."

"He'll be back before you know it, sweetie. You'll have your chance to talk to him."

Even as she reassured her friend, Vonda realized that her own next chance to talk to Bear was probably minutes away. Part of her was always relieved to see him, to have him on the premises with her. The other part of her fought what really lingered behind that relief.

§

The little motel one block over from Club 29 wasn't half bad. Well, yes, it actually was, Danny admitted to himself. But it was what the situation required. This wasn't a James Bond movie, it was real life. He'd filed his notes in an encrypted email to Bear from a new Internet cafe he'd found in Burbank today. It was a pain in the ass to find a new place to file his notes every day, but he couldn't have risked bringing a laptop with him in case someone broke into his room.

He'd eaten a shit dinner and was now slugging back a warm beer. Another time he might have been tempted to watch porn, but not now, not when his mind was half full of calculated worry about what Sonny's next move might be.

Danny had been careful to stay in the shadows. He left it to their local man on the ground to do the legwork inside the club, and to feed him information. The situation was still too hot for either of them to start skulking around Sonny's residence or any other place he frequented. They would only do that if it became absolutely necessary, because the last thing they needed was to tip him off and blow the whole investigation. Danny himself mostly observed the scene around the club, and in the neighborhood. He watched the comings and goings, and looked for just the right key to what Sonny was up to.

It came one day when he noticed that one woman was missing from the group of dancers that usually showed up for work together. He had his contact listen in on talk at the club's bar that night. The contact reported to Danny that it appeared that the dancer's name was Darlene and that she was on an extended leave of absence. He then cased Darlene's apartment until he witnessed Sonny's men entering and leaving it the next day. That night Danny entered the premises to do his own recon. What he found made him more anxious than ever. The day after that, a woman's body matching Darlene's description was found in an alley not far from either her apartment or the club.

Danny wished he could just ice the fucker before heading back to Chicago. Problem solved. But that wasn't how Bear did things. The other half of his mind was on Sioban, but not as a professional would think of his client. He simply hadn't wanted to leave her, even though their best chance of being prepared required that someone get out to L.A., and Bear knew that Danny would never let anyone else do it. He had to see to this himself, though there was no logical reason for him to feel this protective of a woman he'd met less than a two weeks ago, except that the look on her face right before he left melted him. The fear in her eyes made him want to stay with her every moment. It made him want to hold her until she knew that he wouldn't let her be harmed. He wanted kiss the worry from her brow and her heart. He wanted to be the one to help her forget whatever was on the tape that he'd found in Darlene's apartment. Hell, he just wanted her.

If it were possible to clone himself, he'd leave one here on auto-pilot and put his other self on the next plane back to Chicago. Calling Sioban directly with the information he found wasn't protocol, either. Even if he did, who knew if she'd answer. He scrolled through the contacts on his company-issued phone and stared at her number. It sucked, but the best thing he could do for both of them right now was to pay attention to the job at hand, and report regularly—to Bear.

Chapter Eleven

Every man had to face tough decisions in his life. This wasn't one of them. Danny had landed at O'Hare nearly an hour ago, but getting his luggage and then to the truck and finally out and onto I-90 had taken longer than he wanted it to. He should take the next exit and head to Rockford to let Bear know what he'd found out. It wasn't good news, and that made it easier, more critical even, for him to skip that exit and head into the city. He had to see Sioban.

Being gone these past ten days, away from her, had only exacerbated his unrest where she was concerned. Because that was how he felt about it—he had to keep her safe, bless her little vixen heart. He didn't quite understand his reaction to her, but when he got to L.A. and saw Sonny's head still wrapped in bandages, he knew something more had happened than what Vonda had told Bear. And that was when this need to protect her, and get to know her, if he could admit that, had gone into overdrive.

It was past dinner time, which didn't mean anything for the refurb crew; all contractors had been putting in sixteen-hour days at Bear's urging, so that Vonda could get the club open and start making her money back. But the girls might not even be there. In which case he wouldn't bother going to the house. But this way he had the excuse that he wanted to check on progress at the bar without sending Sioban into a tailspin. And discovering a big part of what was behind her sharp tongue and fiery temper just made him want to get to what was underneath that façade more urgently. Because Danny was certain that there was so much more to her—more pain to be sure, but more beauty and joy too. He'd have a hard time explaining to anyone at the moment why he was just as certain that he was the man to do it. But right now, he didn't have to explain himself to anyone. He just wanted to lay eyes on Sioban.

But as Danny pulled up in front of the bar, several contractors, along with a few Rockford personnel, exited the door. Reece Gorman was the last one out, and Danny caught him as he pulled the door closed behind him.

"Gorman." Danny nodded at him as he stepped up. "Where's everybody going?"

"Hey. Dinner break. The guys are on the way to Manucci's. Ms. O'Rourke is inside, but I'll be staying behind. I've got eyes from all the cameras in the van. The guys can bring me a slice." Well, hell. At least with the crew around, he could act more official. But then again, maybe this was the chance he needed. He could let her know what he'd found—Bear would be pissed about that, but it was a chance he was willing to take—and at the same time, try to get her to see that he wasn't the enemy, that he'd help her. He'd be there for her.

"Take off. I'm going to go inside and check on things. *You* can bring *me* a slice, okay?"

"Thanks, Danny. But be warned. She asked to be alone for a while. I think everything is getting to her."

"I won't be here long. Any sign of Ms. Douglas?"

"She stepped out about an hour ago as well, but she'll be back to pick up Ms. O'Rourke."

"Okay, thanks, Gorman. Enjoy your pizza, and don't forget to bring me some," Danny said.

"Will do. It's good to have you back, Danny."

Danny gently turned the key in the lock. The last thing he wanted was to startle Sioban and have her brain him with a piece of equipment. Most of the lights were off inside, but even so, Danny could tell that much had been accomplished since he'd been gone. The pool table and its accoutrements and surrounding seating had been cleared to make room for a stage. Danny smiled to himself as he wondered whether or not Vonda had given in and sold it to Bear. He knew the staff at Rockford would have loved to use it during their down time, but Vonda had probably insisted that Bear take it for free. She hardly seemed to believe that Bear was going to bill her for the state-of-the art surveillance equipment or the extra manpower he'd assigned to both the bar and her home. She probably suspected that Bear had also talked his contractor friends into giving her a deal on the renovation. She was right on all counts. Danny didn't want to be around when she found out that Bear was planning on paying for the overtime needed to finish the renovation in record time out of his own pocket.

As he looked at the newly constructed stage and light box to the left of it, Danny stared in awe at the vision before him: Sioban was standing on the stage with her arms extended over her head to catch the foot of the leg she had stretched up behind her.

Danny's breath caught. She wore a tattered blue sweatshirt with the sleeves rolled up and part of the neckline cut away over a leotard. And good gravy, she'd had her hair cut. It swished in a long shag, with fringed layers that started shorter with her bangs and extended around her head and shoulders, and finally down her back. It moved with every sassy, sexy inch of her, and glowed with a coppery sheen under the single row of track lights that shone down on her. If she'd been beautiful before, she was stunning now.

Sioban reached back to grab the other foot for a brief stretch before she strolled across the stage to turn on a battered boom box that probably belonged to one of the crew members. Danny realized that she hadn't seen him, so he took a silent step back further into the shadows. He finally exhaled as the first notes of a piano sounded soulfully from the boom box. The song, "Natural Woman," was familiar enough, but it wasn't Aretha Franklin singing. Rather, it was the songwriter Carole King. Danny could understand why some people might prefer this version, especially if they ever got the chance to see Sioban dancing to it. King's voice was so wistful, and almost melancholy, but at the same time carried the power of an arrow straight to the heart. Or was that just the way the notes seemed to lift her as if she were a marionette captured in their strings?

As Sioban crossed her arms over her body and traced a semicircle on the stage with her toe, Danny sent up a silent word of thanks that someone, probably Vonda, had had the good sense to put a floor-sized rubber mat over the rough unfinished floor of the stage. He cringed at the thought of splinters tearing into her feet. Every lilt of her arms told him what she needed. Every spin and turn had his blood pumping. She swayed, he wanted to reach out and catch her. She tossed her head, he wanted to turn her face toward him. She took one step, then two quick ones and leapt into the air like a gazelle, with one knee bent and the other leg stretched out behind her, and his heart nearly burst out of his chest.

Too soon, the song faded, and Sioban sank to her knees and let herself fall forward.

"Exquisite..." *Shit*. He said that aloud, and not as softly as he whispered it in his head. The beautiful green eyes that had been closed in the final passion of her dance flew open. Danny knew she'd be pissed, but the panic and downright fear he saw in them made him want to weep.

"Reece?... Reece!—Who's here?"

Danny stepped gingerly out into the light where she could see him. He didn't have a white handkerchief, and he was tempted to put his hands up in surrender. But this was his chance to be himself, his chance to reach her. And it wasn't just about addressing their obvious attraction for each other. In fact, it wasn't even about that at all. Sioban was special, not like any woman he'd met before, not even Caryn. And there was no doubt he wanted her, physically, with every fiber of his being. But after going to L.A. to find out what had happened, and now seeing her dance...he wanted so much more. He wanted to know her, protect her, hell, even love her if she'd give him the chance. He prayed that just talking to her now, just the two of them, would be enough to really break the ice between them.

"It's Danny, Sioban. I just got back from L.A. and I wanted to see how things were progressing here. The guys went for pizza so I told Gorman I would look after you—"

"Look after me?! You scared the bloody hell out of me!" And there it was. It had only taken an instant, and the mere fact that it was him, to send the beet-red flush of anger through her cheeks and make her eyes flash bright again.

"I'm sorry, I should have called Gorman first, or announced myself—"

"Fucking right you should have! Christ, it's been so peaceful these last ten days, and now here you are taking charge again, steamrolling over everyone. Well, see to your business then, and the next time you see me, let me know you're coming so I can fucking run the other way!"

Before he could tell her that he'd had every intention of announcing himself, but hadn't wanted to interrupt her dancing, before he could tell her how flat-out mesmerized he'd been by watching her, she flew down the temporary stairs at right end of the front of the stage, and stomped out of the main bar area toward the office.

Only a few days before, he would have gotten in her face and thrown a retort at her that would have either shut her up or made her slap him. But he knew why she was running now, pushing him away with all her might, or at least he thought he knew part of the reason. But he wasn't going to let her run this time. Danny followed after her, and put his toe out just in time to stop the door as Sioban tried to slam it behind her. Before she could wheel on him, he came up behind her and took her by the arms. He had to make her see that he was here to help her, not hurt her or make her angry. He pulled her back toward his chest.

"Sioban, please, let me just talk to you a minute—"

But in the next moment a new kind of hell broke loose that he was in no way prepared for.

§

Vonda huffed as she balanced the bakery boxes while she tried to unlock the door to Johnny's. She still found it difficult not to think of it as her father's pub in spite of the progress with the renovation. Getting the new sign up would help with that, but that step was a long way off. She'd had some banking business to take care of and then she'd stopped at Delmonico's for some cannoli and a few other treats for the guys, knowing that dessert would be appreciated no matter how much pizza they'd eaten.

As she turned the key in the lock, Vonda glanced at the Rockford van across the street behind her. Of course there were no windows open to the back, so she knew she wouldn't be able to see whomever they had elected to stay behind and keep an eye on the bar—and on Sioban—while she was gone. But she found it odd that whoever was in there wouldn't stick his head out to greet her, if not offer to help her with the boxes, given what gentlemen they all were.

But when Vonda pushed the door open, something primal in her took over. Sioban's piercing screams echoed from the back office. She dashed the bakery boxes to the ground, and didn't stop to close the door behind her. She tore through the bar not exactly knowing what she would find or how she would deal with it. Vonda only knew that if Sonny Coniglione or his henchman had found Sioban, she was going to fight alongside her best friend to the death, hopefully his.

Only the sight of Danny struggling to calm a flailing, crazed Sioban nearly brought her up short. In an instant, she assessed the situation, and her mind raced with how she could intervene without anyone getting hurt.

"Danny! Stop!" When he didn't let Sioban go, Vonda put her index finger and thumb in her mouth and gave a shrill whistle before she called out to him again. They were both reaching exhaustion, which Vonda surmised was what had allowed her to finally break through the chaos and reach them. "DANNY!"

He let her go then, and Sioban stumbled forward and fell against the desk. Jesus Christ. It was no surprise that it was in the office in front of a desk, just like when Sonny attacked her, when she finally lost it. Vonda rushed forward, only putting one arm around Sioban, who was now sobbing.

"Darling, it's Von. Shhh, now, it's all right. Just breathe for me, okay?" Then she turned back to Danny, who stood staring in shock behind her.

"Vonda, I didn't—"

"I know, Danny, just wait for me out in the bar. It's going to be okay." She took a couple of quick steps over to the mini fridge and grabbed a bottle of water, along with a wad of tissues from the desk. She dampened them with a little of the water, and held them alternately against the back of Sioban's neck and her forehead and cheeks.

Sioban was still bracing herself against the desk. She'd stopped sobbing, but she was shaking almost uncontrollably.

"God, what have I done...?"

"You haven't done anything, sweetie. Come sit over here and try to drink some of this water." Vonda led her over to the old couch and eased them both down onto it as she handed the bottle of water to Sioban.

"I just...he came up behind me so fast, and then I was back there, in Jimmy's office, with Sonny—" She choked back another sob, and Vonda rubbed her back.

"Sioban, this is still so fresh. You've only just gotten here to safety. We still have to hear what Danny found out, and you need to talk to someone—professionally."

"I know. Oh, Danny... I've been so bitchy to him, and he only came here to check on things since he's been away. But he didn't tell me he'd come in, and he saw me dancing. I felt so vulnerable, I was so angry with him, and then he followed me back to the office...I know he didn't intend to hurt me. But he put his hands on my arms and then I just lost it. He'll think the worst of me for sure now."

Vonda tucked Sioban's hair behind her ear with sisterly affection. "Oh hon, I think Danny understands more than you give him credit for. You just need to calm down, and maybe you can talk to him."

"I'm going to have to tell Bear the whole story, aren't I?"

Vonda sighed. "I'm afraid so. Depending on what they found, Danny could probably see that you'd done a lot more damage than just pushing Sonny down and absconding with his money. And Bear needs to know what happened so he can determine how best to help us."

"You're right. But that also means that Danny will have to be told. After today, I...I want to tell him myself."

"Okay, sweetie. He's pretty shaken up, though, and he's had a long trip, too. Why don't you collect yourself, and you can talk to him tomorrow after you've both gotten some rest?"

"Okay."

"That's my girl. Try to finish this water. I'm going to go out there and make sure the bar is still standing."

§

Danny didn't hear the contractor guys laughing at the punch line of the crude joke someone had told as they came into the bar, or one of Rockford's men curse as he slipped on a cannoli, or Gorman's "What the fuck?" as he pushed past the other men and rushed over to where Danny sat at the bar rubbing his temples in frustration and anguish.

"Danny!—what the hell, man? The door was open, and where'd those cannolis come from?"

Before Danny could form an explanation, Vonda materialized from the back.

"Hi Reece, it's okay. When I got back, I thought I heard something and panicked. But I ruined the cannolis I got for you fellas for nothing."

Danny eyed Gorman, and tried to signal him they'd talk about it later. Apparently it worked, because Gorman laughed it off.

"Oh, Ms. Douglas, these miscreants will eat anything. Besides, only one or two fell out of the boxes. I don't know what we did to deserve a treat like that."

"Well, all of you have worked so hard, so I wanted to thank you, and I thought we'd celebrate. Let me salvage what I can of dessert, and get some plates."

"Oh, the boys and I will take care of it, Ms. Douglas. Why don't you talk to Danny here about whatever had you so spooked when you came in?" Gorman winked at her, which made Danny roll his eyes. The man was a charmer to be sure, but Danny was grateful Gorman had the sense to distract the other men so that he and Vonda could talk. Gorman laid a pizza box on the bar next to Danny, and as he walked away, Vonda took a bar stool next to him.

"Hey," she said. Bless her, but he couldn't imagine where she found it in her to gift him with such a warm smile after what had just happened. Sioban was lucky to have a friend like her. "Are you all right?"

"I'm...Jesus, I didn't hurt her, did I? You have to believe me, I was just—"

Vonda put her hand on his arm. "Danny, I *know*. You didn't do anything wrong. Honestly, she was bound to have a meltdown. She needs to talk to someone."

"Bear and I are obviously in the dark about everything that went down in L.A." Danny felt bad that she looked down at her hands in embarrassment, but she had to understand that without all of the facts, not only could they not protect her and Sioban as thoroughly, but they also might end up inadvertently doing something to harm them—just like he'd done tonight.

"I'm sorry, Danny. I'll apologize to Bear as well, tomorrow. It wasn't my place to tell him the whole story. I didn't even tell Sioban what I'd done until after I met with Bear. I just didn't think there was anything else I could do, but I had to do something. I had been working out how to encourage her to talk to someone—and either let me tell Bear what happened, or tell him herself. And now you're back, with God knows what to tell us."

Danny sighed and ran a hand through his hair, his fallback gesture of frustration.

"That's just it," he told her. "I did clearly see that whatever happened made Sioban open up a can of whup-ass on Sonny Coniglione."

"At least he's alive, so she won't be facing murder charges. But when I heard her screaming, I thought he'd sent someone after her, or come here himself."

"Exactly." Danny winced, thinking of how terrified Sioban had been. He'd never forget the sound of her screams. "I wanted to talk to her myself, even before I went to see Bear. I know we didn't get off to a good start, Sioban and I, but I wanted to be the one to go to L.A. And God help me, the minute I landed, I wanted to come see for myself that she was all right. I wanted to let her know that Rockford—that Bear and I wouldn't let her down, and that no matter what had taken place out there, somebody would have her back. And yours too, for that matter."

"You're a good man, Danny, and so is Bear. And Sioban is, well, herself. What exactly set her off?"

"Well, I was an idiot. I sent Gorman to eat with the rest of the men and told him I'd take care of her. But when I came in, she was onstage. She started dancing, and...I was mesmerized. I should have stopped her, let her know I was in the bar with her. But I couldn't take my eyes off of her. When she was finished I muttered something about how wonderful her dancing was—out loud."

"I don't blame you for admiring her. She is a wonderful dancer, she just hasn't found the right outlet yet. Until hopefully now. But how did you end up in the office, if I may ask?"

"Of course it pissed her off that someone was watching her, and doubly so because it was me. She stormed away, and I should have just let her cool off. But I really thought if we could just talk, one on one, we could get past this...irritation we have for each other. So I foolishly followed her into the office. I wasn't rough with her, I just put my hands on her arms. When I tried to pull her close to me and talk to her, she went nuts."

Vonda shifted nervously on her stool. "Danny, I'm going to share one tiny little snippet of information with you. But you need to promise me that you won't go to Bear with it until she tells you the whole story herself."

"Okay." Danny was more overcome by the fact that Sioban still wanted to talk to him at all after the mistake he'd made than he was with the anticipation of whatever Vonda was about to tell him.

"Sioban's...altercation...with Sonny happened in Jimmy's office at Club 29." Vonda seemed to will him to understand.

Of course. The office. She'd been standing with her back to him, near the desk. The sonofabitch had tried to pin her to the desk. Danny pushed up off of his stool and let loose a loud string of expletives. The other men, who had been eating cannolis out of the boxes with their hands and trading more lewd jokes, suddenly looked up. Gorman lifted his chin at Danny.

"You all right, man?"

No. "Yeah, never mind. Carry on." When Danny turned back to face Vonda, she melted him with the empathy in her eyes, which only made him feel guiltier about putting Sioban in a situation that triggered her worst nightmare.

"Danny. I'm so sorry you stepped into that without knowing—"

"And I still don't know, not all of it. Jesus fucking Christ. I hope she'll be able to trust me enough to tell me about it, at least enough that can help me protect her and bring Sonny Coniglione down."

"She will. She just needs a little time. Like I said to her, you're exhausted from your trip, and she needs to calm down. You'll both be better equipped to face each other after a good night's rest."

Except there would be no rest for him, he thought, until he could be sure Sioban was safe, and that she understood he was there to keep her that way rather than hurt or upset her.

"For what it's worth, she feels terrible for how she reacted to you, Danny. She wasn't in her right mind."

He wanted to shout again, but he didn't want to stir the curiosity of the others any more than he already had. "Goddamnit," he bit out so that only Vonda could hear him. "She should not feel terrible. She's been attacked, and I just reminded her of it in living color."

"Nevertheless, it was unintentional, and she knows that. Just like you knew that she was reacting to something that had nothing to do with you."

Danny stared at Vonda for a long moment. He'd been prepared to dislike her that first morning at the bar for the simple reason that Bear made him come along. But even though he'd behaved like an asshole to her best friend, Vonda had graciously made allowances for him. Like the way she giving him the benefit of the doubt as far as Sioban was concerned. And wasn't it ironic that Sioban was the one who had driven him crazy and had captured his heart.

Vonda stood then, and reached over the bar to grab a roll of paper towels. "Since nobody's mommy is here, I'm going to see that the boys wipe their hands and faces. I also need to wipe up the floor and check on Sioban."

"Tell her..."

"I'll tell her you'll be ready to talk to her whenever she is. It's going to be okay, Danny."

"I hope so."

He followed Von back across the bar on his way to the door. He gave a chin lift at Gorman, who thankfully didn't try to detain him on his way out.

Chapter Twelve

The ceiling lamp over Bear's round dining-room table seemed almost too bright. There was none of the raucous laughter or good-natured accusations of cheating that accompanied the poker games held at this table. Instead, Bear poured them each three fingers of his best Scotch and pushed a glass across the table toward Danny, who leaned back with one arm over his chair and peered into the glass as he turned it slowly. Bear waited a long moment before he spoke.

"Well?"

Danny looked across the table at his friend and boss, wondering where to begin. Finally, he downed his Scotch with one gulp and leaned in.

"Whatever happened out there, she clocked the hell out of him with something. His head is still bandaged."

"Huh." Clearly Bear was not about jump in with both feet until Danny had said all he came to say.

"I stopped by the bar before I came here." At that, Bear raised his eyebrows.

"And?"

"Gorman was headed to the surveillance van when I got there, said Vonda had gone out, but that Sioban was still inside. I sent him on with the rest of the men to grab dinner, told him I'd keep an eye on the place." He sighed, not wanting to continue his report, but knew he didn't have a choice. "When I came in, she was onstage, preparing to dance. I didn't want to scare her...and then she turned on the music and did this routine...anyway, I must have said something out loud—I did say something out loud by accident, I gave her a compliment. She panicked, and of course she was royally pissed when she found out I'd been watching her without announcing myself."

Danny hung his head. This whole thing sucked. He knew Bear was waiting for him to go on, and as if on cue, he said, "Go on." Bear's voice took on a brotherly tone that let Danny know it was okay to finish his story, that Bear would help him work things out, no matter what he had to say.

"The thing is, I know I've been an ass around her. What can I say, the woman gets under my skin. But I never actually meant to be an ass. I think it was obvious, even without Vonda telling us, that she'd been through something. Then when she asked you for Rockford's help...well, you know all that."

Bear just nodded at him, waiting for him to spit the rest of it out.

"I went to the bar just wanting to talk to her, really talk to her, like two human beings. I was sure that I could convince her that underneath it all, I'm a decent guy, and that I was there to help her, and not just because my boss told me to. Especially after the kind of hurting she'd put on Sonny Coniglione. She stomped off and went to the office, and I was still convinced that I could turn the moment around. I followed her in there, and just laid my hands on her arms. I wanted to comfort her, I swear to you. But she lost it, man. I mean, she went into another dimension. Thank God Vonda came in and knew what to do. At that point, I was just trying to calm her down, but that wasn't happening. I'm not sure I could have restrained her much longer before one of us got hurt. Shit, I was afraid I already had." He paused to gauge Bear's reaction. He still wore a look of brotherly concern. "For Sioban to have clocked him in the head like that, she had to have a weapon, which means whatever he was doing to her was pretty serious. I obviously triggered that experience somehow."

"Listen, it may not have been the smartest thing for you not to tell her you were in the bar with her. But the rest—Danny, it could have been any one of us in that office with her at the wrong moment. Any one of us could have tapped her on the shoulder or come up behind her the wrong way."

"I still doubt she'll ever speak to me again. There's something else...one last piece."

"Oh?"

"There's a surveillance video from the club in L.A. The whole thing is recorded. Obviously I haven't watched it yet, and I don't think we should—at least not until we give her the chance to tell us first."

"Agreed—but how the hell did you come by it anyway?"

Danny filled him in on what he'd found from start to finish.

"Jesus. You weren't kidding about getting lucky on this one. I remember Vonda mentioning that one of the dancers in particular was trouble, but even if she was talking about Darlene, why would Darlene have kept the tape?"

"Blackmail is the only thing that makes sense. She might have been able to turn it into a permanent meal ticket from Jimmy, or even Sonny."

"But it also increases the stakes tremendously."

"Yeah."

"You need to get some sleep. Since you downed that whiskey, I think you should crash on the couch tonight."

"Fine, then pour me another one, and brief me on the rest of the schedule at the bar before I do." Danny scooted his empty glass across the table. Bear poured another small amount into it and added a little more to his own glass.

"You know, you two have both been acting out since you met. But in spite of the circumstances, I think you underestimate Sioban's ability to let you in. She just needs some time."

"Vonda said the same thing. Funny part is, I didn't even know I wanted 'in' until I saw her today."

"But I did," said Bear and laughed.

Between exhaustion and the second Scotch, Danny had just enough energy left in him to stumble out to his truck for his duffle bag.

When the cold air hit him, all the warmth of the whiskey left his body. He shivered as new questions gnawed at him. He wanted to believe Vonda and Bear when they said that things would be okay between him and Sioban. But what if they weren't? What if she wanted nothing to do with him, and asked Bear to assign one of the other team members to protect her? Worse yet, what if, even though a year had passed since Caryn had cheated on him, he still couldn't trust his heart, and he was wrong about what he thought could grow between him and Sioban?

As he closed the door on the last gust of night air that licked at the back of his neck, Danny knew he'd just have to go with it. He'd just have to try. Because no way was his heart going to let him off the hook.

§

The sunlight felt deceptively warm on Sioban's face as it poured through the window. She'd been awake for two hours already, staring and thinking. The memory of Sonny Coniglione's greasy hands on her was still fresh in her mind, to be sure. But not as fresh as that of Danny's warm, silky touch on her arms, or the tingle that rippled through her at the knowledge that he'd seen her dance.

How could she explain it to him, the irrational impulse to fight that overcame her in those moments, when she was still trying to explain it to herself? It was as if she'd been standing outside herself, not just watching, but arguing internally with another part of herself, that was so very frightened and angry, to stop. She'd seen that Danny wasn't there to hurt her, just as she'd seen something in him that she'd wanted to see more of, know more of. It was that confession, even more than recounting the events in Jimmy's office, that had her tied in knots. He'd come to the bar last night with good intentions, that much was obvious. But she'd rejected him time and again with such violent determination, and last night might have been her last chance to interact with him like a normal human being.

Sioban threw back the covers, and climbed out of her bed. She crossed to Von's old vanity table and took a seat in front of it.

"Courage, girl. Courage," she said to her reflection in preparation to face the day.

The little pep talk she'd given herself proved almost useless when she arrived at the bar and saw Danny going over blueprints with one of the contractors. He hadn't seen her come in, and so the tables were turned now, as she listened to him explain to the other man that he had to be mindful of the security cameras that had already been installed, and that all further aspects of the renovation were to be reviewed with a Rockford team member before implementation.

He was strong, sure of himself. And she sensed his toughness, which could be downright scary, just below the surface. But she'd known all along, deep down, that he'd never hurt her, even when he'd scowled at her with all his might that first day. Still, after what had happened last night, maybe she'd really pissed him off now. Before he could notice her, she slipped past to the bar where Von was going over some notes of her own. She looked up and smiled as Sioban approached.

"Hey hon. Didn't you find my note to call me to come get you? I thought you needed the extra rest and I had to get in right away."

"Yeah, I got it, but I didn't mind taking the bus today—I had a lot of thinking to do."

"How are you feeling this morning?"

"If I had to pick one word to describe it, I guess it would be trepidatious. But here I am."

"That's my girl." Vonda winked at her.

"Sorry I'm slacking off this morning. Let me know how I can help."

"Like I said, you needed your rest. Just focus on what you need to get done with Danny today, and there will be plenty to help me with later on. As a matter of fact, before we can start recruiting or auditioning, we need to hire a stage manager. I'm thinking of calling an old friend of mine who'd be perfect, but I'm not sure what he's up to. If I reach him, maybe you can go with me to meet him later."

"Sure, that sounds great. The stage will be finished soon, and it would be good if we had a stage manager already on board to help finish designing the sound and light booth. Count me in."

Sioban noticed Vonda focusing on something slightly to the left. "I think someone would like to talk to you now. I'm going back to the office to call my friend. I'll see you later."

"God willing," joked Sioban before she turned around to see Danny coming toward her. The good news was that he didn't seem to be angry with her, but beyond that she couldn't tell what he was thinking.

"Good morning." His voice was warm, and it reminded her of his hands on her arms the night before.

"Top o' the mornin' to you." Why not? She could try being funny-cheeky instead of obnoxious-cheeky. It worked. Danny gave a hearty laugh. The ice was broken.

"I thought your accent only got thicker when you were provoked," he said.

"Who says I'm not? Maybe I'm just redirecting it."

"Fair enough. Listen, Sioban." But she couldn't let him be the one to start.

"No, Danny, I have to...I have to explain." He paused for a moment, and she didn't think she'd survive the penetrating look he gave her. "Please."

"Not here. There's a coffee shop a couple of blocks over. If that's okay."

"That would be good. I don't mind walking, now I've got a proper coat." She hoped her smile would put him at ease.

"Well, at any rate, it's not far."

Danny gave a few final instructions to the contractor as he put on his coat and hat. Sioban had been content to walk behind him, but he pushed the door open and stood back, holding it for her with the expanse of his arm. He almost put a hand on her back as she walked through, but then shrank as if he were afraid to touch her at all. She found herself wishing somehow that he would.

He glanced over briefly at the van with what Sioban presumed was a signal to whoever was inside, just as Bear got out of his SUV. He waved at them as he crossed the street to the bar.

"Morning, you two. Everybody okay today?"

"Yeah, we're just going to get some coffee," said Danny. "I reminded the contractor to get approval before implementing any steps. The new alarm system is scheduled to be installed today. I should be back before the company gets here."

"Take your time, I'll be here for the rest of the day. Right now I think coffee is more important." He gave them a knowing glance and patted Danny on the shoulder on his way inside.

Oh, he has no idea, thought Sioban. She wished that she could take Danny's hand as they continued down the sidewalk, or that he would take hers. But she knew that she'd have to take it one step at a time with Danny, and she was going to make sure that she didn't take a wrong one today.

§

When Bear stepped inside, he nodded at the contractor, but kept moving. He saw what he was after behind the bar. He smiled at Vonda, but she looked nervously away. He sighed to himself. Well, he suspected she'd be upset about last night, and probably feeling guilty for not telling him the whole story about Sioban when she asked for his help. But it was his job to put her mind at ease, if she'd let him.

"Good morning, Ms. Douglas," he said as he sidled up to the bar and took a stool.

"'Ms,' huh? Sounds like I'm in trouble."

"Not at all. What makes you say that?"

"Oh, I only asked for your help with a very dangerous situation without giving you complete information." She still hadn't made eye contact, but that wasn't going to last.

"Vonda." Bear didn't quite put the mojo on her that he used with his staff. But he wanted her full attention. She met his eyes and wrung the bar towel in her hands. For a brief instant, she looked like she might burst into tears, but he knew better. She straightened herself and stuck out her chin just enough to let him know that he wasn't talking to one of his men. Damn, she was hot when she got determined. "I knew you weren't telling me the whole story when you left that day."

"How?" she asked.

"Honey, I've been in this business a long time, and I know the signs, especially since it was dangerous enough for you to investigate my company's website. I also noticed how anxious you seemed when I found you in the lobby."

Vonda sighed and tossed the towel onto the bar. "I'm sorry, Bear. I really am. I was going to get Sioban to tell you when Danny got back from L.A., or get her permission to tell you myself. I'm just a day late and a dollar short."

"I knew that, too—that one of you would tell me when Danny got back. Vonda, I would never expect you to betray the trust of your friend that way, unless it was life or death, and even then I'd weigh all possible options before I'd ask you to spill the beans on something like that. As it turns out, we hadn't reached that critical mass yet. Had Sonny or any of his people tried to track her here, that would be a different scenario. But Danny confirmed what I suspected would happen when he got out there, that he'd see evidence of some missing pieces. The good news is that Sioban didn't kill Sonny, so we won't have to prove self-defense. Now Danny and I just need to sit down and figure out our next move."

"Thank you for being so understanding. You're right, I wanted to do everything I could to avoid embarrassing her until we knew what Danny would find. I'll do whatever I can to make the rest of the investigation go smoothly."

"Well, in that case, how about pouring me a cup of that coffee back there? It smells heavenly." She returned his smile then, and he knew it was going to be a good day.

Chapter Thirteen

Blessedly, Danny's phone went off as they walked toward the coffee shop. He looked at the caller I.D.

"It's the alarm company," he said to Sioban. "They're installing the new system this afternoon, so I'd better take it."

She nodded her okay. He didn't want to be rude, and he really should take the call. But more than that, he didn't want to say or do anything to break their uneasy truce. Sioban had made it clear that she wanted to be the first to address what happened last night, and she wasn't going to get into it until they were settled in over their coffee. The phone call meant he didn't have to create small talk, or, worse, appear as if he were ignoring her as they walked.

Danny only half heard what the man on the other end said. He tried to pay attention to the important points. Yes, 2:30. Yes, either he or Bear would be on hand during the installation. Rockford would cover the cost and be reimbursed by the client. Thank you, goodbye. The call ended just a few paces shy of the coffee shop. Danny turned to Sioban. She seemed half a world away, but he couldn't stand for there to be silence between them at the moment.

"We've worked with this alarm company many times before. They have superior technical design and their system comes with a lifetime warranty. But they've got a new guy handling installations, and I think he's a tad paranoid."

Sioban made a small sound of acknowledgement. God, he wanted to hold her. And he also wanted to kiss away that furrow in her brow. He didn't know how he was going to get through this day, much less the next several, without touching her.

But he'd do whatever it took to make her feel safe around him and trust him, even if it proved to be sheer torture for him.

When they finally turned into the coffee shop, Danny chose a table near the front, but not directly in front of any of the windows, and held out the chair facing away from the front. This time he was careful not to touch her at all. He'd urged her forward with his hand on the small of her back when they came in. He couldn't do shit like that if he wanted her to trust him.

"Don't like your back to the door, I see. Is that a security-expert thing, or a just a man thing?" Danny could tell she was going for humor, but anxiety still shone in her eyes. And for whatever reason, she was still standing.

"It's a combination of things. Have a seat, and I'll get us some coffee."

"Actually, I'd like to get our breakfast for us. My treat. Please."

Lord, she wasn't making it very easy for him to show her that he could be a gentleman. But he nodded and sat down. At least he could get the lay of the land while he sat there. Sioban returned with a small round tray. On it was a single French press coffee pot, a tea pot with tea already steeping, two mugs, and a plate with two pastries. She set the tray between them and sat down across from him without taking her coat off. Then again, he hadn't taken his off either. Maybe they were both hoping this would go quickly.

"I hope you don't mind French press—I wasn't sure which brew you preferred. And cinnamon twists are my favorite—I got you one too, just in case."

"Thank you. French press is fine," he answered as he poured coffee for them both. "And I wouldn't want you to be the only one eating a cinnamon twist."

141

Except she took neither a sip of her coffee nor a bite of her pastry. When he caught her eye, she just looked down at her lap.

"Sonny almost raped me." Jesus fucking Christ. He tried to think of what to say when she powered on. "I'm guessing Von told Bear what the club was like in general. She had tried to make it a little more legitimate and classy, but there were still a few girls on the poles. And when she left, it didn't take Jimmy very long to turn it back the way it had been before Von had worked there. Only this time he made some other changes. Curtained off the booths for...certain clients and their requests. I was a good hostess, so that kept me off of the poles, for the most part. For a while Jimmy let me maintain the one legit dance number we had, but most of the dancers that Von had hired quit when they realized the direction Jimmy was taking the club in.

"Anyway, one night Jimmy alluded to the fact that I hadn't been called on to perform certain duties. He said I was special and that he was saving me for a special occasion and a special client. Sonny was that client. Jimmy called me to his office that night and Sonny was there waiting for me. Jimmy told me not to fuck it up and left us alone. I turned the music on and thought I could get away with just dancing for him, but he came up behind me and...pinned me face down on the desk. I just couldn't end up...I couldn't let him do that to me without a fight, even if it was the last thing I did on this earth. I saw the marble panther on Jimmy's desk in front of me, and took aim. I knew I had to get out of there, not just the club, but out of L.A. That's why I took the cash, so I could buy a plane ticket without leaving a paper trail. I've been watching too many detective shows, I guess."

"Fuck the money. And fuck Sonny Coniglione." Fury boiled through Danny from the inside out. He noticed his own clenched fists on the table and knew he had to get it under control, or he'd risk frightening her again. He blew out his breath and spoke again. "Look at me, Sioban."

She lifted her chin. She met his gaze, and goddamnit her eyes were brimming.

"You did everything right. You were incredibly brave, not only in defending yourself, but in coming up with a plan on the fly to get the hell out of the club and out of the city."

"I'm sorry I didn't come forward before you went out there. Von told me last night that Sonny's still alive. At least I won't be charged with murder."

"Even if Sonny had died, it wouldn't go down like that. We wouldn't let that happen. It was self-defense. Period."

Sioban wiped at her eyes with a napkin. "Anyway, I would have gone straight to Bear, but I didn't want you to hear it second hand because of...last night."

"Sioban, you have to know, when I came to the bar, I really, genuinely wanted to talk to you. When I followed you into the office, I didn't mean to—"

"I know, Danny. And you have to know that it was the desk that triggered my reaction. That, and the fact that I need to talk to someone professional about this, instead of keeping it bottled up inside."

Suddenly she seemed so vulnerable sitting there, and it killed him. She couldn't let this steal her fire. My god, the woman had clocked a mobster with a marble statue and lived to tell about it. She was something else. And Danny would do everything in his power to make sure she knew it. Impulsively, his hand began to move across the table toward her, but he pulled it back in time.

"I'm so sorry, Sioban. Sorry I didn't announce myself when I came into the bar. Sorry I chased after you to the office."

"It was the desk, Danny. Not you. It wasn't because you...why did you flinch away from me? You put your hand on my back earlier and then took it away as if you'd burned it. And just now, almost reached for my hand, but you held back."

Oh hell. He'd been so careful not to upset her again, and now he'd made her feel like he couldn't stand to touch her. Fuck.

"Did you think I would lose it again, and go ballistic in public?" she asked.

"No, sweetheart." The endearment flew out of his mouth before he could stop himself. But it was how he felt. "I just..."

Suddenly, he saw something, or rather someone, that he didn't like the looks of. A man of average build with short dark hair walked into the coffee shop. Even though the patrons here were ethnically diverse, the man's European style had Danny on alert. He was dressed the part of a young independent professional. But he didn't seem at ease with himself.

"Danny, I—"

"Have a cinnamon twist, Sioban." He took a bite of one of the pastries in hopes that she would follow suit.

"Well, I'm not that hungry at the moment." She was starting to get pissed because she thought he was being insensitive to all she'd just told him. At least the fire hadn't left her, thank God.

"You haven't touched your tea or your pastry. We're in a coffee shop. We need to seem normal. We're going to sip a little coffee and have a bite or two of our pastries, and then we're going to realize the time, and casually get up and leave."

144

He saw understanding flicker across her face. She took a sip of coffee, followed by a bite of pastry. Danny took another bite of his as well. He glanced up at the security mirror near the shelves of merchandise, and noticed that the man was still waiting to place an order at the coffee bar.

"We'd better get going," Danny said, not loud enough to draw attention, but if the man were listening for a cue, he'd hear it. Danny took a final swig from his coffee and stood. Sioban took another sip of hers, and wiped her lips with the napkin, not appearing too rushed. *Good girl*, Danny thought. He came around and pulled her chair back for her as she stood.

Danny himself was trying not to appear rushed, and he was trying equally hard not to touch her again as they walked out. When they'd gotten several steps away, Sioban looked back over her shoulder.

"Keep moving." Danny hated that he'd gone all military on her, but he had to stay focused in order to keep her safe. And bingo, there was an alley just after the next shop entrance. "Step in here."

Once in the alleyway, Danny motioned for her to stand close to the wall on the other side of a dumpster. He stood a bit in front of her where he could remain hidden but still watch to see if the man from the coffee shop had followed them.

"It's Sonny, isn't it? He's come after me," Sioban said behind him. His desire to ease her fear was immediate, but he had to be sure about the man first.

"Give me a minute."

Danny heard her sigh in frustration and hoped she could hang on for him. After a few more seconds, he was rewarded with the sight of the man passing by. He was walking at a good clip and didn't seem to be searching for anyone in particular, which was a good sign. Relieved, he turned back to Sioban. He stepped closer to her and looked at her intently. He wanted to be sure she understood what he was about to tell her.

"First, it wasn't Sonny. There was a man back in the coffee shop who seemed out of place to me. I'm probably being paranoid, but I'm not taking any chances. I wanted to be sure he hadn't followed us."

"And?"

"He walked past the alley a few seconds ago without so much as a glance in our direction. I don't think he was following us." Sioban's shoulders sagged with relief.

"Second," he continued, "there are times when I'm focused. I don't mean to sound rude or brusque. It's not personal, and I need you to trust that and roll with it. Okay?"

"Okay. I know that when you're in work mode, you need your clients to cooperate with you." She shivered then, whether from being cold or from something else he wasn't sure.

And although he hated to admit it, he had to get Sioban back to the bar, where there were other people around and he wouldn't do something neither of them was ready for.

He needed to get out of the alley, and quite frankly, he needed to put some distance between them before he lost all resolve. He turned to lead them out of the alley and back to the bar. They'd only made it a few steps when he heard her plaintive voice behind him.

"Danny?" *Shit*. He turned to face her again.

"Yeah, honey?"

"I just wanted to tell you—I *need* to tell you that I'm sorry, so very sorry for how I've acted since that first day."

"I understand where all that was coming from now. And I'm the one who needs to apologize to you, Sioban. I'm the one who's sorry. More than you'll ever know."

"Oh Danny...when I saw you today, and you agreed to talk with me, I hoped it would mean a chance for me to make things right with you."

"Honey, making things right is the only thing I've wanted to do since I got off the goddamn plane yesterday."

Sioban took a breath as if she wanted to say something more, but then looked at the ground. *Just give her a minute, Sheridan. Don't screw this up.*

"I wanted you to take my hand back at the coffee shop. I thought...but then you pulled away. It's almost like you're at war with yourself."

"Sioban..."

She shook her head and took a step back. She still wouldn't look at him.

"No, I don't blame you. Even if you wanted...even if you felt something between us, Sonny's already soiled me with his hands. That must be a turnoff to you."

No. No! No way in hell was he going to allow her to believe that. The fact that she did made him want to punch a hole in the wall, especially when it had been his own stubbornness and moodiness that had kept her at a distance. He gritted his teeth and tilted her head up as gently as he could. She startled when their eyes met, probably misunderstanding the origin of the frustration she no doubt saw in them.

"You're right," he admitted. "I have been at war with myself since the moment I saw you standing in the middle of the street, but not for the reasons you think. As soon as I left for L.A. I wanted to turn around and come back to Chicago and make sure you were safe.

I can't explain the effect you have on me and that scares me, because the last time I felt this way about a woman...well, it didn't end so well. But I want to work it out. I want to be the one to protect you, and I want to be there when we get to the other side of this thing to explore what's happening between us. If you'll let me, that is."

"I don't quite understand what you do to me either. I feel safe when I'm with you, but trusting anyone is what scares me. When you saw me dancing, that meant you'd really seen *me*. And even in my overwrought state in the office, deep down I knew you didn't mean me any harm. I knew you would have held me if I'd let you. Part of me wants that so much. But the other part of me just wants to run."

It broke Danny's heart to see the tears shimmer in her eyes, tears that she must have been holding back a long time. He took her face in his hands again.

"Well, the next time you feel like running, Irish, why don't you try running to me, okay?"

"Okay."

He pulled her to him, and swayed with her as she cried. "I wanted to hold you like this last night," he whispered as he kissed the top of her head. "I wanted to tell you about everything I've been thinking about while I was away. I'm here, Sioban, and I'm going to keep you safe."

She clutched at the back of his leather jacket, and he held her tighter. The wind had picked up and it was cold as fuck, but he'd hold her like this as long as she needed him to.

After another minute or two, she pulled back to look up at him. "Thank you," she said shakily. He brushed the dampness from her cheeks with his thumbs as he cupped her face in his hands.

"Do you have any idea how fucking beautiful you are? I couldn't speak when I watched you dancing. You took my breath away, Irish."

Her eyes glittered deep green with need and fire.

"You took my breath away," he said again as his mouth came down over hers.

"Danny..." He swallowed her sigh as their lips met, and answered with his own soft groan of relief at the contact.

He heard nothing, felt nothing, except her body against him and the taste of cinnamon on her lips. He'd wanted to devour her mouth all morning, but now he moved over it with his lips slowly, languorously, making it last. He gave her his tongue in hot, lazy strokes, and when she moaned and gave him hers in return, he thought he would burst into flames.

Danny had never realized he could get this excited just from kissing a woman, and his brain could not wrap itself around what it would feel like to make love to her. He heard muffled groans, and realized it was their own sounds of passion. He had to stop, but he couldn't, not yet, it was too good, too sweet. The loud protest of a bus horn finally reached the logical part of his brain, and he tore his mouth away from hers.

"Christ." Danny leaned his forehead against hers. They were both panting, trying to catch their breath. "I'm sorry, Sioban."

"I knew you didn't want this, I—" She tried to pull away, but he held her to him.

"Not sorry in that way. Sioban, that was the most amazing kiss I've ever experienced. I'm only sorry because you deserve more than a make-out session in an alley."

"Oh." She smiled, and a crimson patch spread across her cheeks. "What do we do now?"

"Well, as hot as you are, it's still fucking cold out here. We need to get back."

"But I mean..."

"I know what you mean, sweetheart. There's a lot at stake here, and my first priority will always be to keep you safe until this thing with Sonny is handled. Beyond that, I want to get to know you, Sioban. Physically, I know we're going to be amazing together. But I want a foundation there to back it up. I want to have dates, and talk to you, make out with you, hell, even argue with you. You drive me fucking crazy, you know that?" He lifted her chin, and her eyes darted away again.

"I'm sorry I'm so bitchy. I don't mean to drive you crazy."

"That's just it, Sioban. You're not bitchy, you're...spicy. We drive each other crazy, and it's fantastic."

She didn't seem convinced, so Danny caressed her face and kissed her again, pouring all the tenderness he could into it and hoping she felt it. When he broke the kiss, she gazed at him dreamily.

"All right then," she said.

"All right then. Come on, let's go."

He steadied her carefully behind him while he scanned the area before he took her hand and led her out onto the sidewalk.

The buzz of activity was in full swing when they returned to the bar a short time later. Sioban held her breath as they came in the door, and waited for Danny to let go of her hand. But he didn't, so she didn't let go of his either. She was sure that they were getting looks, especially from Reece and the other Rockford guys, and God only knew what anyone sitting in the surveillance van was thinking.

But she couldn't think about that right now. Her eyes were locked on the bar, where Bear sat talking to Von. Well, he didn't seem to be angry, at least not with Von. That did nothing to change the fact that she had to face Bear herself.

Sioban hadn't realized that she was practically dragging Danny along behind her until he gave her hand a brief tug.

"It's going to be okay, baby," he said as he leaned toward her ear.

"I hope so."

"Well, hello, you two." Bear had noticed them and he gave them a mischievous smile. Sioban did let go of Danny's hand then. If she was going to come clean with Bear, she couldn't cling to Danny while she was doing it.

"I take it you kids worked things out over coffee?" Vonda chimed. Oh for the love of God.

"Obviously." She hated to sound short with Von, but she had to stay focused on what needed to happen right now, and she needed everyone else to be focused too. "Listen, can we just...can I talk to Bear for a minute?"

They all looked at her with sudden empathy, but it was Bear who spoke next.

"Of course, we can talk, Sioban, and we should. If I seemed a little flip, I apologize. I hadn't quite gotten into professional mode yet, and it's just good to see that the semi-permanent scowl on Danny's face has faded, at least where you're concerned."

"Thank you. Maybe we can just step away—"

"Not the office," Danny said, as he put his arm around her again protectively.

"No, I don't imagine that would be a good place under the circumstances. I was thinking that table by the window. I seem to recall you liking that spot."

151

Sioban remembered how she'd separated herself from them that first day at the bar. She hadn't been able to deal with them that day, and she wasn't sure she could handle talking to Bear right now, but she had to do it. She felt the heat of a blush creep onto her cheeks and sought encouragement from Von.

"Go ahead, hon. I'll bring Bear a fresh cup of coffee, and you a mug of your favorite tea. I brought some in to have on hand."

"And since it looks like the contractor is going to shit a brick if no one talks to him, I'll head on over there and see how things are going," said Danny.

"The alarm company will be here soon too, so I won't be long."

Sioban nodded and started to follow Bear to the table, when Danny tugged on her coat sleeve.

"You okay?"

"Yeah. I'll see you in a bit."

"I'll be right over there, if you need me."

When Sioban took her seat across from Bear, she found herself staring out of the window again for her courage to speak. He just sat quietly and waited for her to speak first. When Vonda quietly delivered their mugs of coffee and tea, Sioban took a breath and faced Bear.

"I'm sorry," she said. Bear looked at her with kind and gentle brown eyes. Sioban could see how Vonda would be attracted to him, if the woman would allow herself.

"Apology accepted, because I know it was important to you," he answered. "But I understand completely why Vonda didn't divulge the whole story on your behalf, and why you didn't come forward when you knew she'd met with me."

"Thank you for that. I know I need to tell you now, and I'm prepared to do that. Telling Danny this morning has actually made approaching you easier."

"Sioban, I'm going to stop you there. The next person you should relay the specific details to is any professional counselor you choose to talk to. If you really need to tell me in order to feel better, I'll listen, of course. But Danny can relate any details to me that he deems necessary to your and Vonda's protection, if you're comfortable with that."

Sioban released a breath she hadn't realized she was holding.

"Are you sure? I don't want to take the coward's way out."

"I'm sure. And it's far from cowardly. If I have any questions, I'll ask you directly, but for now, just let Danny be the one to tell me what I need to know. Fair enough?"

"Fair enough."

"All right, well, the rep from the alarm company just walked in, so I'd better go and rescue Danny."

He'd barely stepped away before Vonda reappeared, with a silly grin on her face.

"Don't you start on me, woman." Sioban tried to give her best glare as she took a swig of tea.

"Fear not, we will talk about what happened at the coffee shop this morning. But right now I need you to go over some furniture choices with me, and we're doing an interview tonight."

Another surge of relief washed over her. She was still trying to process the kiss she had shared with Danny; she couldn't even explain it to herself, much less to Von.

"Interview with who? And why tonight?"

"My friend Lex. Remember, the theater guy I told you about. The reason we have to see him tonight is that we're meeting him after his current gig, and I hope to entice him away from it."

§

The canned notes of a recorded track of Dave Brubeck's "Blue Rondelet a la Turk" floated above them as Vonda and Sioban took a small table mid-way back from the stage. The Velvet Room was going to be so much classier than the Starlight Lounge, although Vonda would never say that out loud about someone else's establishment while sitting in it. Sioban knew her friend had too much class herself to do that.

The place was rather run down. The tables were old, and the stage looked like it had seen a million performances. Still, the place held a certain charm. The small table lamps with their cabaret motif lent a certain ambiance, and the band members were dapper in their red tuxedo jackets and bow ties as they took their break at the bar.

A signed, framed photograph of Aretha Franklin singing circa the late '60s caught Sioban's eye from across the room, confirming how long the establishment had been open. Her facial expression showed her in the midst of a full-on belt of whatever song she was singing. That's how Sioban had felt when she danced to "Natural Woman," and as much as she'd tried not to think about it, it was all she could think about—the way the music just took her and spoke its story through her body, through her dance...and how she'd been so furious when she found out Danny had been watching, because really it was Danny she'd been thinking about when she danced. The truth was, she hadn't been ready for him to see her laid bare in her passion for dance, or her

154

attraction to him. No, Sioban hadn't been ready for that. But it *was* what she wanted nonetheless.

The same way she'd warmed under his touch just before the image of the desk triggered the memory of Sonny. The same way she'd wished that he'd taken her hand on the way to the coffee shop that morning, and the same way she was so glad he did on their way back to the bar. The same way she'd wanted his kiss when he finally gave it to her and they both fell headlong into it.

The dim light from the table lamp glowed around her peripheral vision as Sioban stared at the photograph and silently asked Aretha Franklin if this was real—if she'd finally found in herself the woman, the dancer she'd always wanted to be, and finally started to find her way out of a past in which she was bound to her vision of Ava and bound to a mistrust of men. But instead of an answer from Aretha, it was a question from their server that pulled her out of her memory of Danny's kiss.

"What can I get you ladies to drink?" the woman asked.

Von chose a Grey Goose martini, extra dry, but Sioban was feeling girlish and ordered a Bellini. She really wanted a Sex on the Beach—it was her favorite drink—but she knew Vonda was waiting for an opportunity to question her about what had happened at the coffee shop, and she didn't want to encourage it. But Von never needed much encouragement, Sioban remembered when she spoke up as the server walked away.

"So, while we're waiting for our drinks, why don't you tell me where you were just now with that faraway look on your face? Back at the coffee shop, maybe?"

"We worked it out," answered Sioban, curtly, wishing she had her drink already, but knowing that she would probably slam her glass down on the table if she did.

"Come on, Sioban, it's me, why won't you tell me what happened?"

"Because I'm not sure myself!"

"Are you telling me—"

"He kissed me. I kissed him. We kissed!"

"Well that much I figured out. Neither one of you is the type to hold hands and *then* kiss."

"Brilliant, Sherlock."

"Sioban." Vonda looked at her apologetically.

"I'm clear on what happened," Sioban explained. "But I'm having a bloody hard time figuring out how I feel about it."

At that moment, the drinks arrived, to Sioban's great relief. She took a gulp, while Von just sipped at hers, smiling over the top of the glass at her.

"Oh, honey. You've been through so much. Why not just have a little fun, enjoy this little unexpected side adventure?"

"Because I don't know if I can. I mean, it is unexpected, it came out of nowhere."

"True, Danny's truck came out of nowhere. But whatever fuse he lit inside you has always been there, and I suspect it was there for him too."

"Fine, but it's too fast."

"Fast would have been if he'd taken you out to the surveillance van for a quickie."

"Von!"

"Well, did he say anything to make you think he's going to rush things?"

Sioban pursed her lips. Von was so annoying with her wisdom sometimes.

"Just the opposite actually," Sioban confessed. "He said that more than anything he just wanted to get to know me, really know me. Take me on dates and things."

"Mm-hmm. What else did he say?"

"That right now, his top priority would be to protect me until we resolve what happened in L.A."

"Well, that sounds about right. Listen, Sioban, Danny can play the big, scary-looking guy when he has to. But the two of you are so much alike it isn't even funny. You both acted out as a defense mechanism, when it was obvious to me that he liked you the minute he almost ran over you in the street. And I think it was obvious to you too, and that's what scares you."

"Thank you, Dr. Phil."

"So, is he a good kisser?"

"Bloody hell. Yes."

The both giggled into their drinks. But after a moment, Sioban only thought it fair to turn the tables on her dear friend.

"Speaking of obvious things, has Bear asked you out yet?"

"What?" Vonda's face fell. Oh, this was good. It was all fun and games when it was about her and Danny, but shine a light on the goo-goo eyes Bear and Von had been making at each other and trying to disguise as care and concern, and Von had no idea was she was talking about.

"I said, has Bear asked you out yet?"

"Why would he?"

Sioban did laugh then. "Okay. I guess you haven't been paying attention at all to the way the man looks at you."

"He doesn't look at me any way at all." Now the pink heat was creeping into Von's cheeks. Excellent.

"And how he agreed to help with my situation without blinking an eye—because of you."

"He's a good man. He helps people. It's what he does. He would have done it for anybody."

"Hardly. Even so, let's not dismiss all of the top-notch security elements he's gotten you to agree to, and will probably end up paying for himself."

"Because he's very thorough about his work. He cares."

"Yes! He cares! About *you!*"

"I'm saying he would take just as much care with any client."

"He might recommend the same equipment and strategies, but he wouldn't be there on hand to personally oversee everything, especially as pertains to the renovation. He cares, all right. Poor man is just working up the nerve to ask you out."

"Even on the far-out chance that he does ask me out at some point, it's a fruitless gesture. I'm finally arriving at my goals as a dancer, as an artist. I don't have time or energy for anything else. I think that's what's obvious as far as I'm concerned. Or it should be."

Sioban wanted to fire back that what was obvious was how she and Bear were just as guilty of ignoring the chemistry between them as she and Danny might have been. She wanted to ask Von why it was that a little "unexpected adventure" was good for her and Danny, but not Von and Bear.

But she was stopped short when a rather striking-looking man approached the table.

"Vonda Douglas. Good to see you, lady!"

Vonda stood up to embrace him, but Sioban just watched. His brown hair had lighter-blond streaks in it and nearly hung to his shoulders. He had a five-o'clock shadow that would probably be a beard in another day. Judging by the black tee-shirt and jeans he wore, this was Von's stage manager friend. He looked at her with hazel eyes over Von's shoulder and smiled at her.

"You must be Sioban." Vonda stepped back, and he reached his hand across the table to shake Sioban's. "I'm Alex. Everyone calls me Lex. Vonda gave me the very short version of what's happening with her new club, and how you're helping her get it launched."

"Yes, that's right," she answered. His hand was strong and sure, but gentle wrapped around hers. She didn't know what his qualifications were as a stage manager, but he probably managed the ladies quite well. And yet, he didn't seem arrogant at all.

"Well, I look forward to catching up with you ladies after the first set. The show's about to start." He smiled again and hurried off to wherever the light box was.

"Lex is a good guy—and an excellent stage manager," commented Von. "I just hope I can convince him to jump ship and help me out, at least temporarily."

"Is he expensive?"

"Yes, but that's not what worries me. I know we'll build a solid show over time. But keeping Lex interested is another ballgame. I mean, he's done some classy gigs, in New York, even. He's probably only in this place as a favor to the owner."

"Well, he's clearly fond of you, just like everyone I've met. I don't think you have anything to worry about."

As tempted as Sioban was to press Von about her potential feelings for Bear, she didn't want to push too hard. Besides that, in the next moment, the stage lights went down. Lex's voice announced, "Ladies and gentlemen, please welcome the lovely Sahara," and the most stunningly exotic black woman stepped into the blue spotlight. She was tall and elegant, with deep-brown skin and an ultra-short afro. She stood before the microphone with her hands folded in front of her and her eyes cast down. The spotlight was small and only caught the halter top of her white sequined dress. She slowly looked up as the spotlight widened around her. Her minimal makeup was almost unnecessary, because her face was smooth, ebony perfection. Her crystal teardrop earrings sparkled in the dreamy blue light.

Sioban looked over at Von, whose mouth was slightly open in awe. Sahara was a sight to behold for sure, but when she opened her mouth and uttered the first notes of "Here's to Life" a capella, the world, it seemed, stood still. Her voice was at once smoky, like a twelve-year-old Scotch, and sweet, like a woman in love. She dipped and soared along with the piano and the bass, and lifted her hand toward the audience to invite them into the story of her song. She was quite simply an angel come to life.

Sahara carried them along on the wings of her voice for five songs. The applause in between was far less than she deserved, but at least Sioban and Von doing their part. Sioban had learned to whistle when she was still in grade school, and it came in handy just now. She wanted to stand at the end of the set, and she could tell Von did too, but they remained seated. Clearly, Sahara should be in a bigger venue, or at least one with a larger, more enthusiastic audience.

Von ordered another round of drinks for them, and they took turns going to the ladies' room. Within a few minutes, Lex joined them at the table again, with a beer he'd picked up at the bar.

"All right, what gives, mister?" Von asked him. "What's a talented man like you doing in a dive—er, a place like this?"

"Well, the beer's not half bad, plus it's free," he chuckled.

"Von has a theory that you're doing a friend a favor here," Sioban interjected.

"And she'd be right." Lex turned to Von. "How in the world are you, hon? I had no idea about Johnny, or when you got back to town."

"Everything happened so fast. I guess there are still some people who didn't know about either. And then once I decided to start this new adventure, well, I haven't thought about much else."

Von paused and met Lex's gaze. He crossed his arms and waited for her to tell him why she'd really contacted him, which seemed a little bit mean to Sioban. But he did have a twinkle in his eye.

"So, once this favor is done, what's next for you?" asked Vonda cautiously.

"Not sure yet. I'm thinking about going back to New York, got a couple of offers on the table."

"Broadway?" Sioban asked. The man may be talented, but unless he was stage managing the next revival of *A Chorus Line*, he needed to give Von the same consideration he'd given whatever friend ran this place.

"Not quite." He smirked at Sioban before turning back to Vonda.

"All right then. Well, that answers my next question—my little production is no match for whatever you've been offered in New York."

Sioban wished her friend wouldn't give up so easily. She'd probably done the same thing with Bear, assumed he wouldn't help her.

"Hon, you haven't even asked me the question yet, and I'm dying to hear it, I have been ever since you called me. Besides, for all you know, that naked cowboy on Times Square wants me to stand behind him and shine a flashlight on his ass."

Finally, Von laughed. "Okay, you got me. I just hate that I've been out of touch for so long, and the first thing I want when I do call you is to steal you away from whatever you're doing and stage manage my show."

"Steal me, huh?" Lex raised his eyebrows. "You're that close?"

"To opening night, no, but I'd like for you to work with the contractor to get your light box just the way you want it. And I want you to vet the talent for me."

"So now it's *my* light box, is it?"

"Please, Lex? Just get me through the opening, maybe a couple of weeks after that."

"Relax. You had me at 'burlesque show' on the phone. I can start phasing out here, the bet I lost is just about covered. And anybody that wants me in New York can wait a bit."

"A bet?" Von laughed.

Sioban had known he'd say yes as soon as she'd met him. She'd been biding her time to ask her own burning question.

"Speaking of talent, what can you tell me about Sahara?"

"Ah, I was wondering when you were going to get to that. You've got about five minutes before the next set starts, why don't you go see her at the bar over there?"

"Don't mind if I do, Lex." Vonda cut her eyes at Sioban, who stood with her drink. "What? You can't tell me you'd rather have a music track than a performer like that between dance numbers. Hell, she could even accompany the dancers."

"You're right," Vonda sighed. "Try not to promise her the moon, okay?"

"I'll just introduce myself and see if she'll come by and sing for us next week after we've done a little more on the place. Meanwhile, you stay here and keep sweet-talking Lex. We'll slice up the moon and divide between him, Sahara, and any other fabulous talent we can get our hands on."

Sioban winked at her friend, gave Lex a knowing smile, and made a beeline for the bar, where Sahara sat at the end in the shadows.

"Just water for you, then?" Sioban felt silly saying it, but she didn't know how else to strike up a conversation.

"Can't drink during a gig," Sahara answered, without looking at Sioban. "It would kill my voice." Sioban tried not to let her surprise show when she heard Sahara speak. Although she sang in a perfect American accent, she spoke with a rich accent of what must be an African country.

"Right. Us dancers, we don't worry about that, as long as we can do the choreography without falling down, and all."

Sahara leaned a little further into the light. "You and your friend over there are dancers?" Her voice was rich, yet playful. She smiled and Sioban was flooded by the warmth of it.

"Oh, that's Vonda. Yes, we're dancers. I'm Sioban, by the way." She held out her hand to take Sahara's. "We came to talk to Lex about the club Von's opening soon. I guess they're old friends."

"Well, if you're friends of Lex's you must be okay. I haven't known him very long, but I like the way he manages the shows in this place. Applauding like loons that way, though—you'd have to be half drunk," she giggled.

"Yeah, I just met him tonight, and Von hasn't seen him in years, but he seems like a good guy. Von wants him to come and manage her show." Sioban paused to take a sip of her own drink for courage. "As for the applause, the crowd in here needs a fire lit under them, because you were bloody amazing, and I—Von and I, actually, I'm helping her recruit for the show—want you to come meet with us."

Sioban took another sip of her drink. She knew Von's show was going to be fantastic, and she knew that the Velvet Room was going to be a beautiful, classy night spot. But it would be hard to convince a stranger of a vision that hadn't fully come to life yet.

"You mean, come and audition for you, right?" Sahara asked tentatively.

"Well, you can sing for us any time you like, but we don't need you to audition to know how talented you are."

"Okay, then, when do you want me to come there? To the club?"

"How about early next week? Everything should be in order, and you can get the feel of the stage, the acoustics. Here—" Sioban reached for a napkin and dug in her purse for a pen. "Jesus, we still don't have business cards made up yet. I need to take care of that. Here's Von's cell number."

"Thank you. It was nice to meet one of my newest fans."

"You'll love meeting Von too. I'd better let you get warmed up for your next set." Sioban turned to head back to the table, but then remembered one last question. "Sahara. That's not your real name, is it?" Sahara tilted her head and gave Sioban a wry smile.

"No. It isn't. Only my family knows my given Kenyan name. But I might tell you what it is, one of these days, Miss Sioban."

By the time Sioban returned to the table, Von had basically sealed the deal with Lex. He'd come by the next afternoon to put his stamp of approval on the finishing touches to the stage, and the light box. Both he and Vonda were pleased that Sioban had given Sahara a contact number. Lex was certain that any arrangement Vonda could offer Sahara would be much better than what she was experiencing here, and not just in terms of money.

When Sioban and Vonda arrived back at the house, Sioban realized that she hadn't even checked her phone. She didn't want to start expecting things from Danny—they hadn't even really started dating yet—but still she hoped. When she pulled it out and saw two messages from him, she fell back on her bed like a schoolgirl to listen to them.

< Hey, it's Danny. Hope things went well with Vonda's friend, and that you had a good time. Talk to you later.

<Hi, it's me again. Just wanted to know you made it home all right. I know it's late, if you don't feel like talking, send me a text. Bye.

She knew she was grinning like an idiot when she hit the callback button.

"So you do know how to use the phone Rockford got for you." Her breath caught at the sound of his voice.

"Of course I know how to use it! We only just got home."

"Guess you were too busy interviewing that friend of Von's to notice my message."

"Actually, Mr. Know-It-All, it was Von doing the interviewing. Of him, I mean. Lex."

"Lex, huh?

"Will you shut it and listen for half a minute? She did the negotiating with Lex. Don't forget there was actually a show to see, too. We had to make sure the man still knows his way around a nightclub show. But then I actually did something Von's paying me to do."

"And what's that?"

"I recruited the singer there. She's amazing, she's this stunning woman, and I know she could add something special to our show, and—"

"Sioban." Danny's voice went right to her core and melted there.

"What?"

"Thank you for calling in. Are you doing okay?"

"I...yes, I'm okay. Pretty knackered. Thank you for checking on me. I know it's important to do that since you're in charge of my case."

"Yes, I need to know what's happening with you on a regular basis as a client, it's true. But I also want to know that you're safe—I *need* to know that you're safe—for myself too. *Shit.*"

"What's wrong?"

"The needing to know for myself part."

"It's...nice."

"It's fucking complicated."

"Are you regretting our kiss today?"

"Hell no. I want to kiss you again, as soon as possible. So badly I can taste it."

"Um, okay. I mean, me too. I want to kiss you again too."

"Let's work on that, shall we?"

"Yeah. Definitely." Sioban paused, wanting to ask him something else. She could hear him breathing and it was driving her mad. "Danny, did you mean what you said today, about getting to know me, and all that?"

"Damn straight, I meant it."

"So, this complicated part..."

"Yep. So dinner tomorrow night, then. Be ready at seven."

"Wait, hang on, Bossy Knickers! We haven't said...we just..."

"You can pick the restaurant. Okay?"

Sioban huffed out her breath, but she was excited, and he knew it too. "Always have to be in charge of everything, don't you? You know, most women like to be *asked* on dates."

Danny laughed. "True, but I don't want to make it easy for you to turn me down."

"You've got a nerve!"

"And I bet you jumped up off of the bed where you were all stretched out to have some pillow talk with me, and now you've got your hands on your hips, and your cheeks are turning pink. And that's so fucking hot that when I do get you alone, I'm going to put my mouth on you and drink my fill."

Bloody fucking hell. Did he have a spy camera in her room, then? Because that's exactly what she was doing. And the fact that he had her so hot for him right now was no secret to either of them. Was it possible he already knew her just that well?

"And just maybe I'll smack your arse!" She tried to sound irritated, and knew she was failing.

"Well if things go well, we'll get to that over time. Go to sleep now. You need your rest."

"Cheeky bastard! I'll go to sleep when I'm ready!"

Danny only chuckled. "Goodnight, Irish."

She plopped down on the bed again. It wasn't as if she could sleep right now anyway, even if she wanted to. She lay back, and suddenly she recalled the green bustier in her dresser drawer, and how badly she wanted Danny's next kiss, and a whole more than that. In her dreams that night, she got it.

Chapter Fourteen

After two wrong turns and navigating a fender bender that had traffic slowed to a crawl for two miles, Sioban finally turned into the parking lot of the new gym she and Von had joined. Von hadn't joined her today, or many other days yet, because there was too much to do, she said. She hadn't missed a class with Iliana, though, and they both knew their dancing needed to be top notch in time for the opening. Sioban had grown used to Iliana's teaching style and begun to own her own body and relationship to the music as well as the choreography. She was rewarded for her progress by a few nods of approval from Iliana, along with the occasional brief compliment.

But today she was hitting the gym first. If she was to help Von choreograph the show, and teach the routines to the other dancers, she needed strength almost as much as she needed the coordination and artistry she was getting from Iliana. And so here she was, having dropped Von at the bar. She desperately wanted her own car, and it wasn't that she couldn't afford an economy vehicle on her new salary, but Bear and Danny had insisted that she not make any large purchases that could attract the attention of any local help Sonny might have enlisted. As it was, all of her money was deposited into a second business account that Von had opened under the Velvet Room. Vonda herself was still using Johnny's account as executor of his estate; Bear had advised her against opening a personal account just yet.

Once she'd stowed her street clothes in the women's locker room, Sioban made a beeline for the stretch floor, taking a ball and a couple of weights with her. She didn't respond well to trainers, and only endured the free session that came with joining to get some basic workouts that she could continue on her own.

As Sioban pulled out a fitness mat, she took note of some of the other women who were working out. It was a shame there was no way to tell if any of them were dancers. Short of trolling other clubs for dancers to poach, she had no idea how she and Von were going to recruit them. Vonda hadn't been keen on the other dancers in Iliana's class, in part due to feedback from Iliana herself. Most of them had their sights on New York once the ten-week class block was completed, and were only using the class to prepare for auditions. Others just weren't the right fit. Von had said she wanted a certain maturity, along with "something special" that a dancer could bring. And of course they had to be willing to do burlesque. Sioban worried that it would be a two-woman dance revue, with possible live music at intervals if things worked out with Sahara.

An hour later, Sioban was headed back to the locker room when she glanced into one of the studios. Long red sheaths of fabric hung at intervals from metal bolts on the ceiling so that each participant had access to two of them. The instructor was hanging from hers with both arms. She faced the mirror and spoke, and then she stretched up with one leg, twined her ankle around one of the sheaths, and flipped upside down. Now she hung from just one, and by a single leg. As she spun, her arms floated out. She looked like a ballerina, only she wasn't dancing, not in a traditional sense. Without realizing it, Sioban wandered closer to the studio window. There were only six women in the class. It was easy to spot the veterans, because they repeated the instructor's moves without much difficulty. Others had a harder time, and one poor girl wasn't quite strong enough to complete the move. Her leg slipped free, but she managed to put her arms down in time to catch herself before she landed on her head. That would be me, mused Sioban, flat on my arse within five minutes.

Still, she was mesmerized, and by the time the class was over, Sioban had had a flash of brilliance. As the ladies filed out, she edged inside, and waited while the instructor began to pack up her things. She was a tiny thing, Sioban realized. She had short, wild black hair accented with a shock of pink on one side that matched her leotard. But she was all muscle, and she moved gracefully. *Please, God, let her have some dance experience*, Sioban implored silently. Just then the instructor noticed Sioban standing there.

"Ah, you came inside. Next time, we get you on the silks, no?" A lilting French accent only added to her pixie charm, along with the sweet smile she gave Sioban.

"Not even on a cold day in hell." Well, now, here she was about to ruin things at the start. The woman didn't know her at all, and might toss her out on her arse for such cheeky talk. "What I mean is, I'd be scared to. I'm a dancer, I do okay on the ground, but if I tried that contraption—"

"Oh, you are a dancer? Well, it's just like dancing, only you are dancing with the silks."

"Sure, and you made it look that way. It was stunning."

"Merci. It just takes practice. I think you'd be surprised at your abilities. You're welcome to try a class any time, as my guest. My name is Solange." She held out her hand to Sioban.

"Thanks for the offer. I'm Sioban. Not sure how soon I'll be joining your class...but I did have a question for you."

"Of course. Ask away."

"Well, um, can I buy you a drink at the juice bar? It might take a minute."

"That would be very nice. My last class isn't for another hour."

Over green smoothies, Sioban discovered that not only did Solange dance, but that she'd been trained in ballet since she was a small child—and she hated it. Well, not so much hated it as resented it, because her parents were dancers. Or they had been until her mother's injury forced her into an early retirement. Her father sacrificed whatever was left of his own career to open a dance school in Paris. And teach they did, focusing much of their energy on developing their only child as a prodigy. They'd wanted to live the careers they'd lost early through Solange. Only she didn't cooperate. She'd fallen in love with Cirque du Soleil as a schoolgirl. There was no possible way for her to begin training in any kind of gymnastics or other artistry that might have qualified her for auditions. Her parents wouldn't hear of it. But as soon as she was of age, she'd gone to her aunt, her only ally, for money to go to the States. She came on a student visa and never went back. She'd been studying aerial silks as a way to maybe break into Cirque, but had never made it past the first round of auditions.

"But I keep trying," Solange said, as she concluded her story. "At least I can support myself teaching it, and I'm trying to get into a dance arts program that includes the silks. I'm only doing it because of that, not for the dance."

"Is there anything other than ballet in the program?" asked Sioban cautiously.

"Yes, jazz, I think. I suppose it could be okay. It depends on the teachers. I just hope they are not like my parents."

Sioban tried to think of a smooth segue into the real question she had for Solange.

"So, I'm kind of doing double duty here at the gym these days," she began.

"What do you mean?"

"I'm always keeping my eye out for talented women—dancers, to be specific."

"Non," said Solange, and added several more French words that were lost on Sioban. "I'm not that woman."

"Please hear me out. It's not what you think."

"You said you are looking for dancers. This is not what I think?"

"Yes, and no. Let me start over." Sioban related her own story about how she and Vonda had worked together in Los Angeles, and now she was helping Von start the burlesque club. And that yes, there'd be some dancing, but she wanted Solange to show Von what she could do with her aerial silks. "Listen, it would be some extra income. And Von could even help you with the jazz if you needed it. I just know your silks could be a very sexy addition to our show, and the other routines might be fun for you."

"Well, this is...so unusual. I never even considered working as a dancer. I've just been so against it."

"Not a dancer. An aerial silks artist, who happens to do a little dancing. Just think about it, okay?" Von had finally gotten business cards made, and Sioban held one out to Solange. "The number to the bar—soon to be the Velvet Room—is on the front here. I've written my cell number on the back."

"Ça va. I will think about it, as you say."

"Brilliant! Look, I'll make you a deal, which I'm sure to regret. But if you come to audition for Von, I'll take a class from you."

"Really?" said Solange, her eyes growing wide. "Well, that does sweeten the deal, is how you say?"

"For you, maybe," Sioban laughed.

"Okay, well, either way, I will call you soon to let you know what I have decided."

They said their goodbyes, and as she made her way to the showers, Sioban felt a surge of something like pride. At first she'd considered working for Von mainly as charity that she'd been given in order to survive, even the dancing part. But she was finally coming into her own as a dancer, and now she'd just possibly recruited her second person for the show. Von was going to be proud of her. *Danny's going to be proud of me too.* Now where in Christ's name had that come from?

Well, she knew where it came from. She and Danny were getting closer, not just as a client who needed his protection. When she saw him at the bar during the day, he tried to maintain his hard-core exterior, she supposed for the benefit of everyone. But when they were alone, he made her laugh and teased her mercilessly. She guessed it was a side he didn't show to many people. It made her want to share things with him, like meeting Solange today.

And the heat between them intensified with every passing day. The memory of their first kiss still made her blush, and every time they were together since then, Danny seemed to make his mission to make her blush again. Or get her riled any way he could. He'd mercilessly recalled for her that kiss when he picked her up for their first official date, leaning across the dinner table and telling her how much he wanted to do it again as soon as they finished eating. But once he'd gotten the rosy color to rise on her cheeks, he was just as quick to talk to her about anything and everything. He asked her about dancing, and about her childhood in Ireland. He spoke in moderation about himself, mostly about being in the military. That was typically male, Sioban thought, so she didn't mind. It only meant that there would be opportunities for him to share more about himself in the future. He listened intently to everything she had to say, and looked directly at her, even when he was talking. The intensity of his blue gaze soon had her thinking about what would happen after dinner again.

As if his molten kisses weren't bad enough, more than once she'd felt his desire through his jeans as he held her pressed against him. It was clear that they wanted each other. But just as they'd start to consume each other, he'd pull away, and look at her with a searing desire mixed with regret. "Still too soon, Irish," he'd say, and drive her home. Sioban replayed the feel of his mouth on hers, then on her neck, and her collarbone, as the hot water sluiced over her body. Her mind retraced the path of his hands up and down her back, and over her bottom. God, when would it be time? Sioban knew she should be grateful to have met a man that wasn't pushing her into bed with him. But bloody hell, maybe she wouldn't mind being pushed, just this once. Or maybe she'd do some pushing of her own, she thought, as she turned off the water.

She was dressed in record time, and was pressing the call icon on Danny's contact before she even made it to the car.

"Hey, Irish. You done beating the hell out of your trainer yet?"

She'd stopped being irritated with him for calling her that. She'd even stopped reminding him that he was also of Irish descent, because he'd only tell her that he wasn't just off the boat.

"I told you, I don't have a trainer. I got the best of a fitness ball, though."

"Good, if there's no trainer lusting after you, then I don't have to kill him."

God, he could be impossible, but she could give as good as she got. "Whatever. What five-star restaurant are you taking me to tonight, or are we going to McDonald's again?"

There was the briefest pause before he answered, "I thought we could have dinner at my place."

"You're cooking for me. At your apartment. You're not just boiling me some potatoes, are you?"

"Well, no one else has been feeding me all these years, aside from Manucci's pizza and a handful of pubs. I do all right in the kitchen. But if you don't feel comfortable—"

"No, I'd love it! Thank you. That would be really nice. Can I bring anything?"

"Just yourself."

"Okay. Well, I need to take Vonda's car back to her, but I've already showered."

"No problem. I've got everything laid out here. I'll pick you up at the bar in half an hour."

"See you then."

Well, now. Wasn't this a special development. Sioban realized her hands were shaking as she put the key into the ignition. Suddenly, she wished she'd paid more attention to her hair and makeup. At least she was wearing her sexy suede high-heeled boots, and her new suede skirt. But why would tonight be any different? Danny found her to be beautiful anyway, he'd told her so. Because, she realized, tonight might be the night, and if it was, she wanted to be perfect for him, whatever that meant. She was letting that old doubt back in, that old comparison to Ava. But when she got to the bar and he locked eyes with her, she wanted to get lost in them, in him. And when he took her hand and told Vonda not to wait up, her heart did a flip-flop. She'd just have to sit back and enjoy the evening, wherever it led.

§

"So, this is home," said Danny matter-of-factly, as he flipped on a light switch near the door and stood to the side to usher Sioban in.

It was some of what she'd expected and some of what she hadn't. A downtown loft space certainly fit Danny's rough street image. The décor was masculine, clean, with muted colors for the main pieces, with a lot of wood and some chrome accents. The kitchen was all stainless steel, with state-of-the art appliances. Maybe she was in for a tasty dinner after all, assuming he knew how to use it. There were no walls to separate "rooms," yet each space was designated for living, dining, and working out, the latter with a grey modular mat, a set of free weights, and one universal machine with stations for a full-body workout. There was a sizable desk with a computer on the wall next to the kitchen. Sioban's eyes couldn't help darting up to the bedroom area nestled in its own loft space at the top of a short industrial-looking staircase. It was dark, so she couldn't see the bed, and part of her wondered if she ever would.

What she hadn't expected were the stunning choices in modern art, the pops of color in pillows and lamps, and the neatness of the place. Of course, he wasn't a college frat boy anymore. He was a grown man, with a grown man's sophisticated taste. There was so much that he didn't share with the world, so much that he kept hidden behind his toughness. Yet here she was, with Danny, in his home, where he felt more comfortable than anyplace else in the world.

"I...Danny, it's great. Thank you for inviting me," Sioban said, as she tossed her purse and coat on the grey modular sofa.

"Thank you for coming. Can I get you a drink? Glass of wine? Sorry, I don't really have the makings for fancy cocktails. Next time, I promise."

There'd be a next time...Lord help her. Well, if wine was all he had on hand, what she really wanted was to down the whole bottle, she was so nervous. Then again, it wouldn't do to pass out before dinner, or she might miss dessert.

"Wine would be lovely, thanks." She followed him to the kitchen and took a stool at the island. He pulled a bottle of white out of the fridge, along with a beer for himself. He deftly uncorked the wine and poured her a glass, before uncapping his beer and taking a long swig. He reached back into the fridge and pulled out a plate with two thick steaks on it, along with a produce bag with two Idaho potatoes.

"I hope you like steaks," he said. "And don't worry, the potatoes aren't Irish." He gave her a half smile, but something was wrong. Had something happened with her case? Was he upset with her about something?

"They look fantastic. Can I do anything to help?"

"Nah, I'm good. Just relax." He reached for a small tablet in its cradle on the counter. He pushed a few buttons, and acoustic guitar music floated out of the sound system. When he turned his back to scrub the potatoes in the sink, it was almost as if he didn't want to talk at all. Sioban hoped she wouldn't have to carry the conversation the whole evening. At least she had news to share.

"I met this woman at the gym today," she began. "She was teaching this class with these red curtains— silks, she called them—hanging from them and twirling and stuff. It was much more gracious than I'm making it sound. Amazing, really, like she was dancing with the silks. Anyway, it occurred to me that what she does could be a really cool act for our show, something not many other shows would have, I'm guessing. And if she could dance in a traditional way too, well, so much the better..."

Danny had dried the potatoes and started poking them with a fork. But he hadn't said a word. Sure, she was babbling, but he hadn't even looked at her. Come to think of it, he'd hardly touched her, except to take her hand when they left the bar. He hadn't even kissed her yet. Well, to hell with that. Whatever his problem was, she wasn't going to go through the whole evening like this.

"Why haven't you kissed me, Danny?" There, she'd said it. But he just kept stabbing the damn potatoes with the fork.

"I didn't want to kiss you in front of everyone at the bar."

"Well, we're not at the bar now." Sioban took a rather large gulp of her wine. That comment was either going to break the ice or get her thrown out on her arse. Why, why was she so stubborn and mouthy? Here a gorgeous man had brought her to his home and was cooking dinner for her and all she could do was whine because he didn't feel like talking, and hadn't kissed her.

When Danny opened the oven to put the potatoes in, Sioban braced herself for him to slam it shut. But instead, he closed it gently and adjusted the temperature dial. He did look at her then. Lord, if she'd been a potato, she'd be cooked on the spot. She might even have gone up in flames. His blue eyes seared into her, with either anger, lust, or both, and he held her gaze as he came toward her around the island. She turned in her stool as he came to face her. He stepped into the vee she'd made of her legs for him, pushing her skirt even higher up on her thighs. He didn't give her another moment to think before he took her by the hips and covered her mouth with his. But it wasn't forceful. Instead, he moved his lips over hers as if they were the most delicious thing he had ever tasted. They opened for each other and moaned softly at the same time. Sioban couldn't help but push her hips forward as their tongues met, and she nearly cried out again when he pushed back into her, and she felt the hardness beneath his jeans graze her sex through the thin cotton of her panties.

She had been gripping the island countertop behind her, trying to hold on to her control, her very sanity. But now she needed to touch him, or she really would lose her mind. She dove one hand into the hair at his neck and pulled him closer, and clutched his shoulder with the other one. There, that did it. Danny angled his mouth and drove deeper into hers with his tongue. He ate at her lips, pulling on her bottom one with his teeth before molding his lips over hers again, plundering and feasting on her mouth.

"Yes," she whimpered into his lips and clutched him tighter. But then he tore his mouth away from hers, and stared down at her with the same desperate disappointment he'd had in his gaze so many times before since they'd gotten together.

"That's why, Sioban," he said, breathing raggedly. "That's why I haven't kissed you yet tonight. I've been holding back because of what you do to me. And here, tonight, with me in my home...I just need to be sure you're ready."

He still held on to her with his strong, warm hands at the small of her back. She knew she was trembling, but she couldn't stop it. She clutched at his biceps, holding on to her courage.

"I-I'm ready...if I'm enough. If I'm what you want."

A deep, angry frown darkened his face. "What the *fuck* are you talking about? If you weren't 'enough' you wouldn't be here. I haven't had a woman here since...in a long time. Here, now, it's you. I want you so badly I can hardly breathe. You're more than enough, Sioban."

"I want you too. I need this with you, Danny."

His eyes turned passionate again and he leaned in and locked onto her neck with his mouth, half kissing her, half biting her. "Say the words, Irish. Tell me to take you. I need to hear the words." He seared a trail with his tongue down her neck, over her collarbone, between the swells of her breasts.

"Take me, damn you," she choked.

Danny quickly pulled her shirt over her head, barely giving her enough time to raise her arms so he could get it off. While she was sure he'd be deft with her bra, she reached behind and unclasped it in her own impatience. When he closed his eyes and took one of her pink nipples into his mouth, the heat of it shot through her. His moan was almost a whisper, but hers became strangled as her breath caught.

Suddenly, he scooped his hands under her ass and lifted her up. She locked her legs around his waist and arched backward, clinging to his shoulders as he feasted on her other nipple and walked to the couch with her. He laid her down as gently as she guessed his impatience would allow him. She didn't wait for him to tell her to lift her hips when he gripped her skirt with both hands. He brought it, along with her underwear, down over her ankles and tossed them to the floor.

"My boots—"

"Stay on," he interrupted through clenched teeth. Sioban bit her lip and propped one ankle on the back of the couch. Danny hissed a curse and began tearing at his own clothes. She reached for his belt buckle and pulled his hips toward her so she could undo it. He already had his shirt off, and tore at the zipper of his fly as Sioban clawed at the sides of his jeans. He peeled them away, and brought his underwear down with them. As he came free, Sioban gasped at the sight of his member. It was thick, and hard, and jerked when Danny saw her lick her lips.

"Condom," he bit out, and reached down to pluck one out of the pocket of his jeans. He tore at the wrapper, and when she reached for his cock, it jerked again at her touch. Sioban was beside herself. She clutched at his gorgeous ass as he sheathed himself. She really wanted to take him into her mouth, but she'd have to make sure that happened in the near future instead.

Before Danny could descend on top of her, she stood and hiked herself up into his arms, once again clamping her legs around his hips. "I thought I told you to take me."

"Nag," he gritted out, and crushed her mouth again in a smoldering kiss. He spun with her in his arms. His eyes must have been closed too, because he stalked with her in a blind madness to find a place to land. She didn't care, only clung to him and ate at his mouth as he did hers. They swallowed each other's moans as Sioban ground her sex against his cock.

Finally, he found the apartment door and pinned her there. He broke the kiss and stared at her an instant before he entered her with one hard thrust.

"Danny!" she cried at the same time he groaned. She nearly came then, because the shock of it, the raw sexuality between them, took her breath away.

Their eyes stayed locked as he thrust into her again, and again, and again. Sioban couldn't get close enough to him. "Deeper, harder, Danny, God!"

Their moans grew in unison as he bucked against her faster and harder, until Sioban opened her mouth in the onset of her climax. In the back of her mind, she heard voices approaching in the hallway, but she couldn't hold back, not now, not when it was so, so good. Just as the cry tore from her throat, Danny swallowed it with his kiss. He thrust once, twice more before he stiffened. He broke the kiss and threw his head back, unable to stifle his own shout. It was the sexiest, most beautiful thing Sioban had ever seen.

"Fuck," he breathed, and rested his forehead against the door next to her ear, as they both came back to earth. Sioban swore she could hear hurried, retreating footsteps, but she didn't care, and she didn't think Danny did either.

Danny lifted his head and cupped her cheek as he lowered her to the floor.

"You okay, Irish? Tell me I didn't hurt you."

"For a moment, I thought you might have killed me, but I would have died a happy woman." She could see that this wasn't a satisfactory answer. "You didn't hurt me, Danny. I wanted it, I needed it. Just that way."

"Christ, Sioban. Who's killing who here?" He caressed her buttock, her thigh. "Don't even get me started on these fucking boots."

"I'm glad you like them. Um, d'you think anyone heard us, out in the hall there?"

"Don't fucking care."

Sioban giggled. "Me either."

Danny pulled her away from the wall gently and examined her back. "Damn, baby, you have some red marks. Let's get you upstairs so I can take care of that. Can you walk?" He came back around and eyed her with concern.

"Yes, I can walk." When Danny took her hand to lead her upstairs, and held it against his back as he turned, she decided to have some fun. "The question is, can you?" Without warning, she jumped onto his back.

"Wench," he said, and without hesitation, he caught her legs around him.

"What about dinner?" she asked.

"I set the oven on a lower temp. We'll come back down and finish fixing dinner after I take care of your back."

She bit his shoulder as he made his way up the stairs. The bedroom décor was an extension of the living room, with grey bedding and colorful accent pillows. He had a tall, wide locker-like structure for a closet, and a low dark-stained wooden dresser. Sioban nuzzled against the back of his neck as he strolled with her into the bathroom.

"Pony ride's over, sugar." He gently loosened her legs from around his waist and eased her down to the floor. The bathroom was surprisingly large, with a double sink and a cavernous stone-tiled open shower bay with only a half wall instead of a curtain or door. "Sit down a minute."

She sat on the toilet seat, which was a bit cold. It should feel awkward to her that they were both still naked, but somehow she didn't mind. Danny knelt down in front of her and gently unzipped her boots and removed them one at a time, before he pulled her back up and began his second examination of her back. Sioban wasn't sure what to make of herself in the bright light of the bathroom. She was rumpled and flushed, which she knew was supposed to be sexy. But in this light, every freckle seemed to jump off of her skin. Suddenly, Danny was rubbing something cool onto her lower back. It took her by surprise at first, but then the smooth heat of his hands warmed her up again.

"Just a little aloe. Won't take but a minute."

"It's nice, thank you."

"You want to tell me what's behind this 'not being enough' crap?" he asked as he continued his slow, sensual massage. He stepped in closer, and moved in broader strokes over the rest of her back and up and down her shoulders. His eyes found hers in the mirror. Well, this wasn't what she'd expected in the way of pillow talk. But she'd opened the door on this discussion, and she had to answer him now.

"I just never felt very beautiful. Or glamorous. Or talented. Especially next to my mother."

"I see." Danny stopped rubbing her arms, and folded her in his. "Well, I'm here to tell you that you're all those things in a way that no one else could be, not even your mother. The way you laugh, the way your eyes shine when you're speaking your mind, the way you wear all of your colors and sunglasses. All beautiful, and sexy as hell. And when you dance, Sioban? I've already told you how you take my breath away when you dance. And you know when else you're beautiful?"

Danny's hands had moved to her belly and caressed her there. Sioban could only shake her head no. "When you come," he whispered huskily into her ear. "So beautiful. You should see for yourself. I want you to come for me."

He watched her as she clutched his thighs and her chest heaved in growing excitement. But there

184

was more in her eyes than just lust. His heart was impaled by her green gaze and they couldn't seem to look away from each other's eyes. Danny felt the connection between them down to his toes, and he marveled at how his past paled in comparison to this moment, and every moment he'd had with her. He dipped a hand first onto her soft thatch of hair below, and then plunged a finger inside her. A stuttered moan escaped her throat.

"Wet...tight...that's good. Is it good, Sioban?"

"Yes," she rasped, and began moving her hips as she pressed back against his chest. "So good."

"It's about to get better." He worked his wet thumb over her clit and she gasped. "That's it. Come now, baby. Come."

Sioban thrust one hand back into his hair and bucked her hips against the increasing rhythm of the ministrations of his hands. One long whimper became a moan until she cried out as her climax took her shuddering over the top.

"So fucking hot," Danny whispered against her cheek, and bit her earlobe as he held her stomach until her spasms subsided.

Sioban's cheeks flushed as they smiled at each other in the mirror. In the next moment, Danny took her up into his arms and out to the bedroom. He laid her down and gently pulled the covers back from beneath her, leaving her bare. But he lost no time in pulling a condom out of the nightstand drawer and sheathing himself again before he covered her body with his. She was in his bed at last.

"Danny—" She reached up to run her hands through his hair, and he shushed her.

"This may be one of the only times I get you in a state of near speechlessness, and I want you to listen to me."

She only nodded her head and made a small gasp as he entered her.

"Know it for yourself, not just because I tell you. You're beautiful. I desire you. I want you in my bed, in my life. Feel what you do to me, Sioban." He pulled out almost to the tip of his cock and then thrust deep. She made a sound and pushed her hips up to meet him. "Feel how good you make me feel," he whispered.

Sioban felt herself being consumed again, and she didn't want it to stop. Unlike their first time downstairs, their rhythm was slow, burning with a slow heat. The music had stopped and the only sound was their breathing and then their moans as they came together. He stayed inside her for a long moment until he rolled to his side and pressed her against him. She closed her eyes as her breathing slowed again.

"I've got something to say, now," she mumbled against his chest. "You can't stop me."

"I wouldn't dream of it," he chuckled. The sound rumbled through his chest. She had to tell him how amazing that was, all of it. And that he should check on the potatoes and get the steaks going, because she was fucking starving now. In a minute, she thought, and then sleep claimed her.

Christ in heaven, what had just happened to him? He'd known it could be good, that it would be good, but that had been...out of this world, both times. All three, really, if he counted the orgasm he'd given her at the bathroom sink. Unbelievable. He replayed it all in his mind as he seasoned the steaks, which he'd thankfully covered with plastic when he'd taken them out to bring to room temperature. He was still shaking on the inside from what they'd just shared, which was so much more than the orgasms they'd given each other. So many unexpected emotions flooded him, ones he'd only felt a fraction of with Caryn, and that he could build on with Sioban if he took care with her.

She'd fallen asleep almost instantly, and he wanted nothing more than to stay with her, hold her. But he'd heard a text message come through on his phone, and he couldn't afford to miss anything in case there was a development on Sonny. So he'd disentangled himself as gently as he could and left her to rest. He'd check the message and get the steaks started, and wake her when everything was ready.

He'd pulled on a pair of sweatpants and come down barefoot to find a text from Bear, as he'd suspected. But it made him grin:

< The package still with you?

Danny texted back:

< Yeah. I'll deliver it safely in the morning.

The steaks were going, and Danny was scooping out the potatoes to add some mix-ins and bake them briefly again, when Sioban crept carefully down the stairs. She was wearing one of his tee-shirts and even though it hung well past her bottom, she tugged at the hem. He glanced at her panties on the floor next to the couch, and grinned at her.

"Hey, sleeping beauty. Wore you out, did I?"

"Hi. I just...wow, yes you did." He tried not to watch her as she scampered over and wiggled into her underwear.

"Sorry I wasn't there when you woke up. I had a text from Bear, and wanted to be sure there wasn't any new intel on Sonny." Her expression fell as she came over to the kitchen, and he was sorry to have made her worry. He stopped stirring the potato filling and came around the island to meet her. "It's okay," he said, and pulled her into his arms. "He was just asking if you were with me. I answered that you were, and that I'd deliver you safely in the morning—if that's what you want."

"Yes, I want to stay. I...Danny, that was incredible. Thank you."

She blushed a deep crimson and he loved it. He lifted her chin with his thumb. "Thank you, baby, for sharing yourself with me that way. You rock my world, Irish." He took her mouth again, and it was heaven. He could have just stood there kissing her like that for another hour. And then undressed her and taken her again. But the steaks would burn, and they'd never eat, so he reluctantly broke the kiss, and turned back to the potatoes.

"Weren't you saying something about recruiting a girl at the gym today?"

She smiled at him and took her stool at the counter again. He refilled her wine glass as she started the story again. He still wasn't really listening, although he loved to hear her talk. But he was rapt watching her, too. He hoped she learned to understand how beautiful and maddening she was. He still wasn't sure how he was going to convince her of that, but she was here with him, in his life. He had to try.

He started the music again, and pulled a salad out of the fridge to go with the rest of their dinner. They talked—well, Sioban mostly talked and he listened—and laughed. He knew there would come a time when he'd have to tell her more about the past that had him at war with himself, as she had so aptly put it, and he would. But tonight he just wanted to enjoy being with her. They finished another bottle of wine.

And before morning came, when he'd have to take her back to Von's, or to the bar, he made love to her thoroughly, again, and again.

§

Some time well after midnight, Vonda opened her eyes, and something about the house was too quiet. She got out of bed and padded to Sioban's room. It was empty, and Vonda felt guilty for even checking. Sioban was a grown woman, and she'd just started seeing a hot man. Why should she have come home? After all, Danny had said not to wait up, but wasn't he just joking? Vonda shouldn't expect her to report in if she wasn't coming home, and yet with the threat to her still being very real, it wasn't unreasonable for Sioban to send one last text before bed, Vonda argued with herself. Maybe you're jealous, a voice said. And what kind of bitch would say something like that? The part of herself that told the truth, she thought.

Vonda returned to her room to get her cell phone from the nightstand, and shuffled to the kitchen for a glass of water. There was no way she dared to text Sioban to check up on her. But maybe Bear had heard from Danny; they always checked in with each other on the case regardless. Vonda took a sip of her water and sent a text to Bear.

< Are you still awake?

Of course he wasn't. This was her chicken-shit way of contacting him without really contacting him. He wouldn't even hear the phone, and she'd go back to bed, and tell him she hadn't realized what time it really was tomorrow. Within sixty seconds, the phone rang. Uh-oh.

"Hi, sorry to—"

"What's wrong?" he said groggily. *Shit.*

"You're asleep. I'm so sorry. I really thought your phone would be off."

"In my line of work, I never turn the phone off, honey. What's going on? Are you okay?"

"I'm fine. I'm locked up tight, alarm is set, your guys are outside. I'm safe and sound...I'm just being stupid. Sioban isn't home yet."

"No, and she won't be," Bear laughed huskily. The sound hugged her through the phone. "I checked in with Danny several hours ago. I figured she'd spend the night, but we always check in regarding Sioban's whereabouts as part of the case. I'm guessing you knew that."

"I assumed it. Geez, I really am sorry, Bear. I should just trust Danny, and I should trust my friend. I really didn't think you'd answer unless you were still up working on something."

"You can text me or call me any time, whether I'm awake or not, you know that."

"Thank you. I'll make sure it's for a legitimate reason next time." Vonda smiled at the phone, even though he couldn't see her. He had a way of making her smile often.

"I'd say your concern was legitimate, given the threat she's still living under. I think you knew she'd probably stay with Danny tonight, but that's okay too. If something doesn't sit right with you, we're here for you. I'm here for you."

"I'm glad. But I should let you get back to sleep."

"If the house is too quiet, I can come over."

"Uh, you have a man posted in front of the house."

"Right—in front of, not inside."

"The house was quiet for a long time before Sioban arrived, too. I can handle it."

"I know. I'd come if you needed me to, though."

"I know."

"Too bad I didn't know you on those other too-quiet nights." Vonda's knees went weak at that. Damn it, she could tell him to come over right now. But Danny and Sioban complicated things enough right now; it would just be ridiculous for her to start something with Bear— "Anyway, I'm awake now, and if I'm not coming over, the least you can do is talk to me while I make myself a drink so I can fall back to sleep."

The moment had passed. He'd felt her wavering, if not her rejection. She laughed and asked him how his day was, and told him how Sioban might have a surprise act she'd recruited for the show. Almost two hours later, Vonda was relaxed and happy. Bear was so easy to listen to, and talk to, and be around, whether in business or otherwise. And as she drifted off to sleep, she hoped that he wouldn't stop wanting to come over and keep her company on too-quiet nights.

Chapter Fifteen

The next morning Vonda stood with Lex and Bear in the middle of her club, facing the stage. The windows behind the stage, which had been helpful during the renovation, were now blacked out and a standard background wall had been erected in front of them. Lex had lit the stage, and the black curtains were open. Out of sight was the dressing room, for which the builders had expanded several feet onto the back of the building near the office. They'd only lost a few spaces near the dumpster, but the dressing room was perfect.

In the main space, Vonda had refinished the original wood on the bar, as well as the oak floors. Other than that, Captain Johnny's was no more. Round black cabaret tables and wrought-iron chairs with heart-shaped backs and blue velour seats dotted the floor. Along the back wall was a row of booths. Gone were the big-screen television over the bar, the dartboards, and the pool table.

It dawned on Vonda as she stood there that she could no longer call this place Captain Johnny's. It no longer belonged to her father, and hadn't since the night he died. But until today, she hadn't really been able to claim it. She'd hidden in the shadow of his name, comfortable to remain in the transition process during the renovation. But now she had no choice but to claim it as her own. It was the Velvet Room, and it was hers.

"You did it, Vonda. This is incredible," said Lex in awe. He'd already been impressed when he'd come in for the first time the week before to go over the plans for the light box. Aside from a few minor adjustments, he'd found it to be just the state-of-the-art setup he liked, including the ceiling fixtures that would allow for more theatrical elements should Vonda decide to make use of them. He believed that even a small venue should have top-notch technology, because it could do a lot for a show. On the other hand, he'd said, he was also confident that Von's show wouldn't need any magical lighting and sound effects, because it would be stunning on its own.

"Well, let's see if I can hire the talent and get the first show choreographed before my money runs out," Vonda laughed.

"Don't sell yourself short, honey," Bear said, and squeezed her shoulder. "This was the hard part. The rest will be a walk in the park, especially with Sioban at your side."

It wasn't lost on Vonda that he'd called her honey, which normally would have made her smile, except for the testosterone storm swirling around her. The unflappable Mr. Rockford was feeling possessive, it seemed. Well, he'd have to understand that Lex was just a friend, and she was damn grateful to have his help. He would make casting and auditioning so much easier, and she could let him run the technical aspects of the show while she focused on the dancing and costumes.

"And Lex here," she added. "A good stage manager is like gold in this business."

Bear didn't say anything, and Lex took his cue to prepare for their first audition.

"I'm gonna get ready for Sahara," he said, and went to the light box. Vonda turned to Bear.

"You don't seem to like Lex very much. But even though I haven't seen him in a few years, he's a good friend, and he's really good at his job. I'm grateful to have him right now."

"Yeah, he seems okay. He passed our background check." Even though Vonda knew that was standard for anyone she brought in, she suspected that Bear was hoping to find a reason to get Lex booted. "Speaking of staff," he continued, "have you started interviewing bartenders yet?"

"Have you seen any bartenders in here? When have I had time to interview bartenders?" Vonda tried not to sound as irritated as she felt, but Bear's he-man routine was getting to her today.

"I didn't think you had, but maybe you'd brought someone in during the handful of hours I haven't been around. Anyway, I have a candidate you might be interested in. He has a valuable skill set."

"Does he have a good repertoire of cocktails? This isn't the beer-and-nuts joint it used to be."

"Oh yeah. He's been working at a classy hotel lounge downtown for a few years now."

"Why would he leave a good gig like that to come and work for me?"

"Because it's his other skill set that I'm interested in, and I have a feeling he's missed using it in the past few years."

"And what would that be?"

"Jarett was an Army Ranger—briefly. An injury cut his career short. He was a hell of a young soldier."

"How do you know what kind of soldier he was? Besides, it's not like he'll need his M-16 rifle behind the bar."

"I know because he served under me. And I'm sure he'd prefer something a little more practical for this kind of work, like a Glock or a nine-mil. You're not thinking past this situation with Sioban. Think about it, Vonda. This is a burlesque club, and you hope for a civilized audience. But with the nature of the kind of shows you'll be doing, everyone who works for you should have some security skills. It's my job as your security contractor to make sure the place is safe for you and your performers every night, not just after this thing with Sonny has been resolved."

"If you say so. So would I hire him as a bartender, or a bouncer?"

"He'd be a bartender with secret benefits. We'd roll him into your security contract. At least meet him?"

"Great. My ever-expanding zillion-dollar security contract. If you can get him in here, I'll meet him. On one condition: that you be a little more congenial toward Lex. I don't know what 'security' skills he has, but I'm not firing him."

"Like I said, we'll work out your contract. And I suspect that Lex has seen some action in his line of work. I wouldn't be surprised if he's had to boot a few drunks in some of the smaller venues he's worked in. But I want to find out what kind of weapons he's familiar with. I only have the best interest of the club in mind."

Bear turned away, arms still crossed and not giving her much of a chance to argue with him. He was headed for the light box, and she prayed he had listened to her and would ease up on his attitude toward Lex. She mused about whether Danny was this overbearing with Sioban right now. She shook her head in an effort to clear it. While the completed renovation was inspiring, she had to focus on Sahara's audition. She'd called Vonda the day after she and Sioban had seen her sing at the Starlight Lounge. It was really more a formality, since she'd already heard Sahara sing, and Lex had vouched for her professionalism. But, like Bear, Vonda was interested in whether or not she had any other skills, namely dance, of course. It would be great if she were willing to join them for some of the simpler routines, even if she didn't have much experience. That remained to be seen.

At that moment, Sioban blustered in, smiling and shaking snow off of her hair. She glowed, and Vonda didn't ever think she'd seen Sioban so happy.

"Top o' the mornin'," Sioban chimed in a sing-song voice. "Isn't that what I'm supposed to say? I mean, I'm Irish, right? At least Danny keeps calling me that."

"Well, good morning to you too," Vonda laughed. "What...Sioban, you look...happy. I mean really happy, not just in a good mood."

Sioban gave her the biggest, brightest smile Vonda had ever seen on her, and blushed at the same time. She was absolutely lovely.

"Well come on over here, I'll make you a cup of tea before Sahara gets here."

Sioban followed her to the bar and took a stool. Vonda watched Sioban taking everything in, much like she'd been doing a short while ago.

"My God, Von. Would you look at the place?"

"I have been," Vonda laughed. "It's...I can't believe the transformation. But now we've got to hustle so we can open the place before I go broke."

"Don't worry. I wish I could tell you more about my other recruit, but I want you to see for yourself."

"You've piqued my interest. But we digress. Care to tell me about last night? Where is Danny, anyway?"

"He said he had an errand to do. You know I don't kiss and tell—but bloody fucking hell, it was amazing!" They both dissolved into giggles. But it wasn't just the mind-blowing orgasms that burned her memory of night she'd just had with Danny. Sioban had replayed how his eyes held hers in the bathroom mirror and then again, and again throughout the night. She didn't think anyone could make her feel that beautiful, right to her core. And the connection she felt growing between them . . . dare she hope it might be love? It was enough, though, just to revel in what they'd shared, and in everything right now. "Oh, Von...how can I explain? Danny is . . . amazing. And it's more than Danny, it's everything. Dancing, really dancing again, thanks to Iliana. Having this chance at a life I've wanted since Ava brought me to America. And it all started with meeting you and you letting me come here after L.A. I'm so grateful for your friendship and all you've done for me, Von. And now it's all happening."

"Well, don't forget your own part in your destiny, hon. Even before I met you, you never gave up. And your talent has always been there, waiting to blossom. What happened in L.A. was the rather harsh motivator life gives us sometimes when we're not listening to the cues. Me asking you to come here wasn't enough, because you felt trapped, and you didn't think you had the strength to leave. And yet when it came down to it, you knew you couldn't stay, and you got out, albeit in a less than ideal way. Now it's happening for both of us. And don't think I don't need you just as much as you need me right now, every bit of that fire, sass, and talent."

Vonda reached under the bar for a little bottle of whiskey she kept when she needed a little something. It wasn't for customers, but for the health of the owner. She opened it and poured a splash into her coffee and Sioban's tea. "So let's kick ass together."

"You bet your sweet arse, we will," said Sioban as they clinked mugs.

§

Though the door to the light box was open, Bear gave a brief knock on the doorframe, and Lex looked up from his double laptops.

"Hey, welcome to my little kingdom, as it were. Von's lucky, that's one hell of a contractor you brought in, one of the best I've seen. He knew what he was doing even before I got here, and he was quick to get on board with the adjustments."

"Yeah, I've worked with him before. He's the best. Listen, you got a minute?"

"Sure."

"I was telling Vonda, and I'm sure you understand, as her security contractor, it's my job to make sure she and her performers are safe at all times. I feel the nature of the show warrants that her main staff, aside from the bouncers, have certain capabilities."

Lex grinned at him, and rubbed his chin. Bear tried to remember what Vonda had asked of him, but he'd be damned if he was going to compromise on this point.

"I agree. I could be an asshole, kind of the way you've been since you met me. But I get it. Vonda is a good friend, and I want the best for her, all the way around. So I don't have any problem letting you know that I've handled my share of drunks, and while I don't have the military background that you and your boys do, I can handle myself in a fight. As in a real street fight. You need me to elaborate, we can do that over a beer sometime. These days, I just be sure to maintain my black-belt status, and I get in the ring once in a while."

Well. Pretty boy was no slouch after all. He did seem to be pretty cut, and it annoyed him to think Vonda might have noticed that too. But that wouldn't have been any guarantee that he could handle himself if the need arose. "As in mixed martial arts?"

"That's right."

"Can you handle a weapon?"

"Oh, you mean other than these deadly hands—something like this." Lex pulled out an unassuming little Beretta Pico. Okay, not bad. But Bear had one more requirement.

"Would you be willing to work with us to learn our protocols and procedures in case of a code-red event?" Bear knew he was in full operational mode, but he couldn't help it.

"Like I said, whatever it takes for Vonda, although I have to wonder if she's really on board with all of this. Are you going to deputize the bartender as well?"

"She's on board. She knows I only have her best interest at heart. And if all goes well, the bartender will be my ex-Army Ranger friend, who served under me."

"You military boys do stick together, don't you?"

Bear didn't really have an answer for that, but instead answered, "There's more to my thoroughness than meets the eye. Depending on how things develop over the coming weeks, I may need to brief you on a situation that affects the girls. You may need to use that pretty Berretta of yours."

Before Lex could form a response, Sahara walked into the club at that moment. Lex stood and pushed past Bear and went down the four stairs from the light box. Bear followed, feeling mostly confident that he'd gotten through to the man. Time would tell.

When Sahara came into the club, she was just as stunning as she had been onstage. She wore a camel-colored wool cape and black leather dress boots. Her thick brushed-gold hoop earrings were gorgeous against her skin when she pulled the hood of her cape back from her head. Her makeup was simple, and the deep burgundy shade on her lips made her all the more exotic. Vonda probably would have sat there staring for another twenty minutes if Sioban hadn't smacked her in the arm.

"Come on then, she's here," Sioban scolded.

They quickly crossed the room to greet her.

"Welcome, Sahara. Thank you for coming today. It's nice to see you again."

"Thank you for having me," she said, as she took in the space. "This is a beautiful space. So exciting what you have planned." Sioban registered the look of surprise at Sahara's speaking voice on Von's face.

"Yes, it is. I'll put your things in the dressing room for safekeeping. Can I get you something to drink before we get started?"

"Just a glass of water, thank you. Maybe something else after," she said as she pulled off her cape. She wore a basic black wrap dress and a gold chain with a small pendant on it.

When Vonda returned from the back, Sahara was chatting with Lex. Upon seeing Vonda, she handed Lex a flash drive that she'd taken out of her purse. "May I?" she asked, pointing to the stage, where a microphone waited on its stand.

"By all means."

Sioban had refilled their mugs and took a table with Von midway back from the stage. It would be a good distance, Vonda thought, to hear how the sound carried back here. She glanced at Bear, who sat unobtrusively at the bar, and wondered what kind of exchange he'd had with Lex.

After another moment, Lex dimmed the house lights and threw a soft spotlight on Sahara, who gave a nod toward the light box, and stepped in closer to the microphone. As she began, Vonda knew there was music, she heard the notes. But Sahara's voice held her captive, even more than it had the other night. Every word she sang was a string that tugged on the heart, a tear she begged you to cry with her, or a lover's heart you felt beating inside your own. She brought them floating along through "My Funny Valentine," then through "Sunday Kind of Love" and finally "Georgia."

"I brought a few more selections in case you wanted to hear another song."

It was incredible, and it took Vonda a moment to process what she'd just heard.

"Um, no, that won't be necessary. That was great. Why don't you come down here and sit with us?" Then, to Sioban, she added, "Would you mind making a cup of tea for her, hon?"

"Of course. Be right back."

Sahara took the empty chair that faced Vonda and sat down with her back to the stage. "I hope you enjoyed my song choices," she said quietly.

"Oh, mostly certainly, Sahara. Without a doubt you would be—will be, if you want the job—a wonderful asset to the show."

"Thank you so much. I know we need to discuss the terms, but I can tell you at this moment, I'm prepared to give notice at the Starlight."

"And that's good to hear. I just wanted to ask you something. Do you have any dance experience at all? Could you, or would you, consider joining us for one or two numbers? Nothing too crazy..." Vonda trailed off when she saw the panic wash over Sahara's face.

"I...I don't have any dance training, none whatsoever. I'm sorry, but if that's a requirement—"

"No, Sahara, not at all. I didn't mean to upset you. My mind is just in hyper drive right now, with ideas for the show."

Sioban came back with the tea and set it in front of Sahara. "Here you go. Sorry we don't have anything herbal that would probably be better for your voice. Just good old-fashioned Irish breakfast tea. Everything all right here?" She gave Vonda a wary look, as if to say "you haven't blown this already, have you?"

"Everything's fine. I was just about to assure Sahara that we'd be honored to have her be part of the show."

"Oh, well, that's a relief," Sioban said cheerfully as she took her seat again. "And don't worry, give me a list, and we'll get some of the kinds of tea and snacks you like around here."

"Are you sure?" Sahara asked pointedly of Vonda.

"Absolutely, Sahara. Don't worry about the other, I was just curious more than anything. Okay?"

"All right. I, um, need to excuse myself to the ladies' room for a moment."

"Of course, it's right down that hallway," Vonda said, and pointed to where she should go.

Sioban barely waited until Sahara had gotten out of earshot before she launched into an inquisition. "What the hell did you say to that poor girl? She looked like she was about to pass out from shock."

"You know me, I just say whatever ideas come to mind, and I asked her if she'd be willing to dance in one or two numbers, and whether or not she'd had any experience. You would have thought I'd asked her to jump out of an airplane, but I didn't mean to upset her."

"That's strange. Well, don't bring it up again, whatever you do. I'm sure she'll be fine as long as we don't try to press her into anything she doesn't want to do."

"I definitely won't mention it again. When she gets back, keep her company for a minute, while I go to the office and dig out the basic contract I put together. The pay is scaled for dancers. I have no idea what nightclub singers get, but I hope it's enough, at least to start with."

When Vonda returned with the contract, she was pleased to see Sahara laughing with Sioban, who had evidently charmed her out of whatever panic she'd been in. When Vonda showed Sahara the salary figure, she made it no secret that it was considerably more than she was making at the Starlight. Vonda was relieved to hear that, and also that Sahara had become a U.S. citizen recently so that there wouldn't be any hassle with her immigration status. Vonda wanted to take good care of her performers, and Sahara was definitely worth it. But Vonda couldn't help wondering what was behind her panicked reaction earlier. Just as Sahara was signing her contract, Sioban's phone rang. She dug it out of her pocket and smiled broadly as she listened. After a few seconds, she held her hand over the phone and pulled it back from her mouth.

"This is great. Lex! Can you stay a bit?" she called.

"Sure, I can hang."

Vonda was intrigued about Sioban's excitement, but she was heartened to see Lex talking to Bear, and it didn't look like either was thinking of punching the other one in the face.

"Great!" Sioban turned back to Vonda excitedly. "My surprise recruit says she can come over now if we can see her."

"That's fine with me." This would do a lot to temper Vonda's own sense of panic over having to set up auditions. She just hoped this one, whoever she was, could actually dance.

"Okay, I'll tell her."

With the mystery act set to arrive within the hour, Sahara said her goodbyes, along with how much she looked forward to being part of the show. She would give her two weeks to the club, which meant that Vonda had to have the show cast and ready to start rehearsals by then. It was daunting, but she heard Johnny's words echoing in her head again, this time telling her that everything would be fine.

§

Danny couldn't believe he was standing in Lady Eve's lingerie shop. He'd parked several blocks down the street when he came back from his other errands to be sure Sioban didn't see him sneaking in. Hell, so that no one else saw him either. All he needed was Bear or one of those other assholes he worked with on his ass for being in a lingerie store, though he thought of them affectionately. Not to mention it would be an embarrassment to Sioban. They weren't hiding that they were together, but he didn't want to draw extra attention to it either. He really wanted to surprise her, after she'd confessed that she didn't feel beautiful, and he knew just what he was looking for.

The smells of lavender and brewing tea and perfume nearly knocked him over when he walked in. Jesus, what was he doing in here? *Get a grip, Sheridan, this is for Sioban.* A striking young woman stood behind the counter. She seemed an anomaly in this atmosphere for some reason, with her long, straight black hair and ruddy brown skin. And he could see her grey eyes even from there. She looked to be all of sixteen, and when she smiled shyly at him, he hoped she wouldn't be too intimidated by him.

"May I help you, sir?"

Danny wished he had on sneakers, because he sounded like an army as the heels of his boots clunked on the wooden floor. When he got to the counter, he didn't mince words.

"Look, this'll be really easy. A few weeks ago, I saw this emerald-green corset in the window. It had black lace. And I'd like to buy it."

"Oh yes, that one is—"

From out of nowhere a tiny dervish of a woman breezed out of the back.

"I couldn't help overhearing you," she said briskly. "But that was a one-of-a-kind piece from France. We sold it a while back, probably right after you saw it."

Well, hell. He'd had his mind set on that one, and now he'd have to actually stay in this store for a period of time and shop. *Shit*. Not only did he not want to be in there longer than absolutely necessary, but he'd promised Bear he'd be back by lunch. He began to look around in bewilderment, and was about to ask the nice ladies for help, when a text came through on his phone. It was from his contact back in L.A., a member of another security firm owned by a friend of Bear's that Rockford had enlisted to babysit Sonny after Danny left. The idea was that Danny shouldn't stay long enough, or risk bugging any of Sonny's frequent locations, including his house, businesses, or Club 29, and if their contact's cover was blown, he'd only be traced locally and could claim that any one of Sonny's old rivals had hired him in order to spy on Sonny. It read simply:

< Home base mobilizing satellites.

Suddenly, choosing what lingerie to buy for Sioban wasn't nearly as critical as keeping her alive.

"I'm sorry ladies, I'm going to have to come back another day. When I do, I hope you can steer me in the right direction, since the green number isn't available." He didn't give them a chance to answer, because there was simply no time. He dashed out onto the sidewalk and cursed the fact that he'd left his truck parked so far away. His list of Sonny's first- and second-tier connections was in there, and he wanted it when he talked to his contact. He dialed Bear as he ran, so that he could get reports from the posts at the house, and start to implement the next level of their strategy.

"Plan Z. I'll fill you in when I get there."

Danny dialed the contact. Even though he was only a block from his truck, without knowing when Sonny's Chicago connections would strike, he couldn't run fast enough.

§

"Why did you tell him that piece was one of a kind?" Chyenne asked Eve after Danny had gone.

"Because he's stone in love with Sioban, and when he finds out she bought it, it's going to send him over the edge."

"Him? How do you know he's in love with Sioban? How do you know he even knows her?"

"I've been watching the goings-on over there. He's part of the security team working with Vonda. I can see I'm going to have to give you a lesson or two in friendly nosiness. In the meantime, wrap up the blue La Croix. I'll see if I can sneak it to him next door before they leave tonight. It'll be our contribution to the cause." Eve just laughed as she returned to the back room.

Burlesque Bad

Sioban could hardly contain her excitement. Sure, she'd recognized that Sahara would be an asset to the show, and it had been easy to convince Von of that, since she'd seen her at the same time. But this was different. If Sioban was off base, and Von thought she was crazy, well, that would stink. Sioban counted on Solange having told the truth about having some dance experience as she paced the floor.

"You're going to wear a hole in my newly polished floor, young lady," Vonda admonished from the table they'd been sitting at with Sahara, where she'd been making phone calls.

"Sorry." She turned on her heel to retrace her path across the floor, when the door opened and Solange walked in with a duffle bag half her size slung over her shoulder. She brushed snow off of her silver down jacket and pushed her hood back.

"Bonjour!" At the sound of her lilting voice Lex appeared rather quickly from the light box, where Sioban had seen him with his feet up on the edge of the sound board, reading a martial arts magazine. Sioban ignored him and ran up to Solange.

"Hi! This is perfect timing, we just finished another audition." Sioban was reaching to help her with the duffle bag when Lex's hand flew out and caught it in his own grasp.

"Let me help you with that," he said.

He was staring at Solange like a lost puppy, and he wasn't doing much to hide it. Fortunately for him, Vonda breezed up just as Sioban opened her mouth to razz him about it.

"Hello, I'm Vonda. I own the Velvet Room."

"Thank you so much for this time that I can show you what I do," Solange said in her delightful accent.

"Well, Sioban hasn't told me anything, but she's certainly excited you're here too, and so am I. What's in the bag?"

Suddenly, Sioban's stomach dropped. Solange had said she was borrowing silks from the gym, but in her determination to keep the details of this audition a secret, Sioban had completely forgotten to check the setup to see if Solange would be able to hang them. Sioban blew out her breath when she spied the bolts in the ceiling.

"That is my equipment, so to speak. I will need help with it, I'm afraid. We need to hang it—from there." She pointed to the bolts.

"What in the world?" Von asked.

"You'll see."

Lex took that as his cue to get the duffle bag onto the stage. He'd been holding it over his shoulder as if it were a feather pillow. "Let's see what we have here," he said and smiled at Solange. They all watched as he unzipped the bag and pulled the silks out.

"Curtains?" he asked.

"Not exactly," Solange giggled.

"Ah, I see." Lex unfolded them and came upon the thick metal clasps at the end of each one.

"Come on, Lex, you're going to need a ladder. I think the contractor left one in the hallway back there."

"Be right back," Lex said as he smiled at Solange.

"Okay," she said and turned to Vonda. "I'm an aerial silks artist."

Sioban cringed when Von glared at her. "She was also trained as a dancer. Ballet. In Paris."

Solange picked up on Vonda's consternation as well. "Mademoiselle, don't want to waste your time. If this isn't what you're looking for—"

"It's all right, Solange. Sioban obviously witnessed something she knew would be valuable to the show. And you do have classical dance training. Would you like something to drink while we wait?"

"Merci. I'd love some ginger ale if you have it."

"I'm sure there is," Vonda said, softening. "We haven't used much of our soft-drink stock, or any stock, for that matter, since the wake."

Vonda walked toward the bar, and Solange gave Sioban a sad look.

"Her father? This was his place?"

"Yeah. It's still fresh."

"But look what she has now, it's amazing. I'm sure he would be proud."

The men brought the ladder in, and Vonda returned in short order with Solange's drink. It had a cherry in it, which made Solange smile.

"Merci, mademoiselle."

The girl had charm, that was for sure. Vonda was already warming to her and Lex was practically falling over himself. Sioban was feeling more confident as they stood and watched Lex up on the ladder, with Bear spotting. He certainly seemed to be an old hand at this stuff, as he deftly hung each swath of silk. Solange finally took her jacket off and tossed it on the chair at one of the front tables by the stage. She wore a black leotard, with a bright-pink wrap skirt over it. She matched the streak in her hair again, Sioban observed. As Bear and Lex stowed the ladder against the wall by the bar just next to Johnny's picture, she removed her boots and socks, and dug in the pocket of her jacket and pulled out a CD. She ambled up onto the stage, not bothering with the stairs. Lex crossed to her in a few long strides.

"I don't believe I caught your name," he said.

"It's Solange," she said, and pulled at her hair in a nervous gesture to spike it up.

"Well, I'm Lex. What kind of sounds did you bring with you?"

She handed him the CD. "Number nine. I love that song."

Lex reviewed it for a long moment. "What about this one?" he asked, and pointed to another one on the label. "Do you have a routine that will work with that?"

"Sure, I've worked with all of these songs, I use this CD in my class. But you think that one is better?"

"I do. Even though it talks about somebody finding love, there's still a certain...longing about it. Like your first cup of water after crossing the desert— it's so good, it's almost too much."

Solange just stared up at him in a trance. *Lord, the two of them,* thought Sioban. As much as she wanted Solange to get the gig, she was beginning to wonder if it was such a good idea. Bear had said he was going out to the reconnaissance van to get a report, and Vonda was streaming something on her phone while she waited. But Sioban had to get them to snap out of it.

"Ahem! Have we got a world peace summit going up there? Maybe the rest of us should join you."

Solange startled. "Sorry, we were just going over which music I'm going to use." Lex cocked his head, and Solange nodded slowly in the affirmative. She wrapped her wrists around the silks and put one toe behind her before she hung her head in preparation.

Vonda looked up just as the first strains of "At Last" came out of the sound system, and Solange knew her friend was hooked. Solange's body was small for a dancer, but she controlled every muscle, and it seemed that she could send an emotion all the way to her fingertips and toes at any given moment. Her positions reflected the music: a little tortured, a little relieved, and very sexy and in love. More than once, with both arms captured by the silks, she held them out and up, or simply held onto one silk, and her legs floated in sophisticated choreography. She was literally dancing in mid-air. When Solange took her bow, drawing the silks across her and out again, Sioban didn't even want to see Lex drooling on the floor in the light box. Sioban knew what she'd just seen, and that it was magic, something not many other shows like theirs would have. But the question was, what would Von say. When Sioban looked over at her friend, she knew Vonda felt the same way. Von just stared, with her mouth slightly fallen open. Solange released her hold on the silks and stood waiting for one of them to say something.

"That was magnificent, Solange. Don't you think so, Von?"

"Oh. My. Goodness. I guess I'd never really seen this done before, or if I did, it was nothing like that. I mean, she was—Solange, you were—"

"Dancing in the air?" Sioban finished the sentence.

"Yes, that's it! Dancing in the air!"

"So you're not worried about her being able to dance along with us on the ground for a few numbers?"

"Oh hell no! You were right, Sioban. This is something very special. She's in. You're in, Solange! I mean, come down and I'll give you the terms. If they're amenable to you, we'd be thrilled to have you."

As Solange was about to jump down from the stage, Lex came out of the light box and crossed to her.

"That was...incredible," he said.

"Merci. I'm glad I listened to you about the music. It was perfect."

"Yes, it was," he said quietly. She smiled at him and hopped down.

When they sat down to work out the contract, Solange was just as thrilled with the terms as Sahara had been. They all shook hands, and Vonda assured her they would be in touch with the rehearsal schedule when it was finalized. Sioban observed as Lex offered to walk Solange to her car. When she told him that she'd taken the El, he insisted on driving her where she needed to go.

"Well, I guess we just lost Lex," said Vonda.

"In more ways than one," quipped Sioban. It was more than annoying how Von had zeroed in on her and Danny from day one but was oblivious to the instant chemistry between Lex and Solange. And if Vonda ever admitted her growing closeness to Bear, well, just how many love stories could one burlesque show support?

"I was going to invite him to stay for lunch, but I guess he has other plans."

I'll bet, thought Sioban.

They were starving, and Vonda ordered meatball subs from Manucci's. All during lunch, Bear seemed uneasy, and Vonda hoped that he'd worked out whatever differences he had with Lex. They were both good men, and, well, she cared about both of them, and she wanted them to get along. Thinking about how much she'd grown to like Bear unnerved her.

"I'll just clean this stuff up," she said, so she could get up and stretch. She added the trash from dinner to what was already in the bin under the bar, and took it out to the dumpster in the back. She was almost startled to see the second bouncer Rockford had hired standing under the floodlight. She'd forgotten he would be back there. He nodded at her, and she quickly tossed the trash and went back inside. When she got back out front, Bear had brought a huge object wrapped in brown paper packing from somewhere, and stood on the stage with Sioban, who held a bottle of open champagne in one hand, and three glasses between the fingers of her other hand.

"What's going? What are you doing with champagne? We should save that for opening night, assuming we ever get there."

"You will get there, and we'll have more then," said Bear. He was staring at her intently, which only fueled her curiosity. "But you've reached a milestone today, and I have a gift for you that I've been saving to mark the completion of the renovation. I wanted to wait for Danny, but I figure we'd better do this now. Come on up here."

Vonda climbed the stairs to the stage cautiously. She knew it wouldn't be anything bad, not from Bear, but she was still waiting for something to happen.

"Sioban, why don't you start pouring while she opens this. Vonda, just kneel down and tear back the paper. It's too heavy for you to lift, and I want you to see what it is before we stand it up."

"How did you get it in here in the first place, and so quickly?" she asked as she tore gingerly at the paper.

"The sign company had it finished a week ago, and they were holding it until I called them this morning."

Slowly, she revealed what would be her new neon sign for the front: "The Velvet Room" rendered in neon glass script tubing. The Captain Johnny's sign had been covered over with a black tarp, and she'd made some calls that morning for bids on a replacement. Sioban set the bottle down and carefully handed Bear his glass of champagne.

"Bear...I can't believe this," Vonda breathed.

"It'll be blue when it's lit. The sign company will be back tomorrow to take down the old one and hang it. They'll recycle the old one, unless you want to hang it in the hallway or something for posterity."

"It's beautiful, just what I would have picked. But I can't accept it."

Sioban kicked at her. "Are you mad? The poor man has gone to all this trouble, and you're trying to refuse his gift?"

"It's just that you've given me so much already, Bear," she said, ignoring Sioban.

"Vonda, I was sorry to hear that Johnny had passed away. He was a good client and I liked him a lot. And sure, I'd hope to hang on to the account. But you've allowed me to become part of something really special. So this is really my way of thanking you for that. Please let me do this for you."

"Bear, I don't know what else to say, except thank you." Damn it, she was tearing up, the last thing she wanted to do. Hopefully he wouldn't try to take her in his arms in front of Sioban. Had they been alone, Vonda wasn't sure she could resist that.

"Don't cry, honey," he said softly and swiped at a tear on her cheek with his thumb. "This is supposed to be a celebration of your milestone. Have some champagne."

She blinked and took a glass from Sioban, who was beaming.

"To the birth of the Velvet Room!" said Sioban.

They raised their glasses and took a healthy drink of their bubbly. It was real. The Velvet Room was real now. She just had to turn the sign on. And hire another dancer. And a bartender. And put together the first show. And do the PR for the opening. Then it would be real. But boy, was she close now.

"I'll get the guys to help me stand it up over here against the backdrop. It should be okay here until tomorrow." Bear's phone rang then. "Oh, it's the missing man himself. Yeah," he said as he answered the call. Vonda nearly shuddered as she watched Bear's expression turn dark. The call only lasted a moment.

"I'm going out to the van. Stay here. I'm sending the two outside guys in here. DO NOT open the door yourselves for ANY reason. Danny's on his way, and I'll be back soon."

"Wait, what—" Vonda wanted more information. What the hell was going on? She looked at Sioban, who had begun to tremble. Vonda took her hand. "Come on, let's go sit down. I'll make us some tea."

Suddenly, champagne didn't seem like such a good idea.

Chapter Sixteen

Sioban smashed her clothes into the same suitcase she'd brought with her from Los Angeles. It was hard to make out exactly what she'd chosen through her tears as she raked up a pile of socks and underwear from the dresser drawer, and snatched randomly at her jeans and sweaters from the closet. Half of it probably didn't match, but she didn't care.

Lord, would she ever be able to stop crying, would she ever be able to stop running?

Reece Gorman had come into the club and told her and Vonda to come with him, that he would drive them home immediately. They weren't to use Von's car until they could get the under-vehicle search mirror to check for explosives. The only other thing he would say was that there had been a development in Sioban's case, that she was to pack some things because Danny wanted her at his place for the foreseeable future.

"What the hell about Von? I'm supposed to just leave her alone? She's in danger too!" Sioban had fairly screamed at poor Reece.

"I'll be perfectly fine," Vonda had reassured. "I'm sure the guys have a plan that includes me, and we have to trust them."

Well, they'd better, or she'd never take one step to go with Danny. Neither would she let any of them see what a mess she was. She swiped at her eyes, and jammed her suitcase shut. She stopped in the bathroom to throw cold water on her face, and then she heard the doorbell ring. She descended the stairs to find Danny and Bear standing at the bottom. But when Danny reached for her suitcase, Sioban had another idea. She clutched the handle tightly and pulled it back from him.

"I did what Reece asked because I knew he had instructions from you. But I'll be damned if I'm going to just up and leave Von here alone and unprotected while you cart me away."

Both Bear and Von opened their mouths to speak, but Danny jumped ahead of them.

"I know. Don't worry, Bear has taken care of everything here. Vonda will have just as much protection as you will with me."

"Go ahead, sweetie. It's late. Let Danny take you home now. Bear will fill me in on everything."

"I...I know I'll be safe with Danny, I just don't want to leave you like this, everything's up in the air."

"We're only as far away as our cell phones. Call me later if you want to. And I'll see you in the morning."

Von didn't look entirely convinced, but Bear nodded his head.

"All right, just...you call me too if you get scared, or if you hear any noises."

"I will, I promise. Now get going, you two."

Danny and Bear gave each other one of their silent acknowledgements, and Sioban followed Danny out into the night.

As he drove away from the house, Danny tried to take her hand, but she pulled it away. She didn't think she could look at him, either, as he quietly told her the details of what they'd just learned. Bear's contact at another security firm out there had agreed to babysit Sonny after Danny left. If he was compromised in any way, he'd still only have local ties. They'd have no way of connecting him with anyone in Chicago. He'd been able to bug the phones at Club 29, as well as Sonny's locations. He'd finally heard proof in the audio that Sonny was reaching out to his local connections. So far, there was a Russian gun dealer with a base of operation out of a meat-packing warehouse, and possible coordination with another club owner downtown. Specifics had only been discussed in code, making it difficult to pinpoint exactly what the plans were. That was what he and Bear, along with the other Rockford staff assigned to her case, would be focused on, along with air-tight security around her and Von until they figured out what Sonny's next move would be, and, of course, shut it down.

It seemed like he might have had some lingering detail to explain, but she just wanted to get inside and lie down. She flung open the car door as soon as Danny had parked and stalked across the garage to the elevator, leaving Danny to get her suitcase.

"Sioban, slow down. Even though we're home, we still have to take precautions," he called from behind her.

She punched the elevator button hard with her thumb, and Danny was silent as they made the climb to his floor. Thankfully, he didn't want to continue their conversation in the elevator either. It was all Sioban could do not to yank the keys out of his hand and open the door herself. Finally, when he'd gotten it unlocked, she pushed past him and stalked in.

"Sioban. Baby. I know you're upset, but—"

"You think I'm upset? Why, because a mobster is making plans to come and kill me for fighting off his advances? Oh, and to get back the money I stole from him, sure, there's that." She tore off her coat and flung it on the floor as she paced. Danny set her suitcase down and stared at her as she raged on. "But what's really bothering me, what's really got me inside out, Danny, is that I have no life! I keep running around, taking dance classes, helping Von, as if I could just erase what I've done, and who I was before. When really, it's probably all just pretend. Playing house. Because, who am I, really? The daughter of a wasted dancer who could never really get it together. I don't belong here in Chicago, certainly not living in Von's childhood room, riding on the streamers of her dreams. Maybe I don't even belong here with you, either."

"Stop it, Sioban." Danny came toward her, and she turned away from him, but it didn't stop him from wrapping his arms around her gently from behind. "It's time for you to listen to me again," he said, and pressed his lips into her hair. And even though she didn't want to hear the assurance in his voice, didn't want to feel this safe in his arms, she surrendered and let herself go slack as he spoke.

"You're here because it's the safest place for you to be. But you're also here because I need you just as much as you need me. I need to *know* that you're safe every moment, not just hear it from a Rockford staff member. I need to see it for myself. I have to be the one responsible, because I don't know what happened that day I saw you in the road, but whatever it was, it's put you inside me somehow. I need to hold you, touch you. Because if anything happened to you now, when we're just getting started, I couldn't handle it. So, you belong, baby. Here. Now. With me."

"So much for the complicated part," she said with a watery voice. Danny chuckled and tightened his arms around her.

"As for The Velvet Room, it's your dream too, you know," he said firmly.

"Von said the same thing. I'm just not used to believing in myself yet."

He turned her then to face him.

"You'll find it. You'll get there," he said and touched her cheek. "Sioban, there's something else I need to tell you. There's a tape."

Sioban shook her head at him. There couldn't be. Oh...he'd seen it. God. Her legs wobbled.

"Stay with me here, honey. I didn't want to tell you before, but one of the girls at Club 29, Darlene, turned up dead. I'd been watching everything from a distance and had thought about trying to talk to her. I noticed she wasn't at her usual hangouts, and I followed some of the girls she hung around into a bar one night. I overheard them talking, and apparently somebody trashed her place and killed her. I got in there, and it was a stroke of luck that they didn't really know what they were looking for or where to look. I found it in the case for a movie video. It was slightly smaller than a regular VHS tape, so I spotted it right away. That's when I decided to bring it back with me. I'm guessing that's what Sonny wants now; he probably thinks Darlene knew where you went and sent it to you herself. It's not the money you took or the fact that you clocked him on the head. That tape will ruin him, or at least set it in motion, once the authorities have it. Once he's charged with sexual assault, every lawyer in the country who's been trying to bring him down will start trolling out what they've got on him."

"Danny...please tell me you..." Danny gripped her arms to steady her and she tightened her own on his biceps.

"I didn't watch it, Sioban. Neither did Bear. We know what's on it. It was marked with the date on the side, and 'Club 29.' At some point, the authorities will have to view it to confirm. But I don't plan to ever watch it, if I can help it." And he'd keep the cops from seeing it as long as he had to, not only because the thought of strangers seeing what Sonny did to her sickened him, but because cops always screwed up situations like this. He and Bear needed Rockford in control until it was absolutely necessary to call in law enforcement.

Sioban reached for her next words, knowing they would form the most important truth she would share with Danny so far.

"It wasn't that he might have raped me. Sure, a terrible thing it would've been, but I'd have survived it." She paused and closed her eyes. "But what would have come after that...once I'd let Jimmy use me like that, I would have been trapped in that life, just like Ava was trapped. I would have died in that club, Danny. And now I'm still not sure I really made it out."

She'd said it out loud, and Sioban had no more words left. All the tears and uncertainty she'd only allowed herself in brief moments came rushing out of her now in an overwhelming deluge of fear. She could only cling to Danny as he lifted her into his arms and carried her to the couch. She just clung to him as she cried, and he held on to her tightly in his lap. But as the sobs that wracked her subsided, Sioban felt the rumble in his chest as he began to sing "Angel of Hope," one of the newer Irish ballads.

> I search for you each moment
> and wonder where you are
> On summer winds and butterflies
> I've searched from near and far
> But I know you're here to comfort me
> till I can find my way
> and although you speak in silence
> try to hear what you still say
> when a springtime sky
> that's full of clouds
> reveals a patch of blue

and a warming sun comes shining through
I know that can be you

Take me on your wing
together we will fly
let me see your memory through the teardrop in
my eye
Lift my spirit high
till I can touch your soul
take me on your wing
with all the love I bring
my sweet Angel of Hope

This life is full of happenings
that we don't understand
Still you are my miracle
Blessed by God's own hand
And my miracle will be complete
And I'll be truly blessed
When I wrap my arms around you
and hold you close against my breast
Now we have a place for us
that we can call our own
As I gaze upon your smiling face
Sweet Angel of Hope

Take me on your wing
together we will fly
let me see your memory through the teardrop in
my eye
Lift my spirit high
till I can touch your soul
take me on your wing
with all the love I bring
my sweet Angel of Hope

By the time he finished, Sioban had caught her breath, and though her eyes were still closed she ran her fingers over his chest. She opened them when he kissed her forehead, but didn't look at him right away.

"I didn't know you could sing."

"I can't."

"That sounded pretty damn wonderful to me."

"That's only because you're in a state of emotional distress," he chuckled. "You're delusional, you don't know what you're hearing."

"What other talents haven't you shown me?"

"Wouldn't you like to know?"

She did lift her head then and look at him. The way his eyes locked onto her with so much passion—and love, she realized, almost brought her to tears again.

"So, I belong, do I?"

He grabbed her chin, not roughly, but with intent. "You sure as fuck do, baby. All you have to do is own it. Own how the room brightens every time you walk into it. Own how you can flatten anyone with the truth, whether they're ready to hear it or not. Own the talent that's all yours, not Von's, not Ava's."

"And what about you, us?"

"I'm not going anywhere, Irish."

"What about when this thing with Sonny is over? What then?"

"I guess I'll just have to keep showing up every day until you believe me. But you gotta do your part too, baby. Own this, too. Own what we're building together."

She didn't need to be told again. Sioban clutched the hair at his neck and pulled him to her. She locked her mouth onto his. God, she didn't want to let go, and she hoped he didn't either.

Danny leaned her back and ran his hand under her shirt to find her breast as his tongue thrust at hers. She whimpered and pulled at his belt buckle. He broke their kiss and tugged at his shirt. She helped him get her own shirt over her head, and just those few seconds seemed too long since they'd been pressed together. He stretched out over her again, and ground his pelvis against hers.

"More," she moaned against his lips.

They both tore at their jeans and underwear while trying to stay pressed as closely together as they could. It was torture until they finally got them off. Danny lifted her back and she pushed herself up and forward to straddle him. He pulled the straps of her bra down her shoulders as he lay back under her. She reached behind her to unfasten it completely and spill her breasts out into his waiting hands.

"It's amazing having you here, over me like this," he said thickly, and rubbed his thumbs over her nipples.

It wasn't enough. The weeping tip of his cock pulsed just beyond her entrance.

"More," she rasped again as she leaned down and bit the flesh around his nipple. "I need to feel you filling me. I want to ride you hard, Danny."

"Yes, Sioban. Take what you need from me, baby." She was never more glad that they'd talked about protection, and since she was on the pill and they were clean, they'd decided to dispense with condoms.

They both groaned loudly as she brought herself down on his shaft, and he thrust himself further inside of her. Sioban grabbed at his shoulders. If it were possible to pull him any further into her, she'd do it. And then she began to move up and down at a desperate pace.

"Danny...it's so good!"

"Yes, Sioban. Ride me good."

She pressed her hands over his as they gripped her hips and brought her down on him again and again, harder and faster as they reached for a white-hot pinnacle together.

"God, Danny...ahhh!"

She arched her back as her orgasm burst through her. She felt Danny's release fill her as he shouted in the throes of his own climax.

They continued to move together as the last waves of pleasure rippled through them. Finally, Danny lifted her off of him, and Sioban sighed as he pulled her gently to his side.

"That was..." She couldn't quite find the words she wanted.

"Fucking amazing." Danny drew her face up and kissed her again longingly.

"Jesus, Danny. You're making me want you all over again. Right now. And I think it will kill me."

"It's okay, baby," Danny chuckled, and pulled the blanket from the back of the couch over them. "Sleep now. There'll be more where that came from for you when you wake up. There will always be more."

§

"So this is your plan?"

Vonda and Bear stood across from each other in the same place Danny and Sioban had left them. She should have made them coffee. Or a stiff drink, come to think of it. But Bear hadn't wasted any time filling her in on the situation with Sioban's case. Once he started, Vonda was riveted, and not in a good way. The punchline came when Bear announced he'd be staying at the house with her until Sonny had finally been dealt with.

"I don't think we talked about this."

"Um, no, we didn't."

"Meaning, we haven't talked about how there are times in my work when I need to make decisions and I need the client's full cooperation."

Damn if her heart didn't drop a little bit when he said that. So she was just a client to him after all. And wasn't that what she'd been crowing all along, strictly business?

"Especially," Bear added, "when it's not just any client we're talking about."

Vonda crossed her arms and stared down at the floor. What the hell was she supposed to say to that?

"Fine. I mean, thank you. I'm glad that you're taking this seriously, even though Dex is outside."

"Where he'll remain until morning. And yes, I do take my work seriously. Like I told you the other night on the phone, Dex is *outside*. I need to make sure there's someone inside."

"And that someone has to be you."

Bear stepped closer into her immediate space, and she didn't stop him. It was difficult to look into his brown eyes. And yet it was the easiest thing she'd ever done.

"Vonda, I know you're not comfortable pursuing any kind of relationship with me. You've made that clear, even though we haven't ever really broached the subject. I'd never do anything to go against you on that, so give me some credit here. But I think I've made it just as clear that you've become...important to me in ways I don't quite understand myself. So yeah, the man on the inside in this situation needs to be me. *I* need it to be me."

Mercy. "Okay. I'll, um, put some fresh sheets on Sioban's bed for you."

"Not necessary. I'll stay on the couch. I want to hear if anyone makes a breach, and I want to be here to respond to them before anyone even gets to where you are upstairs. Don't make a fuss over me, and try not to worry."

"Right. Can I at least make you a drink?"

Finally, he grinned at her.

"I thought you'd never ask. I'll have whatever you're having."

Vonda exhaled and walked over to the little liquor cabinet next to the TV. She'd heard Bear comment how he liked to settle down at night sometimes with about three fingers of Johnny Walker Red, neat, and that suited her just fine. But since she didn't want to pass out cold on him, she poured herself about two fingers, on the rocks.

When she returned with the drinks, Bear was sitting on the couch. She handed him his drink and took Johnny's BarcaLounger opposite him.

"Thank you," he said solemnly. "Vonda, there's another piece of this I need to tell you about."

Jesus, there was more? Vonda resisted the urge to down her entire drink at once. Instead, she took a fortifying gulp.

"Danny brought back a tape."

If she hadn't been sitting down, she certainly would have fallen down at that moment. The questions swarmed in her mind, but she couldn't seem to find her voice to ask them. Thankfully, Bear answered the first one for her.

"Neither of us has watched it, and we won't," he said.

Deep inside, Vonda knew that, but it was no less of a relief to hear him say it. She wanted to listen to the rest of what he had to say, but suddenly she was so very tired. And it hurt her heart to think of how Sioban had felt when Danny told her, even with his promise that he hadn't seen it. She rubbed her temples, and leaned back as she listened to Bear tell her more about their strategy.

The next thing she knew, Bear's voice was very close, almost as if he were standing right in front of her face. And he was caressing her hand, that was nice. Suddenly she startled awake. Bear was, in fact, kneeling in front her chair. He'd taken her drink and set it on the side table, and his hand now covered hers.

"You need to get some rest, Vonda. Can you make it upstairs, or do you want me to carry you?"

Carry her, yes. No!

"Thanks, I'm good. Sorry, I guess I'm more worn out than I thought. I got all the highlights, though. Sonny's hiring local goons to come after Sioban, and maybe even me; because of that, you're my new roomie for the foreseeable future; and there's a tape, but no one's watching it."

"That about covers it. Come on, let me help you up."

Bear put his hands at her hips and effortlessly pulled her up to her feet. Vonda involuntarily brought her hands to his chest. She felt like she was floating, but that was probably the Scotch talking.

"Um, thank you. I'll just be going upstairs now."

"Keep your cell phone by the bed. If you hear anything, or if you need me, text, don't get up or call out."

"Gee, am I allowed to go to the bathroom, or do you have to supervise that too?" she said jokingly.

"Very funny. Goodnight, Vonda. Sleep tight."

In spite of the reasons Bear gave for sleeping downstairs on the couch, Vonda still believed it was her fault for insisting on such a professional distance between them. But at least, thank God, he was here in the house with her. For all of the bravado she'd given Sioban about being okay alone so that Sioban wouldn't feel guilty about going with Danny, Vonda had been terrified, even knowing that Dex was parked outside. Sioban may have been the one to thwart Jimmy's plans for her and run, but Vonda had been the one to show him up in his own business. He made more money because of her, but that only emphasized that he wasn't a good businessman. And now she harbored Sioban, so in essence, she'd taken a lot from him—too much. Sonny may be after Sioban, but Jimmy had a reason to see her punished as well. Vonda snuggled into her down comforter, more relieved than she'd ever say out loud that Bear Rockford had made her protection his personal responsibility.

§

In Sioban's dreams, there had been a storm swirling outside. Thunder would roll, and when the lightning flashed the faces of people in her past were seen looking in: Jimmy, hard and unyielding, Sonny, angry and cold, Darlene, dead and not gone, and Ava, just sad, so sad. Sioban had wanted to cry out at first but then the sound of the storm stopped. It still raged, and the faces still loomed outside the windows, but she realized that she was safe, and warm. A voice had whispered at one point for her to sleep now, sleep, and she had. Now, with her eyes still closed, she was completely surrounded by the warmth. And the room had become light again, she could tell.

Sioban stirred and opened her eyes. Yes, she had been in a warm place. She was completely ensconced in Danny's arms. She vaguely remembered the darkness of her dreams, and snuggled in closer to Danny. She felt his arms tighten around her. She also remembered that he'd had many more kisses for her when they'd woken up on the couch in the middle of the night. They'd found their way to the bed and made love twice more.

"Morning," he mumbled.

"I had dreams."

"I know. You cried a little bit."

"But you kept me close and told me to go back to sleep."

Danny pulled back then, and lifted her chin.

"You remember that?" Sweet Christ, he was gorgeous. And here she was, wrapped in his arms. To be wanted and protected this way was so far beyond anything she'd ever hoped for herself.

"I think it blended into the dream. But I'm glad that part was real. What gives you bad dreams, Danny?"

Sioban knew she'd taken him by surprise with her question by the way his brows furrowed into a frown. She was risking the good vibe they had this morning, but if he was serious about wanting to know her, then he needed to let her know him, too, especially where his seemingly perpetual frown came from.

"Oh, you know, the usual. An angry father, and a mother who stayed married to him. Takes a toll on a kid."

"So, now you're angry too, much of the time."

He was going for sarcasm, and that was okay. At least he hadn't shut her down completely. He did, however, press a kiss on her lips before he gently extricated himself from her embrace.

"It's not something I'm proud of," he said, as he stood in full naked glory searching for his sweatpants.

This was not the moment for her to get hot and bothered again, but he wasn't making it easy for her to concentrate on what he was saying. "I try to work on it. Bear's been good about it when most would have kicked me out on my ass."

"I want to be good about it too, Danny. It's okay. I'm not afraid of you...well, maybe I was a little bit when you got out of the truck and charged up to me that day."

The look he gave her then went straight to her heart. She hadn't meant to hurt him, but clearly she had. "I hate that you were afraid of me at all."

"Danny, I didn't *know* you yet, at all. Your bad-assery is actually part of what makes me safe, and it's a good quality to have in your line of work."

"I guess. Mind if we talk about something else?"

And there was the shut down, but he'd been soft with it. He needed to believe all the things he told her to believe, only about himself. Including that she wanted to know him and that she wasn't going anywhere. They would just have to work on things together, and that idea made her smile inside.

"No, I don't mind, but if you're not coming back to bed, can I have a tee-shirt? I didn't bring pajamas or a robe. As much as I'm sure you'd like to keep me perpetually naked, I'm prone to chills, even with you close by."

Danny hesitated, and all Sioban could think was that this was how women ruined the morning after for themselves.

"I have something, but it's not a tee-shirt. Sit tight." He pulled the drawstring on his sweatpants and disappeared. She heard him pad across the floor downstairs. When he came back moments later, he handed her a small rectangular lavender-colored box. Lord, it was from Lady Eve's! Sioban sat up in bed and pulled the sheet up around her chest as he handed her the box.

"I planned on giving it to you last night before everything went down, and then I wasn't sure it was the right time. But we can't have you walking around with chills, now can we?"

Sioban tried to stop her hands from shaking as she pried the box open. A thin layer of white tissue fluttered to reveal a midnight-blue lace babydoll gown. She wasn't sure how warm it would keep her, but suddenly she recognized the promise of getting Danny to come back to bed.

"I hope you like it. You can still have a tee-shirt to wear if you'd rather. I just...wanted to give you that for whenever."

"Right now suits me just fine. It's beautiful, Danny. Thank you."

She saw his Adam's apple bob as he swallowed hard. "I'm glad. I'm going to go start breakfast for us. Why don't you come on down when you're ready?"

So that's how he was going to play it, then. Well, she'd make sure that by the time they finished breakfast, if they made it that far, he'd be starving for her again.

He hadn't meant to give her the nightie just now. When he'd gotten back to the bar, Gorman had handed him the box on the sly with a silly grin on his face. Apparently Lady Eve had chosen something for him, since the green corset wasn't available, and it was on the house, according to the Post-it attached to it. He had no idea what Eve had chosen, and he tossed it in the back of his SUV before he went to pick up Sioban. She'd been so distressed when they arrived at his place that Danny had been able to tuck it under his arm as he followed her inside with her suitcase, and she hadn't even noticed. He simply laid it on a small table he kept by the door. He'd wanted to save it for a special occasion, although what that was, he wasn't sure. Perhaps their honeymoon. *Have you lost your mind, Sheridan?* He honestly didn't know what he'd been thinking. Oh, but he did. He'd been thinking how relieved he'd been to bring Sioban home with him last night. And then how good it felt to hold her after the intense love they'd made, and comfort her in the throes of her dreams. Then when he glimpsed what was in that box, all he could think about was taking her again, so he left, or they'd never eat breakfast.

Sioban had caught him off guard when she'd asked him about himself, why he was so fucking moody all the time. She hadn't used those words, but that was what she meant. It wasn't a bad thing. Danny wanted to share with her on that level, and she needed to know what she was getting into with him, both the good and the bad part of it. He'd only given her a sarcastic half answer, because he suddenly remembered how it had felt to reveal himself on that level with a woman—and live to regret it. At some point he would have to tell her about Caryn, he knew that. But he didn't want to spoil things; Sioban had enough to worry about as it was. When this whole thing with Sonny Coniglione was over he would have already proven to Sioban that he truly wasn't going anywhere and that he was hers if she wanted him, and then maybe he could tell her about Caryn. Besides, Caryn was his past, and so far, since she hadn't given any indication that she would use her husband's contract with Rockford to try and get to him, he didn't feel the need to broach the subject with Sioban just yet.

He'd lined up the dry ingredients to make pancakes along the island next to a mixing bowl, and had just turned from the fridge with a bottle of milk tucked under his arm, and fresh blueberries and a carton of eggs in his hands, when he saw Sioban standing there. He nearly dropped it all on the floor. In spite of what she'd said, he hadn't expected her to actually wear the nightgown; not now, in the bright light of morning, anyway. The baby doll nightie was simple, and deceptively sweet. Tiny crystals accented it, and the lace pattern carefully covered some things, but showed enough to bring a man to his knees. And the matching thong nearly gave him a heart attack on the spot. She was stunning.

"Top o' the mornin' to ye, lad. What's for breakfast? I'm starving."

He struggled to find his words for a moment.

"I thought I'd make some blueberry pancakes."

"Fantastic. Need any help?"

Oh, he understood now. When he saw the glint in her green eyes, Danny realized that she planned to taunt him for the entire meal. Well, two could play that game. It was on.

"Nah, I got this. You just relax."

"Okay, I'll just sit here," Sioban said as she hopped up on a stool across from him. Danny had a flashback to the first night they'd made love. They hadn't made it through dinner first, but if her plan was to stall breakfast, she had another thing coming.

For the next forty-five minutes they drove each other mad. She thrust her breasts forward as she peeled an orange from the fruit bowl, and let the juice drip down on them, the minx. But that was okay, because she'd confessed to him once how turned on she got watching him take huge gulps of his drinks. Apparently, she had an obsession with his Adam's apple. So after he poured some of the milk into the mixing bowl, he tipped the bottle and slowly downed the rest of the milk as he rubbed his torso. He wasn't sure, but he might have heard her whimper, and after that, he explained in detail the sensual qualities of cinnamon as he sprinkled it in. He fed her blueberries, and she licked and nibbled his fingers. He watched her squirm as he thumbed a drizzle of syrup off the side of the plate after he poured it.

It would have been easy to take her right then and there, but he wasn't about to let himself lose control now. He brought the plate of pancakes and two forks around and sat on the stool next to hers. They fed each other bite after torturous bite until the plate was empty. Danny wasn't ever one to deny his woman what she so obviously craved. But he wanted to have some fun with her first.

"Well, that was delicious, if I do say so myself. It's late—I'd better get you to the club."

Danny didn't see the pout of disappointment he expected on her face. Instead, she opened her legs slightly on the stool, and said, "Von texted me. She won't be there till later. Besides, I'm not done 'owning this' yet."

"Fuck."

Danny stepped into the vee of her legs and thrust his hand into her hair. He pulled her to him and dragged his mouth over hers.

But before he could lift her onto the island counter to take her, Sioban hopped down from the stool, brushing against the erection beneath his sweatpants as she lowered her feet to the floor. She sighed, and tugged seductively at the drawstring on his pants and reached inside. He sucked in his breath as she took his member into her hand and pumped it twice, slowly.

"Sioban—"

She yanked his pants down past his knees and pushed him onto the stool behind him. She'd never done this to him before, and he was out of his mind with anticipation. He wanted to stop her, make sure she was ready, that it was something she wanted. But she didn't really give him a chance. He groaned when she knelt and took him into her mouth, and he nearly saw stars. Well, alrighty then. It was probably safe to say she wanted this too.

And then he lost every thought in his head as he watched her moving back and forth, with her sweet pink lips stretched over his cock. He felt a surge of the love that he knew he should declare to her, and brushed her bangs away from her face. But she began to move faster and it was too soon and not soon enough before he felt his climax building at the base of his cock. She was so beautiful. She looked up at him and he wanted to hold her gaze when he came for her, but her tongue swept the underside of his shaft once, then twice. He threw his head back and his guttural shout echoed throughout the apartment.

His hips kept pumping of their own accord as he filled her mouth with his come. He knew he should pull out in case she was choking, or couldn't breathe, but her hand clutched at his ass and kept him inside her mouth. He held her head to him as he shuddered through the last wave of his climax.

When he was finally spent, she rose and wiped at her mouth. She reached for a dishtowel on the island, but he grabbed her hand.

"No," he rasped. "I want to taste me on you."

He hoisted her up onto the island and devoured her mouth in a kiss. He could feel himself starting to grow hard again when he tasted the mix of pancake syrup with his own saltiness. It was another hour and a half before they made it out the door and into the day.

§

"We found a way in."

Finally these Russian fucks were doing what he was paying them to do, thought Sonny Coniglione as he popped two more pain pills and washed them down with a cold beer. His head was no longer bandaged, but it still pounded almost constantly. The lingering pain from where that bitch had clocked him with the statue was made worse when he found out that the useless assholes he'd sent to ice Darlene couldn't find the video. Then he'd finally gotten Jimmy to remember where her friend had gone, the one who'd practically taken over Club 29 before she skipped town. Not only did his connections in Chicago find both of them, but they found some two-bit private security firm sitting on them. Without a doubt, that redhead had the tape. But none of them knew whom they were dealing with.

"When do we move?"

"Soon. Piece of cake, as you Americans say. But we have to plan it perfectly, they're sitting on her like an eagle's egg. She went home with her dark-haired bodyguard last night. She had her suitcase."

"Why don't we just get that big ape out of our way?"

"That won't do anything but put two more in his place for us to deal with."

"And what about that other bitch? Jimmy wants her taken care of too."

"Negative. Too much extra clean-up. Let's focus on the original job, yes?"

"Yeah. Fine. Jimmy will have to take care of his other problems. If that Irish bitch has the tape, and we don't get it, he's gonna have more to worry about than how some stupid blonde bested him in the nightclub business."

"I knew you'd understand. Sit tight, and I'll call you again soon."

Sonny hung up, and while the report from the Russians was decent, he wouldn't be rid of this God-awful pain until he had that tape—and the money she stole from him too, come to think of it. That dancer had to pay. Period. In the meantime, it was VIP night at the club again, only this time he'd requested a booth with no security cameras. Plus, Jimmy would have a new girl waiting in it with not so much attitude and an appreciation for earning a little extra cash.

§

Vonda sat at a table in the back going over the plans for the first show that she'd worked up with Sioban. It would be a true soirée, a French-themed show titled "La Vie Jolie"—a beautiful life. They'd open with a reinvented routine to "Lady Marmalade." Three other group numbers would be "La Vie En Rose," which would be accompanied by Sahara, who'd been excited to sing in French, rather than a track, "Zou Bisou Bisou" with Sahara, and of course a can-can number. The three solos would be Sioban's to "Cherchez La Femme," Solange's aerial silks to Streisand's track "What Now My Love," which did have a verse in French, and her own true burlesque number, complete with feather fans and pasties, to Charles Aznavour's "La Bohème." Sahara would do some classic jazz vocals while the dancers reset to give both her and the audience a break from French lyrics. And finally, their curtain call and bows would be to another Piaf song, "Non, Je Ne Regrette Rien."

Burlesque Bad

The Velvet Room was going to have an amazing opening night—Vonda believed and then disbelieved that practically on the hour. It had been difficult to think about all of this with Sioban's situation looming over them both. Then when Bear said he'd help, she'd been able to concentrate much better, and even get excited again about the transformation of the bar, and of her life. Perhaps she'd buried the reality that Sioban's situation might actually get worse before it was resolved, because now that Sonny had made his intentions at least partially clear, and they were all on high alert, the combined pressures of looking over her shoulder twenty-four hours a day and launching her own burlesque club were almost too much to handle. She'd told Sioban to come in later, and she needed some time to herself as well. She knew that as long as she stayed at the house Bear would have stayed there with her. At least here, he'd agreed that putting a man outside the back entrance and having the team in the van out front was enough during daylight hours as long as she kept the doors locked. If she had to go out, Reece would take her.

Just as Vonda was contemplating postponing the whole opening-a-nightclub-dream-life thing and running away to a desert island for the tenth time that morning, she heard the key in the front entrance door. She sighed, wishing for just a little more quiet time. But Bear could have an update about Sonny. Or Sioban could have finally extricated herself from Danny's bed and decided it was time to join the living.

Instead, Reece came in with a young woman who looked like she'd tried to put herself together that morning, but just didn't quite pull it off. Her dull brown hair was pulled back into short ponytail at the nape of her neck. She wore a skirt that was too short and a white blouse. Her makeup was much too bright for daytime, and the fur jacket that only came to her waist, along with the stiletto ankle boots, cancelled out any professional style she might have been going for.

"Reece. What's up?"

"This young lady says she's here for 'auditions.'" Reece's jaw was set, which was never a good sign. The girl just chewed on her lower lip nervously.

"Well, I haven't announced any open calls for dancers. It's invite only. So I don't know how anyone would hear about any audition opportunities."

"That's what I thought," said Reece, taking the girl by her elbow. "I just wanted confirmation that you've never seen her."

Reece started to haul her out when the girl found her voice.

"Wait! I know there aren't any open auditions. I overheard some talk at my gym. The lady who teaches that ribbon-curtain class. Said she got a great dance gig, where Captain Johnny's used to be. So I just came here. If you don't take a chance, you don't get nothin', you know?"

Vonda sighed. The girl was biting her lip again. Reece gave her a look of warning. Sure, the whole thing felt strange. But Sioban had discovered Solange at the gym. And if Vonda could just cross this off her list, adding one more dancer even on a temporary basis...she was just so *tired*. She wasn't sure what to do.

"Listen, Miss—what was your name?"

"It's Tina, ma'am." She leaned forward and extended her hand to Vonda, but Reece pulled her back.

"I'm Vonda Douglas, the owner. Listen, I appreciate you taking the initiative to come all the way down here, but—"

"Please, Ms. Douglas. I really am a dancer, and I'd really like to change my current situation. If you give me a chance to audition, I won't disappoint you."

And how was this girl so different from Sioban? Vonda wondered. For starters, Sioban probably had a hundred times more talent in her pinkie toe. Still, what kind of hypocrite would she be if she didn't at least let this girl audition?

"You aren't wearing your dance gear. Do you have a resume?"

"I was just so excited; I didn't even know if I'd get a slot. You can call Ricky's, I dance there three nights a week."

Vonda could feel Reece boring his eyes into her forehead in the hopes that she'd give a sensible response. Her compromise would be not to make it easy on this girl.

"It's just as well; neither my stage manager nor my talent coordinator is here. Come back at three wearing your dance gear, and bring your resume listing at least two professional references who know your dance abilities. If you don't have those things in order, don't waste my time."

"Yes, ma'am. Thank you."

Vonda rubbed her temples as Reece led her out and locked the door. He walked back to her table and stood there with his hands on his hips, apparently waiting for an explanation from her.

"What? You heard her. She dances. Ricky's is a strip club, but I found Sioban in a strip club." That did nothing to soften the look on Reece's face. "And she found out about us from Solange—or overhearing her, whatever. It's not going to hurt anyone for me to give her an audition. I don't have to hire her."

"Ms. Douglas, you know we would do anything for you. If you wanted to have an open talent call tomorrow, Rockford would have the extra staff in place, and extra hours logged to do background checks on every single one of them. But I have to go on record here that I don't like this at all. It's too easy, something's not right."

"I respect that, Reece, I do. But it's been Bear, along with everyone around me, encouraging me to focus on the show, to make it happen no matter what. And the show feels light to me without four dancers. So, here's one opportunity for me to possibly remedy that. I just want to see her dance. Rockford will have the chance to screen her down to her DNA. I'm not saying I'm going to hire her."

Reece nodded his acquiescence, and turned toward the door.

"And Reece?"

"Yes, Ms. Douglas?"

"Thanks for having my back."

Tina's resume was weak and her audition was less than stellar. Sioban warned Vonda that she wasn't much better than some of the girls they'd tried to train on the fly at Club 29, and that it was going to be a stretch to get her ready for opening night. Vonda couldn't disagree with her, but there was also something about Tina, some sort of determination, that Vonda couldn't ignore. She got Sioban on board with offering her a temporary position as a dancer, with no contract, and the option on both sides to terminate at any time. She didn't miss the glances that went around the room between Sioban, Lex, and Reece.

Rockford's background check on Tina came up squeaky clean, and Bear only reiterated what Reece had said. "We'll cover things, no matter what happens, Vonda." Which was almost as bad as his outright disapproval. Everyone had their reservations about this girl. But Vonda had to do what she thought was best, and in this case, that meant securing a body as a fourth dancer, even on a temporary basis. And she already felt better about her decision. Didn't she?

Chapter Seventeen

Chyenne fingered the lace overlays in each of the corsets for the opening number in the Velvet Room's first show. Eve had special-ordered them from the same company in Paris that made the green one Sioban had bought on her first visit to the shop, and they were stunning. Studding each lace floret overlay were tiny crystals. The solid color of each piece popped under their sparkle. There was black lace on hot pink satin for Solange; midnight-blue lace over matching satin for Sioban; brown lace over copper-colored satin for Tina; and black lace over black satin for Vonda. There were matching headpieces, and detachable feather bustles would make their appearance on the corsets for the can-can number at the end. Chyenne smiled as she remembered Vonda trying to refuse Eve's deep discount on them, so Eve just turned around and said they were a congratulatory gift. She laid them out on the sofa in the dressing room. She wanted to try one on so badly she could hardly stand it. Specifically, the black one. She pictured herself moving across the stage in it.

Next, she gently peeled back layers of pink tissue paper to reveal each of the butterfly costumes for the Edith Piaf number. Eve had subcontracted a local design house to assemble them once she and Vonda had chosen the fabric, a silky lycra blend in a dreamy pastel watercolor pattern that conjured up the Impressionist Gallery of Musée D'Orsay, according to those who had actually been there. The leotards had high mandarin jeweled collars. The sleeves were separate pieces pulled on like gloves, with loose "wings" floating from them.

Vonda had elected simple candy-striper costume rentals for "Zou Bisou Bisou," so all that was left to deal with were the solo outfits. Solange would wear a two-piece garment in black velvet, boy shorts, and a long-sleeved bra top. Her favorite of the three was Sioban's magenta lace teddy. It was going to look amazing with her hair. And there wasn't much to Vonda's outfit. You could hardly call a thong and a set of pasties a full costume. Unless it was a burlesque show, thought Chyenne to herself with a smile. After all, the feather fans were really the main part of Vonda's solo.

Chyenne felt a rush of heat creep up her cheeks. If anyone knew how badly she really wanted to dance in Vonda's show, and how she imagined herself doing a feather-fan solo just like Vonda, she wasn't sure what they'd think. No, not just anyone—her mother was the only one Chyenne feared. No one here really knew the whole story of where she and her mother had been going or why, when their car quit and they ran out of money. They'd been on their way to New York, where Chyenne was going to try to get into Juilliard. As a dancer. But all her mother, Little Dove, had told Eve was that they were getting as far away from their reservation and Chy's alcoholic father as possible.

Eve wasn't one to involve herself in their situation. She'd given them a temporary place to stay above the shop with her, Chyenne her job. Little Dove had been fortunate enough to find a job curating Native American art at a gallery downtown. And Chy knew why her mother had never said one word to Vonda or Sioban about Chyenne being a dancer—because she didn't think that what Vonda was doing with her show was proper dancing. Dancing burlesque wasn't what Little Dove had risked everything for her daughter to do.

Thinking of Tina almost made Chyenne angry. She clearly wasn't as talented as the others. Even Sahara could probably dance better than Tina if given the chance. And there was something off about the girl too, almost as if she felt entitled to be there, to be part of the show. No one understood why Vonda had insisted on hiring her, even on a temporary basis, when she still could have held some kind of open-call audition. Chyenne might have had the courage then to try it, in spite of what her mother would have said. She had almost stepped forward anyway the first time she came to measure the girls for their costumes.

Somehow, she couldn't bring herself to upset the apple cart, not for all the support her mother had given her, and not after Eve had entrusted her with coordinating the procurement of the costumes. Still, there had to be a way. Chyenne would bide her time for now, but she'd be waiting for the right opportunity, and when she saw it, she'd take it.

She checked to make sure everything was ready for the first fitting, when she realized she'd left her sewing basket out by the stage. When she came out into the main room, Chyenne stopped cold at the sight of the man who had just come in the main door wheeling a dolly with several cases of various spirits. He stopped, too, when he caught sight of her, and cocked his head.

"Well, hello, young lady. You seem a little lost."

Chyenne was caught between feeling mesmerized by his green eyes and feeling annoyed at what seemed to her like a patronizing tone.

"I'm not a bit lost. I'm here to do the costume fitting. Who are you?"

"Well, I'm the new bartender. Jarrett Sutter. People call me Rett. I meant no offense, but I've been put on high alert by Rockford security, and since I hadn't seen you before, I was just being cautious."

"Right. I might try to go all kung fu on you or something, and steal the liquor."

"Hey, I've seen smaller girls than you kick ass in the Army. You can never be too careful in my book."

He smiled at her then, and she couldn't resist returning one of her own. Good grief, he was dreamy. His wavy brown hair was cut short, and his crisp white oxford shirt hugged his broad shoulders. Strong hands gripped the clipboard he had in one hand, and with his sleeves rolled up she could see his thick, muscular forearms. His faded jeans did nothing to hide his powerful thighs, and Chy practically swooned at the image of how his ass would look when she saw him walking away. She knew she was staring, but she couldn't seem to find her next words.

"So...what's your name?"

Yes, good. She should tell him her name.

"It's Chy. Short for Chyenne."

"Well, 'Chy, short for Chyenne,' it's nice to meet you. I'm just going to get this inventory checked in, and I'll try to stay out of your way."

"Um, I just came out here to get my sewing kit. I'll be back in the dressing room with the girls, so I won't be in your way, either."

"Fair enough. Let me get this taken care of, and I'll pour you ladies some drinks."

"They mostly just have water, unless you know how to make coffee and tea. But I'll have a lime Rickey—if you know how to make those," she teased.

"I'll have the coffee pot on and the tea selection out on the bar in no time. And as a bonus, I'll set out some cold bottles of water for the taking."

She wasn't sure what to make of it when he winked at her just then. Somehow she didn't think it was because he thought she was hot. Chyenne had always looked a few years younger than she really was, and she should be used to it by now. But this was one time she needed every one of her twenty years to show.

The room filled with a burst of laughter and chatter as four of the Velvet Room's performers came in. Vonda, Sioban, and Solange all had their duffle bags with dance gear in tow. Sahara carried two large garment bags, probably with gowns. She had her own dresses to sing in, but she'd said she wanted Vonda's and Sioban's input on which one worked best with the costumes when they arrived. Of course Tina was late, scoffed Chyenne bitterly to herself.

"Hello, Jarrett. I see you got your key to the place, and that you've also met Chy."

"Yes ma'am. We just got part of the shipment you authorized. And yes, I've met Chyenne. She's given me the low-down on what you ladies like to drink. I'll have it all set up as soon as I've logged in this stock."

"Great. Welcome officially. This is Sioban, my right hand and talent coordinator. Solange is one of our dancers and an aerialist. And Sahara is our vocalist— she has the voice of an angel."

"Nice to meet you ladies."

Just then, Tina half-stumbled in, looking like she'd been ridden hard and put up wet. Chyenne took that as her cue to go back to the dressing room before she said so out loud.

A little over an hour later, everyone emerged from the dressing room, excited about the costumes, and ready to rehearse.

"Afternoon, ladies!" Lex called out from the light box. He'd already lit the stage and set Sahara's microphone.

Sioban carried three mugs in her hands, and started behind the bar to wash them, when Jarrett stopped her.

"Just leave those out on the bar, I'll take care of them."

"Oh, thank you. We're just not used to having anyone else back there. Not that washing up is automatically your job," she answered.

"It is, actually. I keep the bar clean as well as serve drinks. Something else is part of my job, too," he said matter-of-factly.

"Yeah, I heard." Sioban honestly didn't know how long she could remain strung this tightly. As exciting as the opening was, even the rehearsing and the costumes were not enough of a distraction from having to look over her shoulder every waking moment, waiting for Sonny's proverbial shoe to fall on her. And it also seemed with every passing day that yet another person was drawn into the cause of keeping her safe, of keeping Von safe, which was only necessary because of her.

"I just thought you should know that I'll have my eye on things from my little corner of the club over here."

"Well, hopefully this won't last much longer and you can go back to doing whatever it is you really do."

He froze.

"You know, I'm here for the duration. I'm not just in this to remedy the current situation. I'm a bartender with special skills, not the other way around. This is a nice venue. And we're all going to be part of overall security around here. Even your stage manager has been getting up to speed on Bear's protocol, both for the immediate future and the long term."

Sioban suddenly regretted her flippancy. "I didn't mean—"

"I know you didn't. Just know that we're all in this for the long haul, for you, and for Ms. Douglas."

"And we're grateful. It's just been...well, you know."

"Yeah. I know. Take it one day at a time. It will be over, not sure how soon. And it's going to be all right. Danny and Bear won't let anything happen to you or Ms. Douglas. And neither will the rest of us."

"She'll want you to call her 'Vonda,' you know."

"I'll work on that."

He smiled at her, and Sioban turned her attention to the stage. Solange and Von were stretching, and Sahara was warming up her voice. Everyone was in rehearsal mode except Tina, who was held rapt by her phone. God help her, she wished that she had taken a harder line with Von about hiring this girl. Tina just wasn't engaged, and she was barely keeping up with the routines.

"Tina! I suggest you put your phone away, and start warming up. You need this rehearsal as much as the rest of us." It had taken all of her control not to say "more than the rest of us."

She stalked over to the stage and yanked up her duffle bag.

"That was a little harsh, don't you think?" Vonda looked at her pointedly as she stretched on the stage.

Sioban told herself, as she often did, to temper her answer. But she was just about out of patience with Tina and with the whole situation.

"No, I don't. You drew your line in the sand and insisted on hiring her. You rely on me to help teach the choreography and run rehearsals. It's been two weeks and she's still struggling with the steps, which shouldn't be that hard for a professional dancer. So I'm not going to stand here and watch her fuck around on Instagram all night!"

Sioban had planned on apologizing at some point after rehearsal when she'd settled down. Unfortunately, most of the excitement and positive energy had disappeared, making for a very tense rehearsal. In the end, this was one night she was actually glad not to be at Von's. It seemed her escape wouldn't come quite soon enough, though, because Danny was nowhere to be found when she came out of the dressing room. Bear, however, seemed to be enjoying a beer with Lex and Jarrett.

"Excuse me, where the fuck—" They all startled at the sound of her voice. "Sorry. Why isn't Danny here to pick me up? Where is he?" Sioban was wound so tightly that she thought she would snap, as in lose her shit completely, at any moment. Emotionally, she was exhausted with staying alive, with worrying about when the other shoe was going to drop where Sonny was concerned. Added to that was the tension between her and Danny. He had to be just as exhausted with looking after her as she was with being babysat every loving minute of the day. The hell was being comforted by his presence and wanting to get the fuck away from him at the same time, *all* the time. They'd had a huge argument that morning about her needing some time to herself, just one bloody hour alone. He'd of course said it was out of the question, and it had been one grand shouting match after that. She was still feeling the effect of both her anger and his, and now so was poor Jarrett.

"He had to handle a last-minute staff change on the Baxter account. I was already here when the call came in, so he took it. He said he wouldn't be long."

"Great. Jarrett, I need a drink. A real drink."

"No problem. Call me Rett, everyone does."

"Okay, Rett. Then make it a gin and tonic, hold the tonic."

"Yes, ma'am."

Sioban dropped her duffle on the floor, but when she flung her purse onto the bar, she accidentally pushed a manila folder sitting at Bear's elbow onto the floor. When it fell on the floor, its contents scattered. A glossy brochure of some kind fell face down. Sioban noticed a Baxter Industries logo near the bottom of the back cover. A collage of color photos was centered, including several of a man who could only be Rockford's client. But in one of the pictures, the center photo, he stood smiling with a gorgeous woman. Sioban could not believe her eyes. She bent to pick up the brochure. Bear hopped off of his bench to gather up the rest of the papers. She knew he was saying something to her, but the rushing in her ears made it hard to understand him.

As she stared at the photos, the familiar luscious black curls and pale-blue eyes made the identity unmistakable. But the caption confirmed it: CEO and Founder of Baxter Industries Harrison Baxter, and his newlywed wife Caryn at the Chicago Chamber of Commerce Gala. Danny had told her about their relationship a couple of weeks ago. They weren't connected any longer, but he'd pulled her profile up on Facebook after Sioban had joked that she'd Google her on her phone later. She remembered her stomach lurching when she'd seen how beautiful Caryn was. And how much she favored a modern-day Cyd Charisse. Just like Ava had. Danny had been heartfelt about wanting to be open with her about Caryn, and assured her that after what Caryn had done to him, he wanted nothing to do with her again. Except be on call for her husband at all hours of the day and night. And then what was stopping Caryn herself from meeting him at the site, and trying to sink her claws into him again? And if Danny was being so open with her, why didn't he tell her that Caryn was married to one of Rockford's clients? If he'd been afraid she'd go ballistic, well, that was exactly what she was about to do now. Sioban seethed with anger and hurt. She had so wanted to believe Danny, not just his words but the love in his eyes, and in the sincerity he'd demonstrated. Then again, he hadn't told her he loved her yet. He hadn't said *those* words. God, her head throbbed. She just wanted to get away, far away. Bear's voice finally got through to her, though.

"Sioban...I'm guessing by the look on your face that Danny probably didn't tell you about Caryn."

"Oh, he told me about her all right. He just left out the part about working for her husband."

"I'm sorry, Sioban. I thought he would have told you about that. One of my conditions was that interface would only happen with Baxter himself. Danny was only behind the scenes until today. I doubt Baxter even knows about Caryn's former involvement with Danny. Besides, I doubt she would be involved in the security matters of her husband's conglomerate."

Sioban's blood felt like it was boiling in her veins. On top of that she had a huge headache now that would probably never go away.

"You don't know that. Not for sure. I need some air."

"Fine, I'll—"

"Oh for fuck's sake! Leave me be! I just want to go out back for five minutes so I can think, so I can BREATHE. If Sonny Coniglione or whoever is working for him is going to snatch me out from under that ape you've got posted at the back entrance, then none of you are worth your salt to begin with!"

She yanked her purse off of the bar again. She heard Bear reach for the walkie-talkie he'd started carrying. Marcus, stationed at the back door, was already holding it open for her when she got back there. She kept going until she reached the edge of the parking lot. Marcus could still see her, but least it gave her the illusion of being alone for the first time in weeks. Sioban hadn't realized how much she'd actually missed having a little bit of solitude until that moment.

She'd dreaded being alone after Von had left L.A., and then reveled in her company once she got to Chicago. Then, bam! There was Danny, only the stress of keeping her constantly safe had begun to wear on any romantic strides they were making. Standing here now in the dark parking lot with only the sounds of the city around her was almost peaceful.

Until Tina practically gave her a coronary.

"Hey, Sioban."

She whirled around on the stupid girl.

"Jesus! You scared the piss out of me! What are you doing out here?"

"Just thought I'd see if you needed anything. Or maybe you'd like to talk."

Sioban just looked at her with as much incredulity as she could muster.

"That's sweet of you, but short of taking me to beat the shit of out my boyfriend's ex-girlfriend, there really isn't anything you can do. I'd just like to be alone for a few precious moments if it's all the same to you."

"Well, that's exactly what I can do. My car's right over there. I'll take you anywhere you want to go. It's obvious you could use a break from these people, they're all so uptight."

Sioban didn't know this little cuss from a hole in the wall, Rockford's background check on her be damned. Every instinct told her to make Tina leave. But then the same desire to get away herself kicked in, the same rush of adrenaline that she'd had the night she left L.A. The street side of her that Sioban hated to admit she shared with the likes of Tina took over.

"Fine, let's go."

As they moved toward Tina's car, Sioban gave Marcus a friendly wave.

"It's okay, Marcus!" she called. "Tina's taking me to see Danny. I just spoke to him. He knows I'm coming."

Sioban had no idea if Marcus would believe her, or how long they had before the guys were on their tail.

"Hurry up," she said as she climbed into Tina's rickety old Dodge. "Drive. Now."

As Tina peeled out into the alleyway, she asked, "So, we're going to see Danny, then?"

"Of course not. I'll deal with him later. Just get on Riverside. I'll look up the Baxter residence. If that bitch thinks she's getting Danny back, she's got another thing coming."

On some level, Sioban knew she was being irrational. But her every move had been dictated to her for weeks, and she couldn't take it anymore. If Sonny was coming for her, let him come. It felt good to know that she'd be face to face with Caryn, even if it meant she'd make a fool of herself. She wasn't going back to Danny's, either. She'd fire Rockford from her case if it came to that. How could she really trust him now? And if Von was too pissed to let her come back to the house, then she'd get a hotel. She had a salary now, at least for the moment. From now on, Sioban had to take care of herself no matter what.

She turned to Tina, who was answering her.

"That's a good thing, going to see Caryn. Because going to see Danny might put a kink in my plans."

Sioban opened her mouth to ask Tina what the hell she was talking about, but no words came out. Someone had emerged from behind her seat and put one hand around her throat. The other hand covered her mouth and nose with a cloth. The world went black.

§

Tina counted the thick stack of bills before she tucked them back into her bag. Then she checked herself in the mirror. She looked good as a brunette. Lastly, she checked the boarding pass again in her pocket. The man who'd hired her had gotten impatient, even after she'd done everything he'd asked her to. She'd told her story perfectly to the Douglas woman, right down to the part about overhearing that French bitch at the gym. She'd never seen her before the first rehearsal, but her employers had put everything together for her, even a couple of fake references. All she had to do was watch a few Fosse videos so she didn't screw up her audition, and she was in.

Well, the part about getting Sioban in the car with her had taken a little longer. The fucking security dudes had her on lockdown every minute of the day, and her employer knew that. But she came through for them, and had no regrets about bugging out on her dance gig. That Irish bitch had made it difficult for her since the day she got there, and she deserved whatever she had coming to her now. Tina wasn't in the know about that. Besides, she knew that she could make more in tips when she got to L.A. Her employer had set her up with a gig at a joint called Club 29. He said they would keep an eye on her out there. Tina didn't care as long as she had a regular gig waiting for her. She'd take care of the rest herself.

Chapter Eighteen

Danny couldn't think. He'd dragged ass out to Baxter Industries to meet the security supervisor that Rockford had put in place, because one of the night guards, also placed by Rockford, had been arrested on a domestic violence charge. Not the best for Rockford's reputation, but it happened once in a while. Fortunately, Baxter was reasonable about it, so Rockford needed to go over the candidates with the supervisor. Even though it was the last thing Danny wanted to do, he didn't balk when Bear asked him to take care of it, because he was already on that side of town. It would have been a waste of time and manpower for Bear himself to go all the way out there.

Danny knew he was rushing more than he should through this task. But he needed to get back to the Velvet Room and pick up Sioban. She was living a kind of hell, not knowing when exactly Sonny Coniglione would strike. He tried to alleviate her anxiety as much as he could, reassuring her often that he wouldn't let anything happen to her. Hell, it was hard on him too, knowing that at any moment someone might try to take her from him.

The one thing he hadn't done was tell her that he loved her. His mind told him it was too soon, while his heart told him that Sioban was the one and he'd better find a way to hang on to her. But Danny used the current situation as an excuse—for not telling her he loved her; for not telling her that he'd also been helping Bear with his ex-girlfriend's husband's security detail. He kept rationalizing to himself that as soon as this whole thing with Sonny was over, then real life would resume, and he and Sioban would be free to solidify things between them. He ignored the warning from his other voice that this was real life, here and now, and he'd better remember that.

But then as he got into his truck to leave Baxter Industries, his phone rang. The next thing he knew, Bear was asking him to confirm if Sioban had called him to let him know she was on her way to meet him. Then Danny was yelling at Bear for letting her leave unescorted. Then Bear was shouting at Danny for not telling Sioban about the contract with Baxter. Then Gorman interrupted on the walkie to say that he'd lost them. All Danny could seem to say was "What the FUCK?!" He finally realized that Sioban was not on her way to meet him. That she'd only said she was so that Marcus wouldn't question her getting in the car with that other dancer Von had hired. But good man that he was, Marcus did question, and then Gorman followed them, and then lost them.

Danny tossed his cell phone on the seat without disconnecting from Bear. He didn't need to hear anything else Bear had to say at the moment. He just had to get the last location of the vehicle in question, and get there. Rockford had already fucked up, and the cops would only make it worse. Danny had promised Sioban that he'd protect her. He'd failed and now he had to get her back.

As he tore onto the highway, Danny could still hear Bear's muffled shouting in tandem with the crackling of the walkie. He was too far out of range to hear unless he picked up his cell, so he could make out the transmission coming over Bear's walkie in the background.

"What?" he barked into the cell at Bear. That was when Bear told him that Gorman had caught up to the car, and it was empty. Sioban was gone. And that was when he lost the ability to think.

Danny shut off his cell and his walkie, and drove straight to the location of Tina Millstone's abandoned car. Maybe there was some detail they hadn't seen yet. Maybe Sioban had left some kind of clue for them. When Danny pulled up, Bear was standing next to the car talking on his cell phone, which he disconnected as Danny stepped out of his truck.

"Sonny made contact with me, which you'd know already if you'd kept your cell on."

"Where. Where is he holding her?"

"His Russian friends have got her out by the airport."

Danny turned back to his truck without saying another word. He didn't care about how Tina had been involved, or what the plan was. He just needed to start driving in that direction. He knew Bear would have to get in the truck with him, since apparently someone from the team had left him here to wait for Danny.

"Danny, stop." Bear hadn't raised his voice, but he invoked the same tone he'd used to get Danny's attention on countless occasions. The tone that said "I'm still your boss, and I'm also trying to be your friend, so you'd better listen." That tone was the reason so many people respected Bear. Danny stopped at the driver's-side door and looked at him.

"I shouldn't have turned my gear off. I should have told her about Baxter and Caryn. I failed her. I've got to get her back."

"And we will. I've got all hands on deck at headquarters. Sonny gave us two hours to produce the tape. We'll bring a fake one, of course. Reece should have a preliminary plan for extraction by the time we get there. Once we get her out, Rett will deliver the real tape to my buddy at the police department, whom I've briefed. Our friend in L.A. has a bead on Sonny and will sit on him until we can get the tape turned in to be sure he doesn't try to flee the country. And you need to settle the hell down, so I'm driving."

"Who's with Vonda?" Danny asked as he tossed his keys to Bear and walked around to the passenger side.

"Lex and Rett stayed with her at the bar. We asked the other girls to come back there as well until this goes down."

Danny knew that Bear would probably drive in silence and let him stew in his own juices, but he found himself speaking up nonetheless.

"Sioban is so unexpected. She's a gift I never thought I'd be given again after Caryn. Truth is, she's everything Caryn couldn't be, and everything I believed Caryn was, only a hundred times better. I really fucked this up."

"I have a feeling Sioban would have snapped at some point anyway, she just needed a trigger. Even if she'd been with you when she saw that file, something tells me she would have found a way to get away from you anyway."

"I mean, I've really fucked up. With her. With our relationship, if you can call it that."

"I know what you meant. You two have had this tumultuous element since the moment you met. You just haven't had the chance to settle in and get to the deep stuff yet."

"I haven't even told her I love her yet."

"Who's to say she would have believed you at this juncture? We're going to get her back. And then your only job will be to hold on to her after that."

Bear's phone signaled an incoming text message.

"It's a video from Sonny. Shit."

Danny yanked the phone out of Bear's hand, and put it on speaker so they could both hear. The camera focused on Sioban from several feet away. She was tied to a metal chair, and two large men stood on either side of her. Danny knew the look on her face well: scared shitless, but damned if she'd let anyone see it. His jaw locked in anticipation as Sonny began his voice-over.

Much as I'd like to be there to teach this bitch a lesson myself in person, I can't risk incriminating myself by being seen in Chicago. But as you see, I have a direct and constant connection to my colleagues, and so I am entrusting them to carry out my orders. Now, first is the matter of the permanent migraine I have thanks to her. If only I had shipped that statue over for the occasion. But I think my associate can do his job just as well without it.

The man on Sioban's right hit her so hard on the side of the head, the chair tipped over. Sioban cried out, and Danny let out a sound of anguish through gritted teeth. If the goon had hit her with a closed fist, he would have killed her. The man on her left jerked the chair with her still tied to it into an upright position as if it weighed no more than a sack of flour. Sioban moaned, and Danny thought he could see tears on her cheeks. The blow had caught her eye, and it was already swelling shut and turning purple. Sonny continued his sinister commentary.

Now there's also the matter of the money she stole from me. How long has it been, coupla months, at a few hundred percent interest? But look, I'm a generous guy. I think fifty grand ought to cover it. Oh, I know she doesn't have that kind of money, not yet. Especially since she could never draw the big tips like Jimmy's other girls. But I'm sure Rockford Security can float her the dough, especially now that that hotshot

Baxter is one of your clients. I'll even give you an extra hour to come up with the cash. Lastly, I think the boyfriend, what's his name? Dildo? Douchebag? Oh, DANNY. I think he should be the one to make the delivery.

Sioban started to squirm. Shit, she was getting angry. *Just keep your mouth shut, baby. Please don't say anything.* But damn her, she never had the sense to know when to be quiet.

FUCK YOUUUUUUU!

Goon number two hit her this time, catching her right in the mouth. He nearly sent her chair over again, but goon number one caught it this time.

"God damn it!" Danny slammed his own fist into the dashboard. Bear gave a sigh of frustration from the driver's seat, and put more pressure on the gas pedal.

SO. Come alone, or we fuck her up till she's braindead. Screw me over on the money or the tape, and I'll have them both do her the way I wanted to at Jimmy's that night—and then they'll kill her.

Danny's heart stopped as the video went black and ended.

"Call Reece and tell him to liquidate the main account," said Bear unreservedly.

"You can't—"

"We'll recover the money. You heard him, we show up with a duffle bag full of shredded newspaper and he'll kill her. It's the first thing he'll check. The tape is a different story. He won't be able to check that until you get inside, and by then we'll have moved in ourselves."

Danny knew he was right, but that didn't make him feel any better about Bear having to front the money for this sting. Nor did it quell his desire to personally see to it that Sonny was handled. Danny was glad Sonny had requested that he make the delivery. Because as soon as the team moved in, Danny was going to kill Sonny without remorse, whether there was actual cause or not.

§

The taste of her own blood was starting to make Sioban sick to her stomach, as her mouth continued to bleed on the inside where her teeth had cut into her gums from the second blow. Her lip felt about ten times its normal size, and she could no longer see out of her right eye. On top of that, the entire right side of her face still burned from the open-handed blow that first bastard had given her.

Independence was a curse for her now. She'd tried her hand at it, and as usual, her willfulness and her temper had gotten in the way. Sioban could hear Ava scolding her for sassing the nuns in school. It was a memory she hadn't revisited in a long time. All she'd ever wanted was for Ava to be proud of her, to see that if she tried hard enough, Sioban could be just as successful as Ava would have been, had she lived. And finally, she'd gotten away from the life that had killed Ava. She had a real chance to become a dancer. Or so she'd thought. And she'd hooked herself a man too. But her stupidity had forced him and, she was sure, the entire Rockford team to risk their lives to rescue her. She'd been horrible to Von, too. After all, it was Sioban who was riding on the coattails of Von's dream, not the other way around, and she'd put a strain on the whole opening, not to mention added to Von's worry about her own safety.

Sioban was done fighting; she didn't think she had anything left. If she did get out of this alive, she'd have to consider going back to L.A., or maybe even Ireland to see if her aunt would have her. She doubted Von would carry on with her as right-hand talent coordinator. As for Danny, she couldn't imagine being lucky enough to find someone like him again. Someone who could handle her, love her for who she was. Somehow she knew he loved her, with or without the words. She regretted doubting him now, flying into a rage over Caryn, when she knew deep down he'd never go back to her. All she wanted was to tell him she was sorry, which she might never get the chance to now.

She didn't bother lifting her head when a radio squawked and the one who nearly split her head open began speaking Russian. No doubt it was almost time for them to kill her. It was probably too late, but she promised herself to keep quiet and try to stay alive as long as she could.

And then Danny was standing in front of her. She saw his shoes first, the big black boots he always wore. Looking up, Sioban still wasn't able to see him clearly, because she couldn't stop the silent tears from spilling out of her eyes. He knelt in front of her and put his hands on her knees.

"Hey, Irish. Been a rough day, hasn't it? It's going to be okay, though."

Sonny's voice came over an invisible sound system.

How touching. I shouldn't interrupt, though. You should enjoy your last moments together.

Sioban startled, and Danny squeezed her legs gently.

"Just focus on me, Irish," he whispered. Sonny continued.

What, you really thought just because I have the tape now, and some petty cash, that I'll just let you walk? You sealed your fate when you clocked me with that statue, bitch. Your boy here should know that the hostage always gets killed. Criminology 101.

She started to tremble now, despite the warmth of Danny's hands on her legs. *Get ready,* he mouthed. She hadn't seen the monitor they'd wheeled in when Danny arrived. Iron Fist put the tape in, and when nothing but static appeared, Sonny went off.

Son of a BITCH! I told you what would happen if you tried to fuck me over on this! Kill her now!

Before Sioban could process Sonny's order and close her eyes against a bullet to the head, all hell broke loose. Danny actually threw himself on top of her and toppled the chair backward. She braced herself for the impact on her back, and the excruciating jarring of her head again. She saw stars behind her eyes as the sound of gunfire filled her ears. Danny grunted and she felt his body jerk on top of her. Oh God, he'd been shot...he'd gotten himself killed protecting her. A ragged cry escaped her throat. Nothing was left for her to care about, nothing. A voice she recognized from Rockford shouted at Danny to their right. She turned her head and saw a pistol sliding across the floor toward them. Danny stuck his hand out and grabbed it. He was alive...

§

Somehow, Sioban had wandered out into the dark. She wasn't clear on how she'd gotten free, only that Danny was alive, or at least he had been a moment ago. Or an hour ago. She needed to find him, she needed to make sure he was safe. And where was Sonny? What about Von? Were they going to do the show? She should get back to rehearsal. Wait, Danny was calling her. But he sounded so far away! She had to catch up with him, she couldn't let him leave her---

"Shh, Irish. I'm not leaving you, I'm right here. Open your eyes, baby."

It was getting lighter outside. Danny was closer now, so close. Oh. It was morning again, just like the first morning she'd woken up in his arms. He'd chased her nightmares away. Then they were right where they were supposed to be. But when she focused her eyes, it was the harsh glare of the fluorescent lightbulb behind the silhouette of Danny's head as he looked down at her.

"Nooo..." Sioban heard her own hoarse whisper. Her throat was raw, so she must have been screaming louder than she realized during the raid. But Danny was alive, that was the most important thing, not the throbbing of her head, or pain in her lip. "Sonny..."

"Sonny has been taken care of. He can't hurt you anymore. It's over."

She could feel the feather-light touch of Danny's caress on the good side of her face.

"Thought you were shot."

"Shot but not killed. I was wearing a vest. Hurt like a mother, but they'll tape me up and I'll be as good as new."

She reached up blindly and clutched at his back rib cage. He winced and she started to tremble again.

"Easy, Irish. I'm okay. But no more piggy-back rides for a while, all right?" She tried to smile but her lips hurt too badly. "Come on. First responders are here, we need to get you checked out. Put your arms around my neck on this side." Danny leaned in and offered her his good shoulder. She put her arms around his neck and sat up slowly. Danny first got one knee under him and then stood with her in his arms. She knew he was in pain by the grimace he made. But once he was up, he strode out of the building with her almost effortlessly.

Bear was already giving his statement to the police, and he nodded at them as they made their way to the ambulance a few feet away. Danny set her down so that the paramedics could help her inside. She started to panic again, but Danny took her hand.

"I told you, I'm not going anywhere. I'll be sitting right here at the foot of this gurney while they tape up my shoulder and ribs, and take my statement."

She nodded, and lay down gingerly on the gurney behind him. They put an ointment on her lip that stung, gave her an ice pack for her eye, took her vitals, and by some miracle she didn't have any broken bones. One of the medics suggested that she spend the night in the hospital.

"No...fucking no. Danny—"

He was standing now, and turned from the officer he was speaking with as he gingerly pulled his tee-shirt back on over the bindings on his shoulder and around his rib cage.

"Thank you, Officer. I'll be available tomorrow for further questioning if you need me." He tried to climb up inside with her, but Sioban mustered all her strength and scooted down to the end of the gurney.

"Sir, I was just recommending that we check her into the hospital for overnight observation."

"I think the lady was pretty emphatic just now. Any broken bones, or any sign of a concussion?"

"No, sir."

"Then I'll watch for any changes, but I'll be taking her home with me now. Thank you for everything."

The medic held up his hands in defeat, and Danny reached up and pulled her down out of the ambulance into his arms. Sioban reveled there only a moment before she pushed back and punched him on his good shoulder. She'd felt badly about being so angry, but now that she had him back, there was nothing wrong with giving him a bit of business about his ex.

"Why the hell didn't you tell me you were working for Caryn's husband?"

At first he just stood there and stared at her like an idiot. She was thinking she'd have to punch him again when he said, "I love you."

Well, wasn't that just peachy? "I'll tell you why. Because you didn't trust me. All this talk about wanting to be together. What did you think I'd do, kick your arse? Well, I would have, and you'd have deserved it."

"Sioban, I love you."

"And I wasn't coming to see you anyway, I was going to their house, because if that woman had any ideas about getting you back--"

Danny pulled her close again, pressing her against his chest, muffling her outburst.

"Christ, woman, if I could kiss that beautiful swollen mouth of yours, I would have shut you up myself. Will you ever learn when to hold your tongue? Did you even hear what I just said?"

Talking and fussing had always been her defense mechanism, and she doubted that would ever change. She had heard him, but hadn't wanted to believe what he was saying. It was easier to give him hell about Caryn than to think about really, finally having him, having his love. But she reached beyond her fiery temper, looked up at him again, and finally found the only words she knew couldn't get her into any more trouble.

"I love you too."

With astounding gentleness he brushed kisses over her forehead, then her eyelids when she closed them, and finally the lower corner of her mouth where violence hadn't left its mark. He lifted her into his arms again and carried her toward one of the waiting Rockford SUVs.

"I was serious, you know."

"What, that you love me, too? I know."

"No, about going to see Caryn. And after I was through with her, I guess I was going to come kick your arse next."

"I believe you. Sioban?"

"Hmm?"

"Shut up."

She giggled as much as her lip would allow, and tucked her head under Danny's chin again. She'd wake up in his arms again tomorrow, and if the stormy dreams came back to haunt her during what was left of the night, she knew he'd chase them away.

Chapter Nineteen

No one was more surprised at how quickly things seemed to get back to normal after Sioban's rescue. Danny had insisted that she get a proper checkup the next morning. The doctor told her to hold off on rehearsals for a week, but that she could observe and offer feedback, and to help at the club with final preparations for the opening. Sonny had been taken into custody the night of the raid thanks to Bear's quick planning and solid connections. Just when it seemed like he'd beat the attempted-rape charges associated with the video, others came forward with various evidence and accusations, including mob activities. Warrants and subpoenas were obtained, and in the end Sonny was facing up to thirty years of jail time for his combined crimes. As a bonus, since the altercation with Sonny took place on the Club 29 premises, it was shut down and Jimmy was jailed for prostituting his dancers.

Poor Sioban was finally free—free of Jimmy, of Sonny, and of a life that was heading in the wrong direction. Even while her bruises were healing, she looked happier and more radiant than Vonda had ever seen her. Some of that was due to having the love of a good man. Danny was still bossy, and Sioban still shot off her mouth at him. Seeing them drive each other crazy was like watching a modern remake of *The Honeymooners*. But there was an unmistakable tenderness there. Danny did so many little things to care for her, and to make sure she had everything she needed. And Sioban had this way of doting on Danny even while she was slapping him in the arm for irritating her.

As for Vonda, she'd spent so much of her energy on those around her, even on the show, that it was almost uncomfortable for her to focus on her own feelings. Thanks to all of the incredible help she'd had with every detail, the renovation and, now, the final preparations for opening night were proceeding like clockwork. But old suggestions of self-doubt and fear of failure broadcast themselves on a daily basis. With both Sioban and now Bear out of the house, all Vonda seemed to have for company   was   her   own thoughts.

It had taken all of her strength not to throw herself into Bear's arms when he'd finally gotten back to the bar in the wee hours after the raid. He hadn't said much, only that Sioban had been injured, but that she was safe, and that Danny was taking care of her. He'd given the okay for the girls to leave, and turned to her with an exhaustion she'd never seen on his face before.

"Let Lex lock up. I want to get you home safe. I'll stay tonight, until I can confirm that Sonny's in custody tomorrow."

She merely nodded at him, and got her purse. When they got back to the house, she was going to offer him a drink, but he looked like he was going to hit the floor at any moment.

"I've listened to and cooperated with everything you've asked, Mr. Rockford. But tonight, you're going to listen to me. You're not sleeping on the couch. Go up and get into Sioban's old bed." Get into my bed, was what she'd really been thinking. But now wasn't the time for seduction, especially when it could only last for one night. Bear made no argument with her, and walked toward the stairs.

"I'm glad it's over, and that everyone's okay. I just wish...if I hadn't insisted on hiring Tina, none of this would have happened."

Bleary-eyed, he turned back to her.

"Sure it would have. You were just doing what you thought was best for the show, and that's what they were looking for. If that hadn't panned out, they would have found another opening."

"I just hope Sioban forgives me. We argued about Tina so much, and then she turned out to be such a low-life."

Bear reached out and cupped her cheek with his hand.

"No one is a perfect judge of character, and you're not responsible for who she turned out to be. We should get some sleep. I'll see you in the morning."

But morning meant that he was really moving out. He'd offered to drive her to the bar as usual, but she turned him down.

"I'm allowed to drive my own car again, remember?"

"I know. Force of habit." He smiled. He still looked tired, but the strain was gone from his eyes.

"Besides, how would I get back home tonight? I can't have Rockford shuttling me around forever." Neither could she have Bear standing around in her living room forever. "Thank you for everything. I mean, that seems insufficient, but it's all I've got at the moment."

"I'd do it again in a heartbeat. Seeing you and Sioban safe and happy makes it all worth it."

"I confess, I am going to miss having your presence around here. The house will seem awfully empty tonight."

"I'm still just a phone call away. I'll be here anytime you need me," he said softly.

Vonda had hung on to those words for hours after that, days even, wishing she could invent some excuse for him to come back. As much as she wanted to invite him over for dinner, or even have poker night with the Rockford guys, Vonda didn't want to mislead him in any way. Getting the Velvet Room off the ground had to be her only priority, even though it had nearly killed her to watch him walk out her door that morning.

She shook the memory from her mind now, as she sat with Sioban at their favorite table with their tea and the ever-changing rehearsal schedule. Vonda had decided to push the opening out by one week, to give Sioban ample time to heal and get back up to speed with her performance, although her face was almost completely healed now. That had meant having to redo some of the promotional materials and reschedule a few ads, but it would be worth it. Now that Tina had disappeared Vonda really needed the three dancers, including herself, to be in top form. Bear's L.A. contact had reported that Tina had shown up at Club 29 a few days after the raid, but when Jimmy was arrested, she had vanished into the wind. God only knew how horrible she still felt about hiring Tina in the first place.

"It's still not right," Vonda mumbled.

"What?" Sioban looked up from her notes on the last rehearsal.

"I really wanted a fourth dancer. But I guess it's just not meant to be."

Vonda noticed Chyenne out of the corner of her eye. She had just come out of the dressing room and rounded the bar, having just finished the second costume fitting for the girls. Vonda and Sioban had gone first so they could go over rehearsal details while the other girls finished up.

"I know you did. It's not that it's not meant to be ever, you just may not have one for opening night. Besides, anyone we brought on board now would have to practice round the clock to be ready in time," said Sioban.

"Not me."

Vonda looked up to see Chyenne standing in front of the table.

She was almost startled by what she saw in Chyenne's expression. Her eyes were filled with a kind of dark determination, and her expression was all business. Chyenne had seemed so girlish to Vonda, funny and whimsical, breezy and bright. But now, she seemed...womanly. Vonda had gotten the same vibe from Sioban when she was determined, which was probably why they'd fought so much about Tina. And when she glanced at Sioban in this moment for guidance, Sioban only grinned, and winked at Chyenne knowingly.

"Sweetie, I'm not sure where you're going with this," Vonda began.

"Do you know why my mom was taking me to New York?"

"Not really. I just assumed she wanted to get into the gallery scene there. I knew you wanted to start college, too."

"Not just any college." Chyenne pushed her hair away from her face, and took a breath. "I was going to audition for Juilliard. I'm a dancer."

Vonda was speechless. Her mind raced between questions: How much experience did she have? Why hadn't she said anything before now? Could she have found her fourth dancer? But wasn't it impossible? Wasn't she too young?

275

Chyenne laid the two costumes that needed final fittings on a chair at the next table and turned to face them again.

"I couldn't believe it when my mom and I first came to Eve's, and we met you and found out you were opening the Velvet Room. Then the day you brought Sioban, helping her try on that corset and watching you consider having Eve do your costumes was like sprinkling myself in stardust.

"But at the time, that had to be the end of it. My mom trusts Eve, so helping with the costumes is just work. It's safe. I never said anything about dancing, because I knew my mom would never approve of this kind of dancing."

"And now?" Vonda found herself asking. "What's different about today?"

"What's different is that I'm twenty years old. I've already wasted the year and a half it took us to get away from my father. I see a chance to gain experience before I go on to New York that I otherwise wouldn't get. It's staring me right in the face. I've been watching Tina since she first stumbled in here. I knew she'd never cut it, and I just waited for her to crash and burn on opening night to make my move."

Sioban snickered.

"Did you know about this?" Vonda asked her.

"I most certainly did not, but if I had, I would have made you audition her right alongside Tina."

Vonda sighed and rubbed her temples.

"I have to ask—what kind of experience did you get in high school?"

"Well, Miss Vonda, my mom saw that I took as many dance classes as we could get to off of the Reservation. I could tell you how I've worked my butt off to get ready for Juilliard since I got here, and taken more classes on the sly. But the best way to answer

276

your question is to show you what I can do now, here, today. I've learned every routine of your show. I mapped out the steps, and I've been practicing every night in Eve's basement. I just told her and my mom that I was counting inventory and crap like that."

Vonda recalled the past few weeks, especially after Tina had joined them, and they'd started rehearsing in earnest. She'd been too preoccupied then to really register how Chyenne had wandered over to the bar to watch rehearsals whether there had been a costume fitting or not. And she realized now that the girl had always been writing something. Vonda didn't know what she'd thought Chyenne was doing. Maybe that she'd started taking college classes and was doing homework? Clever girl. She had been doing homework, all right.

Sioban was staring at Vonda when she looked over once again for input.

"Has anything about this operation gone the way you've wanted it to? No, it's gone the way it's needed to. Has anything turned out the way you expected it to? No, it's been even better, but only because you've listened and gotten yourself out of the way when you needed to, except in Tina's case, and that was just plain stupid—"

"Okay, okay. Point taken," Vonda said with exasperation. "You're right. Don't let it go to your head. But you finding Sahara, and then Solange, was just...meant to be."

"Not just that, Von. How about our security company turning out to be experts in hiring contractors, not to mention all the James Bond stuff they did to keep us safe. It's all been waiting for you at every turn. So maybe this is the last turn. You'll never know unless you see her dance."

Chyenne was waiting for her response, but not with the wide-eyed look of a Juilliard hopeful. She stood with her hands on her hips, as if she were ready to take on the world, or at least take this chance she was almost demanding by the tail and run with it.

"Did you want to go change?"

"These are stretch jeans. I'll be fine." Chyenne turned to Lex, who was still tidying up the light box. "Lex, can you cue one more song today?"

"You bet!"

"Lady Marmalade, please."

"Well. I don't know what else to say. Sioban's right, of course; my journey to get this place, this show, up and running has been anything but typical. I'm just still so surprised about you. Nevertheless, let's see what you've got."

§

Chyenne took the stage and kicked off her sneakers. She walked in a few circles to clear her head and shuffled her fingers through her hair. She knew she had to push all of the memories of the Reservation away from her now and embrace the moment. She turned to the light box and Sioban mouthed "Ready?" She nodded her head and faced the rear of the stage, since the number started facing away from the audience.

She lowered her head and slowly raised it again as the funky first bars of organ and guitar music sounded. Then she started the seductive quarter turns as Patti LaBelle sang her first notes.

Hey Sister, Go Sister, Soul Sister, Go Sister...

Chyenne was vaguely aware of the other girls wandering out of the dressing room for rehearsal, and of their banter dying as they noticed her on the stage.

She used every curve of her body to show Vonda how she could strut her stuff just like Patti said, and tossed her head with attitude and abandon. Then she was seeing and not seeing Rett Sutter standing behind the bar with his jaw hanging open. She was in the moment, and she brought him into it with her.

Hey Joe, you wanna give it a go?

After that, Chyenne lost herself in the dancer, the woman, she'd wanted to become ever since she and her mother had arrived in Chicago, ever since they'd left the reservation, really, though she hadn't realized it until she saw the beginnings of Vonda's show.

Here it was now: she put a few lunges and deep knee bends from the *Moulin Rouge* version in before raising her arms and throwing her head back on the key note.

Creole Lady Marmalaaaaaaaaaaaaade!...

In the show, the dancers would sashay offstage as the music faded. But Chyenne just did ever-slowing jazz spins, and when she stopped a joy she'd never felt before burst inside and she let the bright glow of the stage lights fill her eyes.

Suddenly, Sioban dimmed the stage lights and brought up the house lights, ending her reverie. Lex had arrived, and stood with his chin resting on his hand. Sahara and Solange seemed confused. Vonda looked like she'd been shot. A glass shattered, and Chyenne turned to see that she hadn't been dreaming after all, that Rett was behind the bar. He wasn't staring anymore, but she heard him mutter a curse as he swiped at the broken glass on the bar top with the towel in his hand. *Oh well,* she thought, *at least I saw my chance and took it. I guess I'll stick to being the costume girl.* None of them seemed pleased, except for Sioban, who was smiling so widely, her face might crack. She was also the first to speak.

"Bloody fucking hell, girl! I can't even believe what you just did!"

Lex just shook his head. "Well, Vonnie, looks like you found your fourth dancer for real this time." He took his post in the light box matter-of-factly and started to re-cue the music for rehearsal.

That was all well and good, but the only person whose opinion really mattered was Vonda's. Chyenne pinned her with her eyes, as Vonda still sat with her hands on her cheeks in astonishment. Chyenne chewed her bottom lip and felt herself slipping back into the scared, uncertain schoolgirl she'd banished for the short three minutes of the dance routine. Maybe, just maybe, she liked it.

Then Vonda finally came out of her shock coma and stood up.

"Yes. Sorry, I'm just...yes, what Sioban said. Yes, what Lex said. I'm just not sure I believe my eyes, Chyenne! You became a different person up there, at least different than the girl I've known all these weeks."

"So...I can have a chance? I mean, I'll understudy, whatever you want. Then maybe in time I'll be ready—"

"In *time*?" Sioban cried. "Are you kidding me? There is no time. We need you now! Um, right, Von?"

Vonda tipped back her head and laughed. "Good grief, yes. I want you—we want you—right now. You've got the basics of that routine, and if you know the rest of the numbers that well, we'll have no problem getting you ready for opening night. Bravo, Chyenne."

Vonda began to clap and was quickly joined by the other three ladies. Lex just smiled from the light box. Sahara and Solange hugged her as she descended from the stage.

288

"Mon Dieu, how have you been hiding this from us, chèrie?" Solange kissed her on both cheeks.

"Welcome to the show, Chyenne," Sahara added. "You must have been nervous, to be sure. We can relate! But you nailed it."

Sioban sidled up to give Chyenne another hug, and Chyenne caught Rett's eye over Sioban's shoulder.

"You all right back there, Rett? Didn't cut yourself on that glass or anything, did you?" Chyenne pulled out of Sioban's embrace to speak to him.

"Nope." His mouth was set in a hard line, and his jaw twitched. He'd already broken one glass; now he looked like he wanted to break another one. Sheesh, and everyone said women were hard to figure out.

"Oh boy," giggled Sioban. "He's not quite as bad as Danny—I mean, face it, nobody scowls like Danny—but he's got something under his skin, and I'm guessing it's you."

Now it was Chyenne's turn to be shocked. In the first place, Rett had hardly said two words to her since he'd started working at the club. He was friendly enough, but how could she have gotten under his skin? Maybe he was peeved because she'd played to him during the song. If that was the case, she'd have to find the courage to apologize to him, or something.

Just then, Vonda came up to offer her own congratulations.

"Welcome to the show, sweetie. Now you'll have to promise Eve that I won't cut into your hours at the shop."

"I'm sure she'll let me adjust my hours. It'll be even easier for me to do costume stuff now," Chyenne laughed. "Speaking of which, I should get busy marking adjustments for Tina's costumes."

"No," Vonda said, almost too emphatically. "Of course, the butterfly outfit can be refitted, and we can order the candy striper in your size. But I don't want any vestige of Tina in my show. Give Eve your measurements tomorrow, and tell her I'll call her with specs for a new corset for you." Vonda pulled back and eyed Chyenne up and down. "I think I know just the colors I want, too. But never you mind, I want it to be a surprise."

"Okay. Thank you so much, Miss Vonda! I can't believe it myself...this is a dream come true for me."

"It seems like the Velvet Room is turning out to be a dream come true for many of us, myself included." But Vonda's next words threatened to crush that dream. "What about your mom, honey?"

Chyenne took a fortifying breath, just as she had a short while ago when she'd asked for the chance to audition.

"I'll deal with my mother."

"I don't doubt it. You're legally an adult, and you clearly know what you want. Just...be patient with her. She'll probably never be ready to let you go completely, but I'll bet she wasn't thinking it was going to be this soon, either."

"I know. I'm more worried about how angry she's going to be."

"She might not understand at first. But she'll come around when she sees you dance the way you did tonight. I can't play referee, but if she wants to talk to me, I'll be happy to reassure her that the sisterhood of the Velvet Room will watch over you. Not to mention the security fraternity assigned to this place."

"Thanks, Miss Vee." Chyenne wondered if Vonda included Rett in that security fraternity she was talking about. She walked cautiously over to the bar. Rett seemed to have settled back into himself, whatever that meant, thought Chyenne. He had his back to her, stacking the same glasses he'd probably been before.

"Hey Rett?"

"Yeah." He spoke without turning around.

"Listen, I'm sorry about before. When I was dancing, and I picked you out—I was just trying to find a focal point out there, I didn't mean...I was just caught up in my performance."

He did turn around then, and Chyenne wasn't that surprised to see the same stony look on his face from before.

"I understand. I know you haven't been out in the real world for too long. You're cocooned next door over there with Eve and your mother. But you want to be careful about the way you dance in front of the men that will be coming to see the show. They're liable to think you're really asking them if they 'wanna give it a go.'"

For the third time that afternoon, Chyenne had to draw on every bit of strength inside of her to rise to what the moment required of her.

"Well, Rett, I'm 'out in the real world'—and it had better be ready for me. Rehearsal's about to start."

She turned on her heel and left him to keep his glasses from breaking.

§

This is it, Vonda thought. She surveyed her proverbial kingdom called the Velvet Room, and tried to comprehend exactly by what miracle she'd arrived at this moment of the final dress rehearsal. It was unfathomable. Yet here they all were. Her club was stunning; all the marketing plans and materials were in place; the costumes and choreography were perfection; her dancers were in fine form, and she was

Nina Day Gerard

in pretty fine shape herself; and she'd never been happier in her life.

But something was slightly off, and it took a moment for her to realize what it was. The girls were warming up on stage, their corsets glittering under the lights. Chyenne had been thrilled when Vonda presented her with her own corset in dark terra cotta lace over deep turquoise silk. The desert colors were a perfect nod to her Southwest Native American heritage. Lex had worked up a light show that popped with the choreography. He had been a godsend to her, and she hoped that he postponed whatever work awaited him in New York indefinitely. Rett was quiet and stoic most of the time, but he was an exceptional bartender, and Vonda was glad Bear had recommended him for his "other" skill set as well, although she hoped nothing ever happened in her club to warrant him using it. He always timed his office work so he could be at rehearsal to prepare their drinks and refreshments. And lo and behold, there were Danny and Bear, pretending to check over the security cameras for the hundredth time, and therein lay the problem. Lex had to be at rehearsals; he was the stage manager. She wasn't even going to think about how he seemed to turn to mush around Solange. And Rett seemed a little overly protective of Chyenne, but they all were, thanks to her mother's concerns. After all, wasn't that part of why he was there in the first place? But she had specifically not encouraged Danny to be there, because, well, she didn't want him losing his cool. At least when the club was open he'd have to hold himself in check when it came to watching Sioban, or watching other men watching Sioban. His only alternative would be to wait in the office until the show was over. As hard as she'd tried to encourage them to stay away, here they all

284

were. She resigned herself to the fact that they'd all see her solo sooner or later. Ultimately, she couldn't be affected by who was in the audience. And as far as Bear was concerned, Vonda knew she shouldn't care whether he was at dress rehearsal or not. But she did. Because she didn't know if she was ready for him to see her in feathers and pasties. There was nothing to do but power through it.

Vonda's costume was nothing short of amazing. She'd kept it hidden, along with the routine itself, even from Sioban until this very moment. She wanted the "wow" factor for everyone, especially her dancer-sisters. If they felt a tenth of the magic she felt when she danced in it, the inspiration they'd soak up would be worth the cost of her secrecy.

Taken singularly, the costume had been one mother of a splurge. But considering that Eve only allowed Vonda to pay for it if she gifted the other bustiers, it was really quite a bargain.

Just before changing into it, Vonda had ushered everyone far enough away from the front of the room so that they wouldn't see her until she had stepped completely out onto the stage. Lex hadn't seen the costume or the routine. But Vonda had given him the music and gone over the cues with him. She'd developed it and rehearsed it under the eagle eye of Iliana. Only once, just after Sonny had been put away and she could stay at the bar as long as she wanted, had she done just that, and rehearsed on her own stage after hours.

She signaled Lex now from her spot just off stage. He smiled and gave her a thumbs up before he initiated an effect of small white lights cascading down the backdrop curtain like a shower of stars, with an overall blue light bathing the stage. He'd already lowered a ceiling mike close enough to be effective, but not to distract the audience from Vonda's performance.

Without meeting anyone's eyes, Vonda stepped onto the stage in a white velveteen hooded cape, with a giant crystal brooch at the neck. The front opened just enough as she walked to reveal part of the sheer panels of her white bustier and her silvery-white shimmering hose. A spotlight captured her just as she arrived at center stage.

Vonda was both relieved and unnerved at the silence when the spotlight came on. She would have been mortified had any of the men made catcalls. At the same time, a little love from the audience would have been nice. If she waited too long, the moment would pass and she'd lose her nerve. She focused on a point at the back of the room and took a breath.

"Is it anybody's birthday out there tonight?" Vonda asked in her sexiest voice.

That did it. Her dancers came to life and called out in a chorus of solidarity.

"Well," she continued slowly, "let's celebrate..."

Marilyn Monroe's "Happy Birthday, Mr. President" came on over the sound system. The girls cheered more as Vonda swept back the hood of the cape with white-satin-gloved hands, and released the snap at the neck. The cape billowed to the floor in a lush pile. The cups of the bustier glittered with tiny crystals and the top edge of the front was feathered along her décolletage.

Whether her audience said anything now or not, Vonda knew she had captivated them. Even though she still couldn't bring herself to look at anyone, she could feel their excitement, and she tapped into it.

In a perfect Marilyn move, she blew a kiss out from the stage and began to remove her gloves, plucking at one finger at a time until she slid first one glove and then the other off of her arms and flung them aside with abandon.

She thrust her arms out toward the audience as she stepped backward over the discarded cape, as if to pull them with her.

Vonda couldn't keep from smiling, a sweet but naughty grin that reflected the sassiness she felt bubbling up from inside her.

For a number with such a slow pace to work, especially in contrast to the razz-ma-tazz of the rest of the show, Vonda had to be clinical in her choreography and impeccable in her artistic interpretation. She danced the hell out of it. The girls would all say afterward that every S-curve she drew with her hips, every lilt of her wrists, and every flutter of her hands was a gift. No, they decided, Vonda herself was the gift, and by the time she turned away from the audience and began to undo the back of her corset, the air was rife with anticipation. The magic was in the special zipper Eve had sewn into it. The back dipped low enough for her to reach it, just where the mass of her curls met the top edge. Her fingers plucked at two crystal buttons like a naughty child stealing forbidden candy. As Marilyn crooned her penultimate "Happy Birthday...Mr...President..." down, down, down came the zipper, which appeared to have opened as far as it could at the bottom edge just as Marilyn sang the "t" of "President."

But then, Vonda gave the crystals a final tug and the corset fell away.

"Happy..." She tossed her head back.

"Birth..." She flung her right arm out and up.

"Day..." Out and down went her left arm.

"To..." She widened her feet to a power stance.

"You..." A shimmy to end all shimmies sent the silver tassels on her nipples in motion.

She danced through the post-verse on the recording, swept up her cape, and sashayed off of the stage as she looked back over her shoulder.

Vonda let the rush of what she'd just done carry her back into the shadows, and before she had time to process it, the girls were swarming around her.

"That was fucking amazing, you know that, right?" Sioban was the first to rush up to her.

"Oo-la-la Vonda, ça c'est magnifique!" Solange added her praise, and after that all of the exclamations over her performance blended together. Only Sahara was quiet. Her smile was one of genuine admiration for her new boss, but it didn't hide the wistfulness she seemed to be feeling inside. Vonda made a mental note to talk with her later in case it was all too overwhelming for her as a singer who had never really danced before.

The chatter finally died down and Sioban lingered while Vonda removed her tassels and changed back into her sweats. She pulled up short when she caught Sioban staring at her.

"What?"

"You've done it. You've put this show together, and done the dancing you've wanted to do your whole life, it seems. Your dream is coming true."

Vonda tried to find words, but couldn't. She just nodded a "yes" and embraced her friend as they both cried.

Out in the bar, the men indulged in less than a minute of stunned silence before they all conjured up work that needed to be done, or places they needed to go. Nobody, it seemed, wanted to look at, or speak to, Bear. Lex wasn't in the mood for Bear's jealousy over him having seen Vonda do that solo, so he focused on resetting the music and light cues starting with the top of the show. Rett announced he was heading to the basement to recount the stock for opening night. Even Danny felt the need to give Bear a moment to collect himself, and said he was going to see if Rett needed any help with the inventory.

As it turned out, Bear did need a minute. He needed several, actually. Bear finally had an idea of how Danny must have felt when he saw Sioban dance for the first time, and he hoped no one had seen his jaw hit the floor as he watched Vonda tonight. He'd purposefully stayed in the shadows himself during her solo, not only out of respect for her request to stay back from the stage, but to avoid anyone clocking his reaction to her performance. He'd known it was going to be good, of that he'd had no doubt. What he hadn't quite expected was for his world to tumble when he saw her dance, and not just because of the nature of what she was doing. He'd seen all manner of burlesque and stripteases and everything in between over the years. But he couldn't seem to find just one word to describe what he felt when he watched her, what he felt about her. She simply brought him to his knees, and he had to check several times during her performance to be sure he hadn't actually sunk to the floor.

He held his breath when she walked out onto the stage. His heart nearly pounded out of his chest when the spotlight hit her, and damn near stopped when she finally released the cape. The corset was only part of what made her so beautiful to him. The way her hair tumbled in a mane of giant curls made him want to thrust his hands into them. She wasn't a tall woman, but her legs—my God they seemed to go on forever. And then when she moved, heaven help him. The way her hands traveled over her own body had him struggling to breathe.

But there was so much more behind her moves than sensuality. He saw in her eyes the moment that she, the music, and the audience became parts of a whole, and knowing that in that moment she was realizing, to a degree, everything that she'd striven for in her life before she came back to Chicago and since then to build this club and this dream for herself, made his heart burst with emotion for her. He didn't think he'd ever seen anything so lovely before in his life.

He'd have to find words of some kind to say to Vonda when she came out again, but he wasn't sure she'd be ready to hear all of what he'd just been thinking, nor was he ready to say all of it. But he'd wait for his chance and do the best he could to show his support for her.

When Vonda finally emerged from the dressing room, Lex brought the lights up to discuss a technical issue. She fought seeking out Bear, but couldn't resist doing it. She caught his eye for only a brief instant before he looked away. It was in that same instant that she realized the real source of her reluctance to begin a romantic relationship with Bear. All along she'd believed that she was the one in control, that she was the one who kept him at bay, when in reality he'd been incapable of accepting what she did for a living. He'd finally seen her in full burlesque mode tonight, and he couldn't handle it. The realization stung the back of her eyes. Damn, and damn again—why had she allowed herself to be wrapped in his kindness, his protection, half hoping that it could be more? Vonda swiped at the dampness in her eyes. She turned back to Lex and tried to listen to what he was telling her, because no matter what, the show had to go on.

Burlesque Bad

The men gathered at the bar as Vonda gave her final notes to the girls. Rett polished the bar top dejectedly with a towel. Bear sat on his favorite stool and stared into his Scotch. Lex strolled over and Rett popped the cap on a cold Corona and handed it to him. Only Danny remained by the stage, waiting for a chance to greet Sioban.

For a brief minute or two their only conversation was a chorus of grumbles and clearing of throats, until Rett finally spoke up.

"Lex, man, I don't know how you do it, watching these women day in and day out. Aren't you afraid Danny's gonna kill you?"

"It's part of the business," Lex answered and took another long pull on his beer. "I just keep things professional. I see them as professional performers, not women."

Bear snorted and cut his eyes over at Lex.

"Don't sit there and pretend you don't turn to mush every time you look at Solange."

"Fine," he said and put his bottle down on the bar. "As long as you don't pretend you weren't ready to start a rumble when you thought I was trying to hook up with Vonda."

Rett gave a long, low whistle of astonishment.

"Boy, are you fellas in deep trouble."

Lex just laughed, and Bear straightened on his stool.

"I shouldn't have to remind you how well I know you, son," he said. "I heard you 'dropped' a glass during Chyenne's audition the other day. I bet if you dropped it any harder, there'd be a hole in the floor."

"Well, I guess we all have our issues. At least we're not totally whipped yet like our boy over there."

Danny held Sioban at her waist and lifted her down from the stage and into his arms. He whispered something in her ear, after which she smacked him playfully on the arm and headed to the back. Danny sauntered over to the bar to join them.

"Well, here he is now, fellas." Lex clapped him on his shoulder. "Aren't you just calm, cool, and collected after watching your woman do her thing up there?"

"Fuck no." Danny tossed back the Scotch Rett had passed to him, and slammed the glass down on the bar for an immediate refill. "I'm just accepting. It's who she is and what she loves to do. And I love her. Period. So, I support her."

"Okay, but we're all dying to know what it was you whispered in her ear that earned you a smack on the arm."

"I told her I plan on being in the audience for every fucking performance, and that if any man in the audience gets within a foot of her, he'll wake up in the hospital."

They all guffawed with relief and raised their glasses in a toast. Each one went home that night with his own secret concerns about the show, and the women in it. And each one knew he'd have to pull his shit together before opening night.

Chapter Twenty

Sioban could see the neon sign of the Velvet Room from almost ten blocks away. Much to Danny's consternation, Sioban had escaped to clear her head before the press arrived.

She cried a little, prayed for the show to go well that night, and thanked the lucky stars that were beginning to glimmer above as dusk became night. When she turned around to go back, she saw the sign glowing in the distance.

Though the question continued to burn in her mind, Sioban knew she couldn't spend too much time wondering how in the bloody hell she'd made it here to this time and place, after all the wishing and all the strife.

Instead she made a last, silent plea to Ava as she walked slowly back to the club.

> *Hi, Mam. It's been a while. I've been a bit busy. I hope you're doing okay, wherever you are. I know you made it to your heaven once you finally got free of this world. Well, I'm free too now, Mam. I got away from Jimmy, away from that hellhole he called a club. I'm dancing with Von now. I know I told you this before, but you'd love her. She's a kick-arse kind of lass, as you'd say, and she saved my life. Well, her, along with a crack team of security specialists, one of them being Danny. You'd like him, too. He's a decent Irish-American lad, although you wouldn't have known it if you'd seen him barreling down the*

street at me in his giant truck. Never mind I was standing in the road! I'm sure I already heard you scold me about that. Anyway, Danny saved me too, and not just by shooting at the bad guys. He gets me, Mam. He loves me for who I am...even though I'm not you. But here's the thing, Mam. I know you're not here. But you know how people always say they'll be with you in spirit? Well, I'm kind of hoping you'll peek in on me from heaven tonight. It would mean so much to me. I think...no, I know, you'd be proud of me, Mam. Miss you terribly. Love you forever.

§

Now, as she finished her last interview, Sioban followed Von back to the office. The doors hadn't opened yet, but a crowd had already gathered outside the front entrance. Several members of the local press had been invited in early, and had each taken a table so that the girls could all spend a few minutes talking to each one. Lex had put on a soft track of Dave Brubeck to set the mood, and the whole place crackled with electric energy.

Sioban closed the office door on the hubbub in the main room. Von had repainted the room, gotten new furniture, and rearranged it all. It bore no resemblance to the way it had looked before, nor to Jimmy's office at Club 29, so she had no qualms about being in there, even when she had occasion to be in there with Lex or Rett.

They both giggled as Vonda popped the cork on a bottle of champagne she'd had chilling in a bucket. Sioban held the glasses steady while Vonda poured.

"You did it, Von."

"Good grief, woman, we did it. How many times do I have to tell you that? I may have come back to Chicago full of pipe dreams, but I could never have pulled it off without you."

"Well, don't shortchange the guys. I mean, I don't even want to think about how things would have been without Danny and Bear."

"Yeah. I know."

Sioban didn't like the sudden shadow that crossed her friend's face, so she forged ahead with a toast.

"To the Velvet Room!"

"To the Velvet Room." Vonda smiled as they clinked glasses and sipped. "And to the best of friends," she added.

Sioban tried to repeat the toast, but her emotions got the best of her.

"Thank you for everything. I love you, Von," she stammered.

"I love you too, hon."

They both dissolved into tears and hugged each other hard. Several minutes later, they'd gone through half a box of tissues, and completed Vonda's toast.

"It's a good thing we don't have our make-up on yet," laughed Sioban.

"Speaking of make-up, we'd better take this party to the dressing room. We've got a show to get ready for."

And what a show it was. Sioban felt her entire power as a dancer. Yet, even as she lost herself to the music in each number, she was absolutely in sync with the others. They told a story together and alone at the same time.

Sioban's curiosity had gotten the best of her before the show about who had reserved the center front table.

"Who do you think?" Vonda had answered.

Danny had quite the explanation for reserving the table for himself when he brought her roses to the dressing room.

"From now on, every night you perform, as long as you're doing this show, I'm going to be sitting at that table, no one else, unless I invite them to sit next to me. That way, if you ever get scared, you look at me. If you ever doubt how beautiful you are up there, look at me. And if any bastard in the audience is stupid enough to rush the stage, I'll be there to protect you."

When she stepped out for the first number, all trepidation about seeing Danny sitting at that table vanished. She performed for the audience, but neither could her connection to him be severed. Whenever she needed a face to smile at, or toss her hips at, or wink and give a come-hither glance to, she had Danny. She was completely safe. And when she danced her solo, she felt wrapped in his loving gaze, even when she was in her most vulnerable poses, or she couldn't make eye contact with him. It was a love affair hidden in plain sight. It might have been obvious to anyone if they had been watching Danny, but every set of eyes in the house was riveted on Sioban.

Like most events of that magnitude, once it started, it moved at a lightning pace. Suddenly, their encore can-can was over, and they were taking a final bow before thunderous applause and a standing ovation.

Thank you, Mam.

Burlesque Bad

There were a thousand pictures to be taken, it seemed, by professional photographers and audience members alike. Then the catering staff broke open the cases of champagne for an equal number of toasts. That meant that at least poor Rett could take a break and enjoy the party for a little while.

Sioban wanted desperately to find Danny. She finally caught his eye, and he winked at her. Christ in heaven, he looked delicious. He was dressed in all black, a suit with a black silk shirt that he wore open at the neck instead of a tie. The electric blue silk handkerchief in his breast pocket made his cobalt eyes light up like stars.

As she moved to leave the stage and come to him, he motioned for her to stay put, and leaned over to say something to Lex. And when Lex went back into the light box, her stomach dropped. She couldn't have moved if she tried. Danny's blue gaze pinned her in place as he made his way toward the stage, while Lex helped clear the way for him over the sound system.

"May I have your attention, ladies and gentlemen? If you could make way for that dapper man in black you see clawing his way toward the stage, he has something he'd like to say."

Like magnets, all eyes went to her. It seemed their connection was more obvious than she'd thought. Von and the girls smiled devilishly at her from the other side of the stage. Eve and even Iliana stood rapt in the audience below her. Every man in the room let loose with whistles and catcalls at Danny as he mounted the stage. Sioban was temporarily relieved as he pulled her in close to his side. But when he began to speak, her nervousness about what he had planned returned. The crowd fell hushed in anticipation, and his deep voice filled the room.

"Hello, everyone. Like my friend Lex said, I've got something to say—but first things first." Another wave of appreciative noises rolled through the crowd as he turned to her. "Great show, baby."

The crowd roared as he brought his mouth down on hers, with just enough tenderness to be decent, and just enough heat to leave no doubt how much he couldn't wait to get her alone. Her head swam and she felt her cheeks burn as he broke the kiss.

"Now where was I? Listen, I suck at talking in front of people, so I'll make this quick. Sioban," he said, and her legs almost gave out when he looked at her. "The day I met you, you'd taken the biggest chance of your life, and done what you had to do to leave the past behind and begin something new."

"You mean, the day you nearly ran over me with that beast of a truck you drive?" she laughed nervously. The remark won her a smattering of laughter and a "you tell him!" from somewhere in the audience. Danny just grinned.

"Well, that's your version, baby. I could never have hit you, because your beauty stopped me cold." Everyone clapped at that. "And when you opened your ever-loving Irish mouth, I knew I'd met my match. I also knew I wanted to spend the rest of my life kissing it."

Sioban couldn't believe what she was hearing. The raucous responses seemed to fade and a rushing sound filled her head as Danny bent in front of her on one knee.

"Since day one, you've had me in a tailspin, Sioban. I fought what I knew for a few days, and bungled my way into being in your life. Now that your dream as a dancer has started to come true, I hope you'll make my dream come true. I need you in this life, Sioban. You turn everything upside down and make it right again at the same time. I decided tonight was it, for you, for me, for this. Will you marry me, Irish?"

She knew he'd pulled a box out of his pocket and opened it as he held it out to her. But she couldn't tear her eyes away from his. This was all real, *he* was real. Sioban couldn't believe she'd ever doubted that he was the one for her. She'd never be able to love anyone else with so much fire, and passion—the same way she loved dancing. Jesus, everyone was waiting on her to answer him.

"Yes, Danny. My God, yes!"

"Thank fuck. I'd better kiss you before you change your mind."

He did kiss the living daylights out of her for all the world to see, at least the part of it that was in the Velvet Room that night. There was more champagne, and a multitude of kisses, hugs, and well wishes from everyone. He finally put the ring on her, and she nearly started to cry all over again when she really looked at it. The marquis-cut sapphire was the perfect size for her hand. It was flanked on both sides by two trillion-cut diamonds, and set in platinum.

"Danny, it's amazing. I'm sorry I didn't let you put it on me right away. I'll cherish it, but more than anything I wanted to be looking in your eyes when I said 'yes' because I had to be sure it was real. I love you so much, Danny."

"And I love you, Irish."

She finally pulled herself away long enough for the girls to giggle and squeal over the ring, but eventually, Danny's impatience took over. She feigned panic as he swooped up and locked his arms around her from behind.

"Come on, baby," he whispered into her ear. "I need to be with you. I need to make love to you."

"Then take me home, Sheridan," she whispered back.

§

As the after-party died down, Vonda glanced over at Johnny's picture. Its permanent home would be in the back hallway outside the restrooms along with other photos of her and the girls. But tonight she'd taken it down off the wall over the bar, and put it back on the easel where she'd had it for the wake. She'd definitely felt his presence with her tonight.

I did it, Johnny, she thought.

Not without a lot of help, and everyone who meant something to her, and had been part of bringing the Velvet Room to life, was there tonight. There hadn't been much room for the general public by the time everyone she wanted to invite showed up, and the after-party was supposed to have been invite only, but the whole audience stayed, and Vonda didn't mind. If she'd done her marketing right, word would get out about the show and those who couldn't get in on opening night would be back for the next one.

She made a mental inventory of the highlights of the evening: champagne and laughter, costume malfunctions, Lex heroically coming up with new light combinations on the fly when his computer program crashed. Among her biggest thrills had been seeing and hearing the audience go wild for every single performer. Sahara wrapped them in the magic of her voice. Solange mesmerized them with her silky machinations. It had been amazing to see Sioban blossom onstage with the passion and talent that she'd known was always there. Chyenne had been the biggest surprise of the night. Her exotic beauty was the subject of many conversations Vonda had overheard at the party. Chy had choreographed her own solo based on her tribe's native dance. She'd chosen Native American flute music, and designed her own costume. The solo tugged at something primal in the souls of every person in the room. Even Chy's mother Little Dove had smiled proudly at her daughter from her table near the stage.

As for her own work, Vonda humbly accepted Iliana's measured praise for the show from top to bottom, and of her solo. It was the only kind of praise Iliana gave, and it really meant you'd reached a pinnacle if you received it. Eve had rejoiced with her, making Vonda so glad she'd taken Eve's offer to help her with costumes. Vonda hoped that the postcards on the tables announcing that the corsets had come from Lady Eve's next door would have her store flooded with new customers the next day.

Vonda's bond with the girls was now forged in the blood, sweat, and tears they had all put into the show. The tears and toasts they'd shared before the show were nothing compared to the triumph they shared in after the show. They huddled laughing and crying just offstage for a few precious moments between their last bow and greeting the throng in the main room. After that, they referred to themselves as the Order of the Velveteen Sisterhood.

Now that Danny had swept his fiancée away, the girls had floated happy and glowing into the night with Lex following behind them, and all of her closest friends had left; only a few remaining catering staff and Rett were left in her company. It was then that she realized that the one person she hadn't really seen was Bear. The disappointment she'd felt at seeing his reaction to her solo at the final dress rehearsal hadn't really done anything to stop her from wanting to see him tonight, from wanting his approval on some level. She knew he was there, because she'd seen him come in. But she never found him in all the festivities. She finished placing all the flowers she'd received on the bar and picked up her purse, thinking to let Rett lock up. But she turned to find that he already had his jacket on.

"Hey, boss lady. Congratulations, great opening."

"Thank you, Rett. I hope having the catering staff allowed you enough time to enjoy the evening."

"I enjoyed it very much, on both sides of the bar. I'll see the rest of the catering people out. I think there's somebody over there that wants to see you."

Of course, it was Bear, sitting on his favorite stool in the shadows, his face dimly lit by one of the tiny lamps on the bar. Vonda walked toward him slowly, unable to read his expression.

"Good evening, Mr. Rockford. Glad you could make the show." She drew herself up onto the stool next to him and faced him.

"I wouldn't have missed it."

"I wasn't sure. I mean, you didn't say very much after the dress rehearsal."

Bear sighed and pivoted on his seat to look at her.

"You might need to give some of us—me—a chance to get used to this, is all. I'm just...in awe, and that's the truth. What you do out there is one of the most beautiful things I've ever seen, Vonda. Doesn't mean those of us who are used to being in control don't need to get our Tarzan protective bullshit in check. Can you understand that?"

"I can. I do. After everything that's happened to get to this point, feeling your disapproval was hard for me. I thought I'd lost your support."

"Not gonna happen, honey. I just needed a minute, so to speak. I thought you were...let's just say I couldn't take my eyes off you, not in rehearsal, and not tonight."

Well, that got her attention. If she'd wanted appreciation from her audience, particularly from Bear, the way his deep-brown eyes smoldered with both desire and affection left no doubt about his opinion either of the show or her part in it.

"It's nice to know you were watching me from afar," she demurred as she felt the heat rising in her cheeks. "Everything went smoothly from a security standpoint, don't you think? The crowd was respectable, and I didn't hear any reports of anything getting out of hand."

"I concur. I'll get the report and the tapes from my boys in the morning to confirm that. I was a little surprised to see some of Johnny's friends here tonight. Doesn't seem like their kind of thing."

"Oh, I'm sure it was just a case of curiosity about what Johnny's little girl has done with the place. Ray Connigan brought a group of his buddies that used to hang out here. I hadn't seen him since the wake, and I was glad they got seats."

"I just hope their curiosity stays friendly."

It always alarmed her a little bit when Bear expressed his little insights and concerns. But she'd also learned to trust that if they ever became big concerns, he'd tell her right away. Danny's speech about tonight being a night of beginnings, and then his proposal to Sioban, had Vonda gearing up to tell Bear what was really on her mind. She wasn't even close to wanting to explore a serious relationship with him, much less one that would lead to a proposal. But for the brief time she'd thought herself to be without his friendship and support, she'd felt alone and empty. Aside from Sioban, she really didn't have anyone to share this night, this achievement, with. She realized she wanted to share it with Bear, as friends, if that was something he could accept. She wanted him around the bar, she wanted to have lunch with him, and maybe even dinner sometimes. She wanted to run things by him, and she liked listening to him talk about things he knew a lot about. Like Danny, there was no time like the present to ask him for his friendship.

"Bear, I...I can't tell you how glad I am that you're here, and how grateful I am to you for everything. You've gone above and beyond to make sure the club is safe, that I'm safe. And you've also been my friend."

"I'm glad you realize that. It's all I've been trying to tell you, be for you, all along."

"I'm just not ready for anything more, Bear."

"I understand. But I'm hoping you'll let me keep being here for you, as your friend."

Vonda's heart soared.

"Yes, that's exactly what I hoped too. It would mean so much to me, having you around. Not just as my security contractor, but as my friend."

"I'd like that, Vonda. And I'm not going anywhere. It's late, want me to drive you home?"

"Ah, that's tempting. I think I can drive myself. Walk me to my car though?"

"How about I walk you to your car, and meet you for lunch tomorrow?"

"Deal."

By the time Vonda finally crawled into bed, it was just a few hours before dawn. She pulled the covers up to her chin and reached for her cell phone. Bear had told her in no uncertain terms to call him when she was safe at home. She had to admit that she didn't mind one bit that his voice would be the last thing she heard before she fell asleep. He answered on the first ring.

Burlesque Bad

"I was getting a little worried."

"Sorry, I've been home a little while. I headed straight for the shower."

"And now you're all tucked in." Boy, was she ever. Vonda wondered what bedtime story he'd tell her if she asked.

"Yes, safe and sound. I thought I'd be too keyed up to sleep, but I think I'm finally fading."

"Well, I'm sure you'll sleep well. You've done an amazing thing, Vonda. I'm proud of you, and I know Johnny would be too."

"Thanks, Bear. I'd better let you go. It'll be light in a few hours."

"Yes, and I'm really looking forward to having lunch with you."

"Me too. Sleep well."

"Thanks for calling, I'm glad you made it home safe. I'll see you soon. Sweet dreams."

The instant she ended the call, Vonda sailed into the delicious oblivion of deep sleep with a smile on her face. Maybe she could make a little room for what her heart wanted after all.

Epilogue
The following Christmas Eve

Danny stared at his bride as she made her way around the different tables. He was supposed to be with her, greeting the guests, but he'd gotten sidetracked by one of his buddies from college. He knew he should get back to her, but he'd be just as happy to stand here and gaze at her all day. He'd thought he had an inkling of how beautiful she might be today until he'd seen her coming down the aisle at the cathedral, and then he wasn't sure if he'd ever breathe again. He'd heard the girls describe it during dinner as a Celtic peasant-style dress, but to him she was nothing less than an angel descended from heaven. He was no fashion expert, but he knew fine satin when he saw it. The sleeves came off her shoulders, leaving them deliciously bare, and came to her elbows, with flowing sheer extensions. The top was embellished with lace and tiny pearls and crystals. The pale cream color of the gown complemented her skin perfectly. But the corseted back was his favorite, and made him think of how much fun it would be to get her out of the dress later that night. She'd fixed her hair in big, loose curls, and thankfully she'd chosen a crown of pale pink and white roses instead of a fussy veil. He'd been able to look at her beautiful green eyes the entire time she walked down the aisle to him.

I'm one lucky bastard, he realized as he made his way toward her. It was a small affair, but everyone who mattered to them filled the Velvet Room for the reception. His dad and brother had come, and whether or not that was a good thing depended on how drunk his dad got that night. But Danny knew he could count on his Rockford brothers to handle anything that came up. Sioban's aunt Rose had cried tears of joy when Sioban called her, but hadn't been able to make the trip, even though they'd offered to help her with travel expenses. Sioban had been crushed, but Danny wasn't too worried, because his plans for their honeymoon would go a long way to remedy that. Other than that, the only people they considered family were the people they spent the most time with: Danny's Rockford mates, and Sioban's Velvet Room girls. She hadn't wanted a large wedding party, which was just fine with him. He wasn't that close with his brother, so Bear stood up for him, and Vonda, of course, was Sioban's maid of honor, in a silk dress similar in style to Sioban's. They kept calling the color 'chartreuse' but it looked green to him, very fitting for the season. Vonda was lovely in it, and he caught Bear staring at her. The poor man had to be in pain, because Vonda was still keeping him at arm's length. Danny knew they had lunch together a few times a week, and that Vonda had gotten Bear into playing video games with her, of all things. Bear didn't seem to spend much time at the house with her, but she'd started hosting poker night for them here at the club. Lex and Rett made lively additions to the usual Rockford bunch.

Danny stopped near the table where Sioban stood talking to Sahara, Solange, and Chyenne. Each table had a one-of-a-kind mini wedding cake. A special table for four had been set up onstage for the wedding party, where they'd eaten their dinner. The main cake, a delicate two-layer masterpiece, waited on its own table on the other side of the stage. Sioban looked up and Danny crooked his finger at her.

"Time for dessert, Irish. At least the one we can eat in public."

"Danny!" As fiery as his new wife was, he could still make her blush, and he loved that.

He took her hand, and led her up onstage. He'd thought about doing the messy thing that everyone did, but he just couldn't see smashing cake into that angelic face of hers right now.

Flashbulbs went off as they cut their first slice together. A chorus of "awws" rippled through the audience as he gently fed Sioban a piece of the cake, leaving only a tiny smear of frosting on the corner of her mouth. He wanted desperately to lick it off of her, but instead wiped it gently away with a napkin.

Sioban's eyes glittered as she broke off a piece much bigger than the one he'd fed her. Well, shit. So much for being a gentleman. His Irish lass had never been able to resist causing trouble. Only this time she did it without saying a word. Instead she shoved what little of the cake would fit into his partially open mouth. She smeared the rest, mostly frosting, all over his chin and lower face. Some of it even pushed up into his nose. Everyone cheered her on, but Danny was going to give as good as he got this time. The cheering only got louder as he yanked her toward him and crushed his mouth over hers. He felt her smile as their tongues lapped at the frosting and each other in the messy kiss. Yeah, he was one lucky bastard.

§

It was a magical Christmas Eve. Her best friend had just gotten married, and she was surrounded by everyone she loved in her new club that she had launched. And yet Vonda still felt an emptiness, because everyone was there except Johnny. It was her second Christmas without him, and she still missed him. As Danny and Sioban cleaned each other's faces off, Vonda slipped away. She leaned against the wall across from Johnny's picture in the back hallway. In one of her "what would he say if he were here" moments, Vonda knew without a doubt that he'd be proud of what she'd created here, how she'd transformed the old place, and of her success as a dancer. But she could also hear his voice admonishing her for something else she already knew. *It's not just me that you're missing, is it, princess?* No, Johnny, it wasn't. Vonda had worked hard to manifest her new life here in Chicago, and cope with the loss of her father. And she knew that she couldn't hide behind her work and the Velvet Room forever. Nor could she go on pretending that her little lunches with Bear were enough. *How do I do this, Johnny? How do I let him in?* Vonda pleaded silently. For almost her whole life, it had been her and Johnny, then her and her best friend Sioban trying to make their way in the world. Sure, she'd lost her virginity the way many girls had, in a less-than-memorable way, and she'd only had one or two semi-serious "relationships" since then. All Vonda knew was work; she didn't know love. She was scared. *You don't have to be afraid of Bear, princess. He's a good man. Let him love you.*

"It's almost time for their first dance."

Vonda nearly screamed, she was startled so badly. Bear had come in from the bar and was standing at the end of the hallway.

"I didn't mean to scare you. I was just hoping for a dance when they open the floor."

Her heart nearly pounded out of her chest. His brown gaze seemed to penetrate to her core. It warmed her and stripped her bare at the same time. Somehow he must know of the longing and loneliness she tried so hard to hide.

"I was just...I wanted to take a minute. Christmas, you know. I still miss him." She nodded at Johnny's picture. "But yes, of course, a dance. I'd like that. I'll try not to lead, it's a thing I have."

Bear chuckled as he moved toward her.

"If you want to lead, I have no problem with that. But I have a present for you first."

"A present? But why? I didn't get you anything—"

She'd felt his intent before the words were out of his mouth. He seemed to move in slow motion and yet before she could take another breath, he'd wrapped his arms around her waist and taken her mouth with his own.

At first she dared not breathe, for fear of breaking the spell. He tasted of champagne and cake, and he was slow and deliberate with his mouth, destroying her sensibilities as his lips pressed, and caressed, and slid over hers. They didn't devour, but rather opened for each other hotly, quietly, breathlessly, taking small touches with their tongues, retreating, and finding again. Then Bear angled, coaxed her open more widely, and dove deep with his tongue, hard and hot, before he broke the kiss. She would have collapsed had he not been still holding her. Vonda had never known anything could feel that good, that hot, that right.

"Merry Christmas," he whispered, and gently set her back from him.

"M-merry Christmas," she said.

"I love every minute with you, having lunch, playing those stupid video games. And I love playing poker with the guys in here while you play hostess to us. But today, I just wanted you to have a little taste of what I've been feeling and wanting all these months, and I think you want it to. I want you to know what's waiting for you when you're ready. Like I said before, you take the lead, on and off the dance floor, for as long as you need to. I'm a patient man. But I know that you have needs, Vonda. So I'll wait, because I want to be the one to fulfill every last one of them."

"Um...okay..." Lord, what else could she say? A dreamy man who had been her protector and her friend, and who'd now kissed her senseless, called out her desire for him, and told her he'd wait until she got her act together and acted on it? There was nothing she could argue with.

"As for not getting me a gift, there's that dance I asked for a minute ago—and I want you to have Christmas dinner with me tomorrow night. Come to my house and we'll cook it together."

Holy moly. She really did have everything she ever wanted for herself right here, not only in what she'd created for herself, but apparently standing right in front of her too.

"I'd like that...a lot."

She wanted to say more, to thank him, to reassure him that she would come around eventually, to explain why she'd been so hesitant to explore the chemistry between them. But that would only ruin the magic of the moment. Strains of music rose from the bar, and he held out his arm.

"We'd better go. We don't want to miss the happy couple's first dance—or ours."

They emerged from the back just in time to see Sioban run from her corner of the dance floor to take Danny's outstretched hand as he met her in the middle, and the notes of the Celtic-sounding version of "Jesu Joy of Man's Desiring" from Amy Grant's Christmas album filled the room. Danny had said there was only one time he'd ever be caught dancing, and that was at his own wedding. None of them had known he could dance an Irish jig this way. He made a proud show of it, whether Sioban had coached him prior to the wedding or not.

Danny and Sioban bowed at one another on the last boisterous note, and everyone cheered briefly, before Lex made the request over the sound system that everyone join Danny and Sioban on the dance floor that had been laid for the evening. He'd told them it was foolish for them to hire a DJ when he could run the whole show from the light box, but even he crept down to grab Solange for a dance as the next song began. Reece, Dex, and a few of Danny's other Rockford buddies swept up the other ladies for the dance, including Iliana and Eve, who Vonda knew was missing Johnny just as much as she was tonight.

Bear pulled her out onto the dance floor before the first bars of "There Is Love" had finished. There was indeed love, and Vonda wasn't afraid of how heavenly it was being held in Bear's arms for the second time, if you counted the earth-shattering kiss they'd just shared.

After the song ended, Vonda signaled to Lex as she made her way up onto the stage. He asked for quiet over the sound system, and she grabbed a white envelope tied with a pink ribbon sitting next to her empty plate at the wedding party's table before taking center stage.

"Hey, everybody, I hadn't wanted to do this when I toasted my best friend and her husband earlier, but before this party really gets out of control, I want to give Sioban my wedding gift to her."

Sioban blew her a kiss from where she and Danny stood on the dance floor.

"When Johnny died and I came back to Chicago, I asked Sioban to come with me, to be part of what I'd planned on building here. It didn't work out immediately, but eventually she made it, albeit under tough circumstances. But the point is, I knew from the day I met her what a powerhouse she is, how smart and talented she is, and that I wanted her to be part of whatever I fancied myself doing as a dancer. None of us would be standing here in the Velvet Room, and none of what I've accomplished in the past year would have happened without her. She's been on the payroll since she arrived, but I realized that the best way I can thank her for all she's meant to me is to really share everything with her. In this envelope are legal papers, signed by me, making Sioban a full partner in the Velvet Room. All she has to do is sign."

For once in her life, the girl was speechless, and Vonda came down from the stage to give her the envelope.

The dancing and drinking lasted well into the night, just as it had on opening night here at the club. And just like that night, Vonda was the supreme hostess until Danny drove Sioban off in his truck, which had been decorated by a secret brigade of friends, and the last guest had departed. Bear was also the last one waiting to walk her out. When they got to her car, he repeated a familiar ritual, with something new to look forward to at the end.

"Call me when you get home?"

"You know I will," promised Vonda.

"And I'll see you tomorrow?"

"I wouldn't miss it."

"Good," he said, and kissed her lingeringly on her forehead. She'd rather he kiss her lips again, but she knew he was honoring his promise to take things slow. Vonda would have to be the one to let him know when she was really ready to take things to the next level. Physically, she'd been ready for a long time. But emotionally, it was a different story.

When she glanced at her Charlie Brown Christmas tree on the coffee table on her way up to bed that night, she decided to take it with her to Bear's tomorrow. Maybe he'd even use it as a centerpiece for their Christmas dinner. It had been a year of both sadness and triumph, loss and gain. But Vonda's sleep came with the peace of dreams achieved, and the joy of the possibilities awaiting her in the New Year.

§

Sioban tossed her crown of roses away as Danny carried her across the threshold, much the way she'd tossed her bouquet away with happy abandon. She'd been hoping Vonda would catch the bouquet, but the woman avoided love like the plague. Then again, the way she obviously relished dancing in Bear's arms might mean there was still hope for her.

"I'm going to kill those bastards," Danny grumbled as he kicked the door shut and lowered her gently to her feet. "Somebody better cough up to get my truck washed."

"As opposed to having to get a limousine cleaned before returning it?" Sioban had insisted that they leave the wedding in Danny's truck rather than a limousine, for posterity. "I figure if you almost ran me down in that thing, it wouldn't hurt to have it spruced up when you drove me away in it."

"So you put them up to this, then?" he asked, feigning aggravation.

"No, I just gave them the keys," she giggled.

"Well, then you should be the first one punished." He growled and administered love bites along her neck as he backed her toward the stairs leading up to the bedroom. Another thing Sioban had insisted on was coming back here for their wedding night. Not only did it seem ridiculous to her to spend hundreds of dollars on a hotel room for one night, but she wanted their first time making love as husband and wife to be here, at home, where she felt safest and happiest in all the world.

The honeymoon was a different story. They were leaving tomorrow, and Danny refused to tell her where they were going. All he'd said was that he hoped she didn't mind that they weren't going to a tropical climate. She didn't care if they were going to the dark side of the moon, as long as they were together. But she was finding it difficult to focus on anything at all with him ravaging her this way.

"Need to get this dress off," he said, and took her mouth in a searing kiss.

She agreed, but could only claw at the buttons on his shirt as she became lost in his kiss. He'd ditched his jacket and tie after the last formal pictures were taken by the photographer. God only knew where they'd ended up, but it didn't matter as long as the rest of his clothes ended up off as well.

Sioban felt his restraint in loosening the corset strings on the back of her dress, and finally he found enough give to ease the dress off of her shoulders. He gasped appreciatively as it fell to the floor and revealed the pale pink set of underwear, including the garter that attached to her silk stockings, all from Lady Eve's, of course. She'd managed to get all of the buttons on his shirt undone, and she licked her lips at the sight of his bare, hard chest, just waiting for her hands to caress it. She never tired of looking at him, or loving him.

"I've never seen you more beautiful, baby," he groaned, as he stepped forward and cupped her breasts in his hands.

Sioban closed her eyes as he nuzzled in the crater between them created by the delicate strapless bra. He moved his hands around to expertly finesse the clasp open, freeing her breasts to him at last. She tilted her head back and sucked in her breath as he licked at one nipple and then tugged it into his mouth. His other hand slid down her side and came to rest on her upper thigh.

"Ohh..." she moaned, as he thumbed her sex through the thin lace of her panties and drew her other nipple into his mouth at the same time.

When Danny grabbed her buttocks and held her pelvis directly over the hardness of his cock straining through his pants, it was she who reached for the last snippet of her own restraint. She pushed hard at him to get enough momentum to step back. They were both panting, and his look was one of frustration and confusion. She put a finger on his lips before he could protest.

"You've got my dress off, and now it's time for me to get my wedding present to you."

"Don't need it now. You're my present. I need you."

God love him, and she needed him just as much. She knew that technically her surprise could wait, but she'd fantasized about this ever since Danny had proposed. At the risk of killing them both with her denial, she pressed on.

"It'll be worth it, my love, I promise." She took a step backward, over her dress pooled on the floor. In a gesture to reassure him that he really wasn't that far from getting what they both wanted and needed, she unfastened the garters and sashayed out of her panties. "Meet me upstairs in one minute. And be naked when you get there."

She flung her panties down and darted up the stairs as fast as she could. Danny growled where she'd left him and tore at his belt buckle. She snatched her bottom dresser drawer open and pulled her tissue-wrapped surprise out from its hiding place beneath her tee-shirts. Just as she heard Danny on the stairs, Sioban threw the door to the bathroom closed.

"Your sixty seconds are almost up, Mrs. Sheridan," he called from the bedroom. "Don't make me come in there after you."

With less ceremony than she'd planned, Sioban tossed the tissue paper to the floor and kicked off her shoes. She then peeled off the stockings and stepped into the green corset. She hadn't worn it again since the day she'd tried it on in Lady Eve's and purchased it, knowing all along she wanted Danny to be the one to see her in it. She managed to get it zipped, though it was an effort of futility once she revealed herself. She opened the door and stepped into the bedroom to find Danny waiting for her without a stitch of clothing, his erection straining toward her.

Without warning, he tipped his head back and laughed. Her heart sank. All she wanted was to wear this for him, to be sexy and beautiful, and he found her choice laughable compared to what she'd worn under her wedding dress. She could just die on the spot.

"Oh, Irish," he said, and smiled as he came to stand in front of her. "Never, ever stop surprising me the way you do. I'm laughing because when I went to buy this very garment for you just before the first time we made love, Eve told me that it was a one-of-a-kind corset, and that someone had already bought it. She sent over that nightie I gave you before."

Sioban had to catch her breath again before she spoke.

"You did? She did? So...you like it?"

"Baby, I love it on you, just like I knew I would when I tried to buy it for you. And I love you, Sioban, above all else, no matter what you're wearing. So how about I make love to you now?"

"Yes, Danny. Yes."

He kissed her again, and she was lost. They did many things to each other before Danny finally got the corset off of her. But once he did, he laid her down with tenderness and covered her naked body with his.

"I love you, Irish."

"God, I love you too, Danny."

They spent the rest of the night demonstrating their love for each other, first with a slow, rising heat as they held each other's gaze and came together, then later clutching at each other's bodies and feeding on one another until dawn threatened to break across the sky outside.

They shared a Christmas brunch with their friends, once again hosted by Von at the Velvet Room, before heading to the airport. Sioban had cried and thrown herself into Danny's arms when he revealed where he was taking her on their honeymoon. And when they saw the next sunrise from their honeymoon suite at the Shelburne in Dublin, her heart burst with joy. They'd spend the next two weeks there taking in the sights, making love, and getting to know her aunt Rose again, who lived outside the city. As she stood with Danny looking out at the Dublin skyline, Sioban laid Rose's letter on the glass table next to the window. She smiled, knowing that all her dreams had finally come true.

About the Author

Nina Day Gerard considers herself an Accidental Romance Writer. While she's been writing stories since grade school, and trading romance novels with her girlfriends since high school, it wasn't until 2012 when she had a V8 moment: "Hey, I can do this---I *should* do this!" And she never looked back. Nina lives in Los Angeles with her husband. The memory of her muse, a little Calico named Celine, still surrounds her.

§

For more on Nina and her books, visit www.ninadaygerard.com.

For a free exclusive excerpt of *Burlesque Baby: Book Two of the Destiny of Dance* series, join Nina's mailing list. She'll never spam you, just send you announcements of new releases!

www.ingramcontent.com/pod-product-compliance
Lightning Source LLC
Chambersburg PA
CBHW061933170626

46813CB00006B/2378